"*My beautiful little skeptic,*"

Hank murmured huskily. He put his arms around her. "Haven't I shown you in every possible way how I feel about you?"

Briana had to admit that he had. He'd shown her how much he desired her. With his kisses he'd shown her how much he enjoyed her response, with his caressing hands how quickly she could arouse him, with his magnificent body how they could soar together into ecstasy.

But it wasn't enough.

Just three words—*I love you*—would have made all the difference. And two more—*marry me*—would have obliterated all her doubts.

Dear Reader,

Welcome to Silhouette **Special Edition** . . . welcome to romance. Each month, Silhouette **Special Edition** publishes six novels with you in mind—stories of love and life, tales that you can identify with—romance with that little ''something special'' added in.

April has some wonderful stories in store for you. Lindsay McKenna's powerful saga that is set in Vietnam during the '60s—MOMENTS OF GLORY—concludes with *Off Limits,* Alexandra Vance and Jim McKenzie's story. And Elizabeth Bevarly returns with *Up Close,* a wonderful, witty tale that features characters you first met in her book, *Close Range* (Silhouette **Special Edition** #590).

Rounding out this month are more stories by some of your favorite authors: Celeste Hamilton, Sarah Temple, Jennifer Mikels and Phyllis Halldorson. Don't let April showers get you down. Curl up with good books—and Silhouette **Special Edition** has six!—and celebrate love Silhouette **Special Edition**-style.

In each Silhouette **Special Edition** novel, we're dedicated to bringing you the romances that you dream about— stories that will delight as well as bring a tear to the eye. And that's what Silhouette **Special Edition** is all about— special books by special authors for special readers!

I hope you enjoy this book and all of the stories to come!

Sincerely,

Tara Gavin
Senior Editor
Silhouette Books

PHYLLIS HALLDORSON
You Could Love Me

Silhouette Special Edition

Published by Silhouette Books New York

America's Publisher of Contemporary Romance

SILHOUETTE BOOKS
300 East 42nd St., New York, N.Y. 10017

YOU COULD LOVE ME

Copyright © 1992 by Phyllis Halldorson

ISBN: 0-373-09734-4

First Silhouette Books printing April 1992

PHYLLIS HALLDORSON

At age sixteen Phyllis Halldorson met her real-life Prince Charming. She married him a year later, and they settled down to raise a family. A compulsive reader, Phyllis dreamed of someday finding the time to write stories of her own. That time came when her two youngest children reached adolescence. When she was introduced to romance novels, she knew she had found her long-delayed vocation. After all, how could she write anything else after living all those years with her very own Silhouette hero?

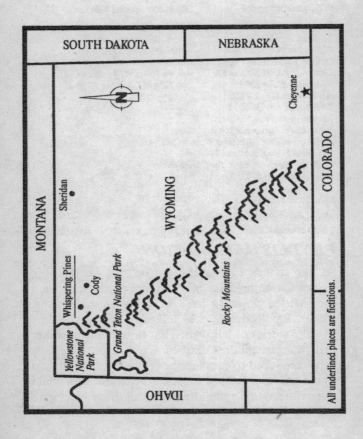

Chapter One

Briana Innes stood in front of the big colorful calendar in the dental office where she worked and felt the familiar agony of despair.

Yesterday had been the last day of January, and today the calendar page must be flipped. It was a pretty calendar with a different Norman Rockwell painting reproduced for each month. January's featured a group of brightly dressed circus performers playing chess.

Safe enough, but what about February?

She finished buttoning her white lab coat and reluctantly reached out to turn up the page. February was represented by a preschool-age girl clad in pink drop seat pajamas peeking through the keyhole of an enormous double door. Her hair was parted down the back of her head and braided on either side, but the little face was hidden.

Briana felt a wrenching pain at the symbolism. How appropriate that the child's face was turned away from her.

Her gaze moved slowly downward to the first numbered square. Friday, February 1.

Four years ago they'd told her the memory would fade and February first would be just another date, but they were wrong. It might as well have been circled in red and announced with blaring horns and firecrackers.

Each succeeding February 1 was as painful as the last, and she suspected it always would be.

Heavy footsteps coming down the hall alerted her that her time for grieving was long past, and she turned to greet Allen Wainwright, D.D.S., the town's only dentist and her employer.

Dr. Wainwright was a tall thin man in his midfifties with brown hair and eyes, and a confident smile that put even his most fearful patients at ease. "Good morning, Briana," he said cheerfully. "Sorry I'm late. With the subzero temperatures last night, I had trouble getting the car started—even with the new engine starter."

He took off his sheepskin-lined overcoat and hung it and his hat in the closet. "We'd better get moving. I've got a full schedule booked, and Paula just told me we'll have to make room for an emergency toothache before lunch."

Briana affected a grimace, but her eyes smiled back at him. "I'll bet it's someone who hasn't been coming in for regular checkups and now can't understand why his tooth hurts."

He eyed her suspiciously. "You're right, but what makes you so sure it's a *he?*"

"Because men are the ones who put off going to the dentist until their teeth start to hurt, then they want to be seen immediately."

He laughed. "Well, you're on the button. Hank Robinson hasn't had a checkup for two or three years. I remind him of it every time he brings his little daughter in for hers, and he always promises he'll make an appointment, then never does. He couldn't have picked a worse day, either. Eleanor has to leave at eleven o'clock to drive Frances to Cody for her monthly checkup."

Their chairside assistant, Eleanor Wainwright, better known as Elly to everyone but her parents, was Dr. Wainwright's daughter, and Frances, her mother, was recovering from a recent heart attack.

This time Briana's grimace was real. "And you want me to assist." It was a statement, not a question.

He looked down at her from his great height and assumed a pleading expression. "Yes, please, if you don't mind, Ms. Dental Hygienist," he teased. "I know it's beneath your dignity, but what can I say? I'm desperate."

She couldn't hold back the chuckle that bubbled from her throat. He was more or less right. In school she'd been taught that a dental hygienist does not pinch-hit as a chairside but practices independently as a paradental, cleaning teeth, taking X rays and doing preliminary examinations.

The rules had to be bent when you worked in a small town like Whispering Pines, Wyoming, population 3,435.

"Okay, but you're gonna owe me," she said with a toss of her raven ringlets. "Right now, though, you've got an extraction in the first operatory, and I have a cleaning in the second, so I'll see you later."

At eleven o'clock, Elly took off, and by eleven-thirty there was only one man left in the waiting room—obviously the emergency toothache.

Henry Robinson closed his eyes and tried to ignore the throbbing pain in his jaw as he leaned his head against the wall next to the uncomfortable chair in the dentist's waiting room. The pain had started yesterday afternoon, but being the optimist that he was, he'd assumed it would go away.

It hadn't, and he'd spent a sleepless night taking aspirin and applying an ice bag, but nothing helped. Damn, he should have heeded Allen Wainwright's warnings and made appointments for regular checkups.

He didn't hear the door open, but a low, husky voice lifted him gently out of his musing. "Mr. Robinson, I'm sorry you were kept waiting, but the doctor will see you now."

The words were impersonal, a simple business message, but the voice was warm and soft and seemed to envelope him in a soothing caress.

Slowly, reluctantly, Hank opened his eyes, afraid his illusion would be shattered by reality, but he couldn't have been more wrong. Standing in the doorway was a young woman whose looks fulfilled all the promise of her voice.

Roughly five foot six with a cloud of loose ebony curls that framed her delicate face and brushed her shoulders, she had almond-shaped green eyes and a mouth made for kissing. His fascinated gaze lowered to high, full breasts, a tiny waist that he was sure he could span with his two large hands, and firmly rounded hips and thighs. Under an unbuttoned white lab coat she wore a snug-fitting brown skirt, a fluffy sweater in the exact shade of leaf green as her exotic eyes, and on her feet, calf-high boots.

Hank knew he was staring, but he couldn't help it. Never had he had such a strong first reaction to a woman. In fact, for the past three years, he'd been lucky if he could work up any enthusiasm for them at all.

So why did that this one make him ache just to hold her?

Briana had stood in the doorway, silently watching the dozing man for a minute or so before she spoke. What was it about him that drew her attention so insistently? He was big, but she'd known plenty of big men. According to her chart, he was thirty-two, but age had never mattered to her. He was dressed like all the other men in town—in jeans, boots and a plaid wool shirt—so his clothes didn't set him apart.

Maybe it was the suggestion of vulnerability. He looked so uncomfortable squeezed into the small chair with his shoulders and head leaning against the hard wall. His eyes were shut, but even from a few feet away she could see the dark shadows under them and the lines of pain on his rugged face.

When she spoke she startled him and he opened his eyes. They were beautiful. A smoldering green, almost the color of her own, that connected with her gaze and wouldn't let go, but probed past her calm exterior and stirred to life a sensual awareness she hadn't felt in years.

She tried to blink and break the spell, but her eyelids wouldn't respond. It was as though she were being drawn into his very psyche, and she wanted nothing more than to let it happen. A feeling of rightness and inevitability seemed to flow between them, even though they had never seen each other before.

She wasn't sure which of them finally managed to tear their gazes apart, but she felt as if she'd been released from a magnetic pull.

He stood, and she noticed that he looked as dazed as she felt. She glanced around in an effort to pull herself together and saw a heavy leather jacket and a Stetson on the chair next to the one he'd been sitting in.

"If you'll bring your jacket and hat I'll hang them in the closet," she said, and was embarrassed when her normally husky voice sounded even sexier.

He still didn't speak but picked up his things and followed her.

She led him into the second operatory and seated him in the chair, then introduced herself. "I'm Briana Innes, and I'm a dental hygienist," she said with a smile. "I'm trained to do some of the routine dental care and free Dr. Wainwright for more important procedures like fillings and extractions."

His attention was concentrated on her mouth, and almost before she'd finished talking, he raised one hand and gently stroked her cheek. "My God," he murmured in a tone tinged with awe, "you even have dimples."

A fine tremor ran through her, and she caught her breath. His fingers were rough, the texture of a man who works with his hands, but his touch was feather soft, the touch of a lover.

Before she could gather her scattered wits about her, he snatched his hand away and his expression changed to chagrin. "I'm sorry," he said, clenching his fist in his lap. "You must think I'm some kind of nut. Would you accept a plea of temporary insanity?"

The smile that lit his face was as beautiful as his eyes. "I must have been dozing when you came in," he explained, "and when you spoke, you startled me. I wasn't expecting . . . I mean . . ."

He frowned and ran his hand through his straw-colored hair. "Oh, hell, I'm making a damn fool of myself. I'm Henry Robinson. My friends call me Hank. You'll have to excuse me, but I didn't get any sleep last night, and this tooth is about to drive me crazy. I promise you that next time we meet, I'll be perfectly rational."

Briana looked down at him and allowed herself to touch his slightly swollen jaw. "Don't apologize, Hank," she said softly as her fingers absorbed the smooth-shaven texture of his weather-beaten skin. "I understand. Now, about that tooth. Which one is it?"

It was nearly one o'clock before Dr. Wainwright and Briana finished replacing the filling Hank had lost. She lowered the chair so he could get up. "There, now that we've got that exposed nerve covered, it should feel better."

Hank fingered his jaw. "It does. Now I can't feel anything, not even my tongue."

She chuckled. "That's true, and you'll have to be careful not to bite it or the inside of your mouth before the Novocaine wears off. Better stick with soup for lunch."

He stood and looked down at her. He was at least a couple of inches over six feet tall, and she was much too aware that his broad shoulders and chest tapered to a surprisingly slender waist and hips.

He reached out as though to touch her again, but quickly withdrew his hand. "Those dimples do the damnedest things to me," he said hoarsely. "Have lunch with me, Briana?"

She had no will to refuse. "All right," she whispered.

Hank took Briana to Kasey's Kitchen, the newest and classiest of the two cafés on Main Street. It had a homey decor with maple tables and chairs and ruffled blue-and-white-checked curtains at the windows. Kasey, a plump, affable woman of indeterminate age who functioned as owner, manager and cashier, greeted them cheerfully. "Hey, Hank, haven't seen you around lately. Been out of town?"

He grinned. "Yeah. January's kind of slow in the lumber and construction business so Crystal and I drove down to Tucson. We visited my sister, Shirley, and her family and soaked up some of that Arizona sun. We were gone about three weeks."

Briana knew from the conversation between Hank and the dentist that Crystal was Hank's four-year-old daughter, whom he was raising by himself. She didn't know whether he was divorced or widowed.

Kasey eyed him teasingly. "I see you didn't waste any time checking out the new gal in town when you got back." She turned to Briana. "Hi, Briana, how do you like Whispering Pines by now?"

"I love it," Briana said. "In just five weeks I've gotten on a first-name basis with almost everybody in town, and they're all so friendly. You can't really appreciate that unless you've spent most of your life in a place the size of Los Angeles like I did."

"Yeah, I know what you mean. I've been around, but when I decided to settle down, I came back here. It's home to me. Always has been and always will be." Kasey turned and waved toward the dining area. "Just pick out a table and sit down. Naomi'll be with you in a minute."

They hung their wraps on the coat tree in the corner and slid into one of the blue, vinyl-upholstered booths along the wall. "In L.A., we wouldn't dare hang our coats in a public place," Briana commented. "They'd be stolen before we could sit down."

The corner of Hank's mouth turned up in a one-sided grin. "Wouldn't be worth the trouble to steal something in Whispering Pines. We all know each other. If anyone stole my jacket and wore it in public, everybody who saw it would tell me.

"The crime rate around here is practically zero," he continued. "Our police department consists of the chief, two officers and a secretary. We have two jail cells, but there's seldom anybody in them except old Ollie. He's the town drunk and has to be locked up sometimes in the winter to keep him from passing out in an alley somewhere and freezing to death."

The waitress arrived and after some good-natured bantering with Hank, took their orders and poured coffee into mugs already set on the table.

When she left, Hank took a sip of the scalding hot liquid and looked at Briana. "Tell me about yourself," he said softly. "Before I left for Arizona I'd heard that Allen Wainwright had a new young assistant who was... uh... gorgeous."

Briana laughed. "Are you sure *gorgeous* was the word?"

He had the grace to look flustered. "Well... you know how men talk, but the description could definitely be translated as gorgeous. Every man in town must have been coming in for checkups."

Now she was the one who blushed. It's true she'd gotten a lot of admiring glances and comments from a good share of the male population, and she'd dated a couple of the single ones, but none of them had caused her heart to pound and her breathing to accelerate the way Hank Robinson did. "Hardly every man, but I have been kept busy."

"I'll bet you have," he drawled. "How on earth did you find your way to Whispering Pines, Wyoming? We're just a tiny dot on the map."

She stirred cream into her coffee and began the explanation that she'd found usually satisfied people's curiosity. "I was born and raised in Los Angeles, and took my dental training at a community college in Denver. It was there that I met Dr. Wainwright's daughter, Elly, and we became close friends. After we graduated, she came back here and I got a job in Denver, but we kept in touch. Then, when her father's practice grew to the point where he couldn't comfortably handle it alone and decided to take on a dental hygienist, Elly urged me to apply for the job. I did, and here I am."

Hank looked puzzled. "But why would you leave a city like Denver to come to this little nowhere community? We're not on a main highway, and we're so far up in the mountains, we get snowed in sometimes."

Briana had hoped he wouldn't ask questions, but Hank obviously wasn't one to be content with a condensed biography. She shrugged. "I'm not especially fond of cities, and Elly made Whispering Pines sound like a nice place to live. She was right."

"But how about your family?" he asked, digging deeper. "Are your parents still in L.A.? Do you have brothers and sisters? How about boyfriends? Surely there's a special man in your life."

Briana felt the beginnings of panic. She hadn't expected so many questions so soon from this overwhelming man. He wanted to probe her roots, and all she was prepared to give him was the blossoms, the highlights of her twenty-three years.

To her relief, Naomi appeared just then with two steaming bowls of split-pea soup and a plate of biscuits with honey. It gave her the distraction she needed to change the subject, which she did as soon as the waitress left.

"Okay now, enough about me. Let's talk about you for a while." She split one of the biscuits in two and buttered it. "Are you a native of Whispering Pines?"

"Sure am," Hank said as he stirred his soup to cool it. "I've lived here all my life, except for the four I spent at the university in Laramie. I'm a partner with my mom and dad in the family lumber, hardware and feed business."

A picture flashed into her mind of a large warehouse-type building surrounded by stacks of lumber in the spacious yard. "Of course, Robinson's Lumber and Feed. I didn't connect the names. I guess I've never met your parents."

He nodded. "I have the one sister, Shirley, and that's about all there is to tell. Life in Wyoming isn't near as exciting as it is in California."

He hesitated, and when he spoke again, there was a cynical melancholy sadness in his tone. "Once the novelty wears off, I doubt that you'll stay here long."

Exciting! That wasn't exactly the word she'd use for her life in Southern California. Wretched, maybe. Despairing, certainly, but she'd had all the so-called excitement of city life she could tolerate. If Hank only knew what a haven Whispering Pines was to her.

"Don't be so quick to jump to conclusions, Hank," she said carefully. "*Excitement* is another word for stress, and I had enough of that to last me a lifetime while I was growing up. I love the peace and quiet here."

She quickly changed the subject before he could pick up on what she'd said and ask questions. "Tell me about your daughter."

His face lit up at the mention of his child. "Are you sure you want to hear about her? I warn you, I'm a proud father and I brag a lot."

She'd have known that by his expression and by the devotion that radiated from his voice. It told her that this was not only a loving father, but a special kind of man. "Of course, I want to hear about her. Does she look like you?"

He grinned. "Naa, Crystal's a little beauty. Long brown hair, big blue eyes and a smile that lights her up from the inside out. She's smart, too. She can read parts of her little books already, and can add simple numbers."

"That's great," Briana said with forced cheerfulness—in spite of the desolation his joy in his little daughter caused her. "Does she go to preschool?"

"No, there aren't any around here, but my mother keeps her during the day while I work, and she's teaching her. Crystal's going to kindergarten next year."

Briana pushed her empty soup bowl aside and picked up her coffee. "I like her name. Crystal. It's different."

Hank's glow dimmed a bit. "Yeah, I guess. I would have preferred something more traditional, like Catherine or Elizabeth, but her mother was hell bent on naming her Crystal, so I gave in. After all, what do I know?"

Briana heard the bitterness that tinged his voice and wondered about Crystal's mother. This was the first time he'd mentioned her, and Briana debated about whether or not she'd be out of line to inquire about her. Maybe if she did it with as much finesse as possible...

She twisted her hands in her lap. "Did you...uh...lose your wife?"

Hank's short laugh was a bark of rancor. "Yeah, I guess you could call it that, although I didn't actually misplace her. She left Crystal and me three years ago and went off to Hollywood to pursue a career in acting."

"Oh." Briana felt as if she'd had the wind knocked out of her. Did that mean they were still married? He wasn't wearing a wedding ring, but a lot of married men didn't.

She tried again. "Then you're just living apart because of her career?"

For a moment he looked startled, then he reached down and took her hand. "No, Briana, we're not just living apart. I filed for divorce and custody of Crystal. DeeDee didn't contest either action."

The relief his words sent coursing through her was frightening. She'd known him for all of two hours. It shouldn't matter to her what his marital status was, and she shouldn't be tingling with pleasure just because her hand was nestled so securely in his. What was the matter with her? The last thing she wanted was to get involved with another man. Her encounter with Scott Upton had taught her well that men were seldom what they seemed and should never be trusted.

She moved her head and her gaze collided with Hank's and melded. He'd moved closer, and the look on his face told her that he wanted to kiss her. It came as no shock, but seemed a natural blending with her desire to be kissed by him, to feel their lips moving together....

The voice of the waitress finally penetrated their mutual absorption. "Hey, you guys want some dessert?"

Briana jumped and pulled her hand from Hank's. Dear God, had she lost her mind? If they hadn't been interrupted, she'd have kissed him right here in a public restaurant! What must he think of her? Worse, her reputation in this small village would be mud if word got around that she was seen making out with one of its leading citizens in broad daylight.

Hadn't her experience with Scott taught her anything? She should know by now that it was always the woman who came out of such a scandal with her name blackened and her life in tatters. Somehow, the man usually emerged with his macho image enhanced. After all, boys will be boys, but girls are supposed to be angels.

She looked at her watch. It was long past time for her to get out of there.

"No, no dessert," she said to the waitress, then turned back to Hank, but avoided getting entangled in his magnetic glance again. "I really have to get back to the office. I'm already late."

She picked up her purse as he stood. "Yes, of course." He sounded disoriented, and she could tell that he was as shaken as she. "Just let me settle the bill and I'll drive you."

"No! I—I'd prefer to walk. It's only a couple of blocks and I need the exercise. Thanks for the lunch."

Before he could reply, she'd charged across the room, grabbed her coat and fled.

Hank watched her leave with a mixture of disappointment and relief. Dammit, the woman must be some kind of witch. She'd cast a spell over him that melted his resolves and scrambled his brain.

He tossed some bills onto the table and strode out of the restaurant. It was only when the wind, with its below-zero chill factor, struck him that he remembered his jacket hanging on the rack inside. He shivered and ran toward his pickup. To hell with it, he'd stop by the house to get another and come back for that one tomorrow. He was in no mood for conversation with anyone.

Inside the truck, he started the engine and turned on the heater. He must be suffering some kind of hormone imbalance, he mused. Everything had been going so well lately. He seldom thought of DeeDee anymore, and his life had been so filled with work and Crystal that he wasn't often troubled with the desire for a woman.

At first that had bothered him when he thought about it, and he'd wondered if DeeDee had psychologically gelded him. He found out, though, that he functioned fine when the need struck, and the rest of the time, he was glad not to be bothered.

Driving away from the curb, he headed in the direction of his house. That's what made his attraction to Briana Innes so upsetting. He could handle it a lot better if it were just an overwhelming sexual urge he felt, but it wasn't.

Not that he wouldn't like to bury himself deep inside her and build up to the explosive release that coupling was sure to create. Just thinking of it made him shiver, but somehow, he knew that if he ever got involved with Briana, good sex would only be the tip of the iceberg. His need for her would go all the way to his soul, and he couldn't risk that.

Chapter Two

The following week was a busy one for Briana. The heavily laden clouds that had pelted the northwestern mountains of Wyoming with snow since she'd been in Whispering Pines magically disappeared—to be replaced with bright sunshine. The temperatures no longer plunged to below zero, but seemed almost warm as they hovered in the high teens and low twenties.

It was weather for skiing and sleighing and snowball fights in a wonderland of glittering white.

Briana had never felt so euphoric—a condition partly due to the nearly six-thousand-foot altitude and the clean pine-scented air, but also to the peace and tranquility she'd found in this friendly little town.

She loved the old-fashioned Main Street, the first one she'd ever seen that twisted lazily upward instead of laying straight and flat. When she was growing up in the concrete canyons of Los Angeles, trees that got in the way of urban sprawl were chopped down, but this quaint village built on the side of a mountain had charted its business district to weave around several irreplaceable centuries-old pines.

The town was named for them. Indeed, the area around Whispering Pines was so heavily forested that it seemed to be in danger of being taken over by the towering lodgepoles and their dense underbrush.

Briana hadn't seen or heard from Hank Robinson since her hasty exit from the café and she was both relieved and disappointed. Relieved because she didn't want another intimate relationship with a man. She'd learned her lesson well from superhunk Scott Upton, her first and only lover, who'd deserted her, leaving her to make the most heartbreaking decision a woman could be asked to make. She wasn't going to repeat that mistake.

On the other hand, not even Scott had had as strong and disturbing an affect on her as the lightning response Hank evoked without even trying. It was scary! This man was dangerous to her peace of mind, but still, she'd felt strangely rejected when he hadn't gotten in touch with her again.

She shook her head to banish that disquieting thought and slid the yards of the stiff white petticoat over her head. It was Saturday, and she was going square dancing with Luke Odell, youngest son of the local banker and much sought after by the single women of the town. He was a nice man in his late twenties with dark hair and eyes and a pleasant personality. They were double dating with Elly Wainwright and Elly's steady boyfriend, Ted Thurston, who was in charge of home mortgages at the bank.

Briana adjusted the petticoat, then put on the bulky red-and-white-checked full-skirted dress and zipped it up the back. This would be the first time she'd square danced in Whispering Pines. She'd joined a singles dance club when she was working in Denver and had enjoyed it. It was a great way to meet other people her own age, and she'd made lasting friendships.

She was tying the ribbons of her red ballet-type slippers around her ankles when Elly's distinctive knock on her apartment door was followed by the sound of it opening, and Elly's voice rang through the rooms.

"Briana, okay if I come in?" An irrelevant question since she was already inside.

It had taken Briana a long time to get used to not having to latch her door when she was home. In the city that would be unthinkable, but in this tiny, isolated mountain community, locking yourself in your home was almost a rebuff to friends and neighbors who might stop by.

"Be right with you," Briana called back from the bedroom as she hurried through the small kitchen to the living room.

She resided on the second floor of an ancient rectangular, box-type house that had been remodeled into four apartments, two on either side of the middle stairway. They were all alike with a living room, kitchen and bedroom in a straight row one after the other. The closet-sized bathroom opened off the kitchen.

"Ted called to say they'd be about twenty minutes late," Elly said as she removed her warm, down-filled, quilted jacket and slung it across the back of the sofa. "So I told him I'd come on over and they could pick us both up here."

"Fine. Oh, I like your dress," Briana said as her gaze took in the bright green Tyrolean-print garment fashioned much like her own, with a scooped neckline, short puffed sleeves, tightly fitted waist and the prerequisite three-tiered skirt over a ballooning petticoat. "Did you make it?"

Elly smiled, but her brown eyes didn't reflect gaiety as she pirouetted to show off the skirt. "No, I bought it in Cody. I love the color."

Briana grinned. "You should. It really sets off your flaming hair."

Elly had the brightest red hair Briana had ever seen in an adult, and the light complexion and freckle-sprinkled nose to go with it. She was small and cute and cuddly, and had been an instant hit with the male students at college, but all the attention hadn't changed her a bit. She'd dated and had a grand time, but after two years when she'd graduated with an AS in Dental Assisting, she'd happily packed up and returned to her home in the remote mountains of Wyoming.

Something had happened to her since then, though. She no longer had the carefree demeanor that had once been so much a part of her personality. She was quieter, more thoughtful.

Of course, she was twenty-two years old now, two years older than when she and Briana had graduated from college. It could just be that she'd matured, but Briana didn't think so. Maturity didn't usually change a bouncy, extroverted personality into an introvert. Elly seemed more sad than mature. It could be that she worried about her mother's health, but...

Briana's musing was interrupted when Elly chuckled at the reference to her hair. "Talk about red, you're sure dressed appropriately for a Valentine dance. Better watch it, Luke's apt to want you for his very own."

Briana shook her head. "No way. This is only our second date. He's a nice guy, but not really my type."

"Oh?" Elly sounded curious. "And just what is your type?"

The question sobered Briana. "I'm not sure," she said thoughtfully, "but I'll know him when I see him."

Or would she? Briana had been so sure that Scott was her ideal, but she'd been a hero-worshipping teenager then. As it turned out, she couldn't have been more wrong. Now the specter of Hank Robinson intrigued her, but she didn't want to get involved, and apparently he wasn't intrigued by her.

"We might as well sit down and catch up on all the latest gossip that we don't have time for at work," Briana said as she motioned Elly to a seat on the couch, then sat down beside her. "We'll start with you. Tell me what's been bothering you lately."

Elly looked startled. "Bothering me? I—I don't know what you mean. Nothing's bothering me."

Briana knew she should back off, but she wanted to help if she could. She reached out and touched Elly's shoulder. "Look, don't try to con a good friend. I know you too well. If there's anything I can do—"

"There's nothing wrong," Elly interrupted as she jumped to her feet. "I'm just overworked. All of us in the office are. We need another dentist in this town, but it's impossible to find one who's willing to settle down in such a remote community."

She began to pace. "Oh, it's lively enough when the park's open, but that's only a few months in the summer. The rest of the time we're pretty isolated."

The park she spoke of was Yellowstone. It was less than thirty miles from Whispering Pines to the east entrance, and the town had a brisk tourist trade during the summer months. Nothing to compare with Cody, however, which was bigger, more accessible and the home of the Buffalo Bill Historic Center.

Briana had to admit that Dr. Wainwright's practice was unwieldy, but none of the others in the office had complained of fatigue. Could there be something wrong with Elly's health?

Briana decided to drop the subject for now, but she intended to pursue it later.

Half an hour later, the two couples walked into the cavernous old town hall where the square-dance party was being held. The hall was decorated with paper hearts and red and white balloons, and the dance was already in progress. There was live music instead of the usual records.

They left their parkas in the cloak room, and Briana could hardly keep her feet still as they listened to the caller and waited for the set to finish. The hall was crowded, and the tempo was too fast to see anything but the swish of voluminous petticoats and the colorful Western attire of the men as they whirled around the floor.

At last the music stopped, and the newcomers were greeted by the dancers close to them. Briana knew quite a few, and Luke now introduced her to others. All made her feel welcome, and when the music started again, she and Luke got into a square with three other couples.

"Honor your partner," the caller chanted, and the men bowed while the women curtsied. "Join hands and circle left all the way around. Allemande left with your left hand, here we go with a right and left grand. Swing your partner and let her go, then proceed with a do-si-do."

Briana could feel the bouncy rhythm in every fibre of her being as she pranced and twirled to the commands. Her feet responded automatically to the steps, and her heart pounded with the pure joy of abandon as the melody and the beat and the warm, happy smiles and handclasps of the others in the square all came together to fuel her exuberance.

All too soon the call to "swing your partner and promenade home," signaled the end of that square. There was a pause to let the dancers catch their breaths before swinging into the round-dance mixer. In these, the couples formed a huge circle and danced in waltz or two-step time with the ladies moving up one at certain intervals, thus changing partners several times. Briana recognized this as an old one, a dreamy waltz.

Luke took her in his arms as the romantic melody set the mood. Minutes later she'd changed partners a number of times and was paying more attention to the music than the men as she moved up once more into the arms of still another when a low familiar voice murmured in her ear, "I've been telling myself all week that you couldn't possibly be as beautiful or as sweet as I recalled, but you're everything I remembered and more."

It was Hank Robinson. A shiver ran through her as he cradled her against his hard, muscular body. She melted into his embrace, but before she could gather her wits and answer, the music stopped and the round dance was over.

He didn't release her immediately, but continued to hold her as the other dancers swarmed by them on their way to the chairs lining the walls where they could sit for a few minutes and rest.

"I—I didn't know you were a square dancer," she stammered, knowing she should pull away from him, but not having the will to do so.

"And I didn't know you were," he said. "Are you . . . uh . . . involved with Luke Odell?"

She looked up at Hank and quirked one eyebrow. "Involved?"

"Are you dating him on a regular basis?"

"No."

"Good." Hank took her arm and escorted her over to where Luke stood talking to several people.

Luke smiled and reached out to take Briana's hand and tuck it in the crook of his elbow. "Hi, honey," he said. "I was wondering what happened to you. I should have known that Hank, here, would find the prettiest girl in the room. I gather you two have met."

He grinned at Hank, but there was a note of possessiveness in his tone that annoyed Briana.

Hank grinned back, but it didn't reach his eyes. "Sure have," he assured the other man. "She assisted when I had a tooth filled last week."

Then Hank looked up and his smile became genuine. "Here comes Molly," he said as a tall thin blond woman wearing a purple dress trimmed with rows of white rickrack joined them. "How about changing partners for the next dance." It didn't sound like a question.

Briana knew Molly Phelps, a beauty operator at the Cut 'N Curl salon on Main Street. According to Elly, she'd been divorced twice. That probably accounted for the cynical expression she habitually wore. Apparently she was Hank's date for the evening.

"Do you two know each other?" Hank asked.

"Yeah, we've met," Molly said. "She cleaned my teeth last time I went to the dentist for a checkup. How are you, Briana?"

"Fine, thank you," Briana replied.

The music once more called them to form squares, and Hank reached for Briana's hand while Luke took Molly's arm. Hank escorted Briana to a square that already had three other couples, and Luke and Molly continued on to another one.

Briana frowned. "Why do I get the feeling that I'm being politely but firmly abducted?"

Hank chuckled. "Because you are. I couldn't wait to dance with you again, and I didn't want Luke in the same square where he could glare at me."

She couldn't help but laugh. "Well, at least you're honest, but really, Hank, that wasn't very nice. What will Molly think?"

"She'll think I want to dance with you. There's nothing wrong with exchanging partners, it's done all the time...."

His last few words were drowned out by the caller as he began his patter. "Honor your partner. Now the lady to your left...."

They twirled and do-si-doed and formed a star, and every time Hank's arms went around Briana, he hugged her close to him. Her heart pounded and not just because of the strenuous footwork. She marveled that a man as big as he could be so agile and light on his feet. He didn't miss a step.

When the music ended, he again clasped her to him and murmured in her ear. "Come to the workshop with me next Friday."

"Workshop" was the term for the weekly dance sessions each club held for its own members, while the "parties" were held the second and fourth Saturdays of the month and were open to the public, with the two different clubs in the area taking turns sponsoring them.

Tell him no, her good sense warned. *You know what's going to happen if you get involved with this big, rugged bear of a man. You'll lose your heart as well as your precarious serenity.*

He brushed his lips against her temple and whispered, "Please."

She felt the gentle friction of his mouth against her skin all the way to her core.

Stop him! her good sense screamed. *Don't let him seduce you right here on the dance floor. Tell him you don't want to go out with him, and run back to nice, safe Luke.*

"I—I'd love to go to the workshop with you," she heard herself saying instead. "But I'm not a member of the club."

He hugged her even closer. "That doesn't matter. Membership's open, and we'd be happy to have you join. I'll pick you up at seven-thirty."

Briana overslept the following morning and awoke to a dark, overcast sky and gently falling snow. She sighed and reached for her warm, fuzzy robe. Although she'd spent the past four years in Denver before coming to Wyoming, she still missed the year-round sunshine of Southern California.

As she pulled on her fur-lined slippers and headed for the bathroom, she chided herself for her ambivalent loyalties. Los Angeles was the last place she'd ever expected to miss. As far as she was concerned, the sunshine was all it had going for it.

A prick of her conscience reminded her that she wasn't being fair. The first eight years of her life had been happy ones for her and her older brother and two younger sisters. It wasn't until a virus damaged their dad's heart and the paychecks stopped coming but the babies didn't that they started their descent into poverty and welfare.

The wave of pain that always accompanied her brief forays into nostalgia swept over her, and she grimly pushed all thoughts of the past from her mind. A glance at her watch told her that if she hurried, she could still make it to church for the last service. After that, she'd have Sunday dinner at Kasey's Kitchen and then maybe catch a movie matinee before coming back to the apartment to write the weekly letter to her mother. That schedule should keep her too busy for gloomy reminiscences.

By one-thirty, the snow had stopped falling as Briana turned the corner and headed toward the theater situated in the middle of the block. Her apartment was only three blocks from Main Street, and she preferred to leave her car in the garage and walk to the business district. She was young and healthy and enjoyed the exercise, but her Chevy was past its prime and tended to stall if it was parked for too long in the open.

As she neared the theater, she glanced at the marquee to see what was playing. Oh darn! She'd forgotten that the Sunday matinees were family movies, and today they were showing the rerelease of a vintage Disney classic. Not that she had anything against G-rated films, but she'd seen this one and it was too juvenile for her taste.

She hesitated at the door, trying to decide whether or not she wanted to go in when a familiar voice spoke. "What's the matter? Aren't you a Disney fan?"

She turned to find Hank standing just behind her right shoulder. A rush of elation made her grin. "Well, yes and no. *Sleeping Beauty* was a visual delight, and *Fantasia* a symphony in motion, but I draw the line at flying Volkswagens."

Hank's eyes sparkled as he chuckled. "Come now, where's your imagination? If Peter Pan can do it then why not a VW Beetle? If you're not here with anyone, join

Crystal and me. We'll let you share our supersize box of popcorn, won't we honey?''

Startled, Briana looked down to see an approximately three-foot-high child clinging to his hand. She was warmly clad in a blue snowsuit with overshoes, mittens and a thick, hand-knit stocking cap. All that was visible of the youngster herself was a delicate little face that beamed with excitement.

Briana blinked and fought back the stab of longing that always tormented her when confronted by a child this age. So this was Hank's daughter. He'd been right when he'd said she didn't look like him. She had high cheekbones that tapered down to a narrow chin, bright blue eyes and a small, turned up nose. Much too pixielike to resemble her robust father, but a beauty in her own right.

"We're going to have sodas, too," the little girl said happily. "You can have some of mine."

Briana's heart melted and her lips trembled through her smile. "That's very nice of you, Crystal," she said. "My name's Briana, and I'd be pleased to sit with you and your dad."

"Okay, but I get to be in the middle," Crystal said as she pushed the door open and plunged into the lobby.

Hank groaned audibly while Briana laughed. "She means it, too," he groused as they headed for the ticket booth. "There's no privacy for me to go courting with her around. I suspect that I'm doomed to spend the rest of my life as a single parent."

"Don't bet the farm on it," Briana teased. "Any woman with an ounce of determination knows how to get around a child."

His glance caught hers. "And are you determined?" he asked softly, with no trace of mirth.

A small gasp escaped her before she could stop it, and she tore her gaze from his.

"Not yet," she murmured, but knew that if she continued to see him, she would be. The question was, is that what she wanted? And more important, was it what *he* wanted?

When they'd chosen their seats, Hank removed Crystal's heavy wraps, and Briana could see that the child was slender and had long, curly dark brown hair. Briana couldn't help but wonder if she looked like her mother. If so, Hank must have been badly torn up at losing his beautiful wife.

Crystal bounced and squirmed through the first half of the movie, then crawled up on her daddy's lap and promptly fell asleep. When that happened, Hank motioned for Briana to move over into the seat next to him, then reached for her hand and entwined his fingers with hers.

He tucked their joined hands against the side of his chest and returned his attention to the screen, but the soft texture of his plaid flannel shirt and the steady beating of his heart under her bare skin was far more distracting than the movie. When it was over and the credits started to roll, she had no idea how it had ended. She suspected from the way his heart had speeded up that Hank hadn't been paying attention, either.

When he found out she was walking, Hank drove Briana home, but declined an invitation for him and Crystal to come in for a snack. "I'd love to," he said regretfully, "but we're due at my parents' house for supper in less than half an hour. Look, why don't you come, too? Mom would be happy to have you. She always cooks more than we can eat in one meal."

Briana didn't want to meet Hank's parents. Not yet. It was too soon. The very idea scared her to death. What would they think of her? They'd be sure to ask questions about her background. Questions she couldn't— wouldn't—answer. Later, maybe, but not now.

"I'm sorry," she said, "but I had a full meal at the restaurant before the movie." She unlatched the door on her side of the truck, then turned to look at Crystal strapped into her car seat between them. "Goodbye, Crystal, I had a great time with you and your daddy. Thanks for inviting me."

The little girl stared at her. "You can go with us again," she said as Hank opened his door and started to get out.

"Oh, no, Hank, don't bother coming to the door," Briana hastened to admonish. "You don't want to leave Crystal in the truck alone. Thanks for the movie—and the popcorn and the ride. I really enjoyed it."

She stepped out of the truck as Hank got back inside. "Are you sure you'll be all right?" he asked anxiously. "We'll wait here until you get inside the house. Don't forget, you're going square dancing with me Friday night."

"I won't," she assured him, and shut the door. "Bye, Crystal." She raised her arm and waved, then turned and was inside the house before she heard the truck pull away.

An hour later, Briana was curled up at one end of the couch, writing a letter to her mother, when she heard the front door close and footsteps on the stairs, then a knock on her door.

Her heart actually leapt. Could it be Hank? Had he left Crystal with his parents and come back?

A glance out the front window dashed her unrealistic hopes when she saw Elly's white Toyota Celica, a gift from her parents on her twenty-first birthday last year, parked on the street.

Before Briana could put aside her stationery and get up, the knob turned and the door opened just enough to admit Elly's head. "Where have you been all day?" she blurted as she swung into the room. "I've been here twice and called three times."

Briana was dumbfounded. Sweet, even-tempered Elly was not only being unreasonably demanding, but it was evident that she'd been crying. Her face was pale, and her eyes and nose were pink.

Briana jumped up, spilling her writing things onto the floor. "Elly, what's the matter? Here, let me have your coat."

She took Elly's coat and tossed it across a chair as she motioned toward the couch. "Sit down and tell me what's happened," she said as she picked up her paper and pen before settling down again on the sofa.

"Ted Thurston asked me to marry him last night," Elly replied.

"And?"

Elly looked up. "What do you mean, *'and'*?"

Now it was Briana who was confused. "I mean, *and* what happened to upset you so? You've been dating Ted pretty steadily since I came here, and he seems like a nice guy. A proposal shouldn't send you into hysterics."

"I'm not hysterical," Elly snapped, "and I never intended for Ted to fall in love with me. I didn't mean to hurt him, I just wanted people to think of us as a couple so they wouldn't guess— Oh, never mind. I shouldn't have come. I—" She covered her face with her hands.

"Elly, please, I want to help you," Briana said as she caressed the other woman's shoulder, "but first I have to know what the problem is. Try to pull yourself together while I get us a drink.''

Briana went to the kitchen and poured them each a whiskey and soda. Apparently she'd been right on target last night when she'd insisted that something was bothering her friend. She hadn't pried when Elly denied it, but today she wasn't going to be put off.

''Here, sip this,'' she said when she returned to the living room and handed Elly one of the glasses, then sat down beside her. ''I said last night that you could talk to me if you were troubled, and I meant it. Surely you know that you can trust me not to reveal any secrets—if that's what's holding you back.''

''Yes. No...Oh, I don't know.'' Elly's tone was more of a cry than a statement. She took a swallow of her whiskey and tried again. ''I shouldn't have come here. It's time I started working out my own problems, but I just keep getting in deeper.''

A tug of apprehension made Briana catch her breath. Dear heaven, what had Elly gotten herself into? She was only a year younger than Briana, but Briana was a lifetime ahead of her in plain old street smarts.

''Look, honey,'' Briana began tentatively. ''Everybody's entitled to help when the going gets rough. I was raised in one of the poverty pockets of Los Angeles and I've seen people mess up their lives in more ways than you can imagine. I'm not going to be either shocked or judgmental, if that's what's worrying you.''

Elly sat quietly turning her glass around in her hands, and Briana leaned back to give the other woman the space she needed to make a difficult decision.

Finally Elly looked up and gazed directly at Briana. ''I can't marry Ted because I'm in love with Quentin York.''

Quentin York? The name was familiar to Briana, but she couldn't put a face with it. Quentin York... Oh, yes, now she remembered. He was the principal of the high school whom she'd met at the party last night. He and his wife...

Wife! Quentin York was married!

Chapter Three

Briana made a massive effort not to let the consternation that tore through her show on her face. So much for her smug assumption that she was shockproof! Not that playing around with a married man was all that unusual, but for Elly to do so was unthinkable.

No wonder she'd lost her sparkle and her sense of fun. Elly was the most morally straight young woman Briana had ever known. As the only child of two puritanical parents, who were middle-aged when she was born, she had been raised in the protective bunting of handpicked friends, early curfews and outdated dress codes.

During the two years she was in college and away from them, she had become more flexible, but she was still a virgin when she graduated. It had been her choice. She'd said she wanted her husband to be her first lover.

Briana stifled a moan at the possibility that some middle-aged, married philanderer had robbed Elly of that innocence.

"All right, go ahead and say it," Elly said stoically. "Falling in love with another woman's husband is a despicable thing to do. I won't blame you if you hate me."

She looked and sounded so guilty that Briana hurried to reassure her. "Oh, Elly, I could never hate you. You just surprised me. I hadn't expected—"

"You didn't expect me to confess that I'm having an affair with a married man," Elly snapped. "Well, neither did I. I sure never set out to—"

"Affair!" Briana couldn't keep the anguish out of her tone. "Elly, are you sleeping with him?"

"No!" Elly shouted, then paused to lower her voice. "Not yet, but it's getting so hard to resist—" A sob cut off her ability to speak.

Briana put her arms around her friend's shaking shoulders. "Go ahead and cry," she said softly. "Get it all out of your system, and then we'll talk. We don't always pick the men we fall in love with, and few of us can withstand the temptation to go to bed with them. I suspect that you're punishing yourself a great deal more than anyone else would." *Except probably his wife,* she amended silently.

Elly shook her head and blew her nose. "You don't know how vicious the gossips in a small town can be. They can and do tear a reputation to shreds with their recriminations and rumors and insinuations. Quentin is a school administrator. He'd lose his job if it ever got out that he was...uh...seeing me."

"Yes, I imagine he would," Briana agreed. "I gather the two of you have been meeting somewhere?"

Elly nodded. "Yes." Unable to sit still, she rose and started to pace. "Oh, God, I know it's wrong, and I hate myself afterwards, but when he calls and asks me to come I—I just leave whatever I'm doing at the time and go to him."

"Where?"

Elly stopped pacing, but it was several seconds before she answered. "In a storage room in the basement of the high school."

"The school!" Briana couldn't believe she'd heard right. "Good heavens, Elly, whatever possessed you to pick the school? It's nearly always in use with classes during the day and activities in the auditorium at night."

Elly started pacing again. "I know, but it's the place where Quentin is expected to be, and he has a key, so no one is surprised to see him there at any time."

Briana sighed. "Do you still insist that you and Quentin aren't making love?"

Elly stopped and looked directly at Briana. "Of course, we're making love," she said with a touch of scorn. "Even I have to admit that, but we're not...not going all the way, if you know what I mean."

"I know what you mean," Briana said sadly, and she bit back a stronger warning about the chances they were taking. Quentin would have thought of that since he had the most to lose, so they must be taking reasonable precautions against being caught.

She picked up Elly's drink from the coffee table and held it out as she patted the cushion beside her. "Here, sit down and drink this while we talk. It'll help calm your nerves."

Elly raised the glass to her mouth while Briana settled back on the sofa. "How did you ever get involved with this guy?"

Elly, too, leaned back and seemed to relax a little. "He was hired last summer to replace Mr. Polhemus, who retired. I met him when he came into the office with an abscessed tooth. Dad managed to save it, but Quentin had other teeth that needed work, so he was in the office a lot."

She sat forward and drank the rest of her bourbon and soda. "We didn't intend to get involved." Her voice was strained. "You've got to believe that. It just happened. We were attracted to each other right from the beginning, but we didn't do anything about it until..."

She paused as though unwilling to go on, but then sighed and sank back again. "It—it was the square dancing that threw us together. He and Janelle, his wife, came to the beginning classes the club held last fall. The new dancers paired with experienced ones to make it easier to learn the steps, and Quentin and I just seemed to—to gravitate toward each other. I know now that we were playing with fire, but it felt only a little wicked at the time."

To you, maybe, but you can bet Quentin knew what he was doing. Briana wasn't willing to give him the benefit of the doubt. If he'd really been falling in love with Elly, he'd have stayed as far away from her as he could get. Honorable men didn't play games with naive women almost half their age, but pointing this out to her wouldn't do any good right now.

"By the time I woke up to what was happening, it was too late," Elly continued. "Whenever Quentin put his arms around me, I—I just melted. I couldn't help it. Especially in the round dances that have more body contact and are slower."

Briana could relate to that. She'd had the same reaction last night while dancing with Hank. But Hank wasn't married!

Damn Quentin York. He had to be in his late thirties. Old enough to know what he was doing, and he was a real jerk to seduce an innocent like Elly. She not only didn't know how to play the game, she didn't even know it *was* a game.

Again Elly stood, too distraught to relax. "It's not as if I was responsible for breaking up their marriage." Her voice was tight, almost self-righteous. "It's been a sham for years. They haven't been...you know...intimate for months."

Briana almost groaned aloud. The old my-wife-is-frigid bit. Dear Lord, men were signing that line before language was invented! She bit back an unladylike oath and reminded herself to go easy with her opinion of Quentin or risk pushing Elly even closer to surrender. "I'm sorry his marriage is an unhappy one, but if it's that bad, why don't they get a divorce?"

"Because his wife is a bitch who makes his life miserable, but won't let him go," Elly said through clenched teeth. "She's threatened to file for sole custody of the children with no visitation rights if he leaves her."

"Children!" It was a cross between a yelp and a screech that slipped out before Briana could stop it. She took a deep breath and prayed that she could sound calm. "You didn't tell me there were children."

Elly nodded miserably. "Two. A boy, twelve, and a girl, ten. Don't you see? They're old enough to get the wrong impression if they found out about Quentin and me. Their mother would be sure to make our love sound like something cheap and dirty."

Elly, my artless, unsuspecting friend, how can you be so trusting? Open your eyes and take a good look at what's going on before this man breaks your heart and ruins your life.

Briana pressed her lips together to keep the words from exploding out of her. It wouldn't do any good to rail at Elly, she was feeling guilty enough. The only way Briana could help her was to find out what was going on in Quentin York's devious mind and try to put a stop to it.

Elly was pacing again, and it was obvious that she was too upset to go into this any further tonight. Briana stood, too. "You need some sleep," she said gently. "Why don't you go home and go to bed? Otherwise you won't be worth a darn at work in the morning. Come over for dinner tomorrow night, and we'll talk more then."

Elly agreed, but it didn't quite work out that way. She still lived with her parents, and when she didn't come to work the following morning, Dr. Wainwright said she'd awakened with a bad cold. At first Briana was afraid it might be an emotional breakdown that she was hiding from her parents, but later that afternoon, the dentist told her that his daughter had been to the doctor, who'd diagnosed it as the flu. She probably wouldn't be able to come back to work for a couple of weeks.

Briana wanted to visit her, but Dr. Wainwright asked her not to. "I'd have to close the office if you got sick, too," he warned.

With Elly out, Briana was swamped trying to pinch-hit as chairside assistant as well as keep up with her own duties, and she didn't see Hank again until he arrived for their date on Friday evening.

She'd been looking forward to this all week, and when she heard his footsteps on the stairs and his knock on her door, her heart sped up. She couldn't contain the happy smile that lit her face as she opened the door and saw him standing there looking like a burly giant in boots, tight-fitting jeans and a heavy, sheepskin-lined jacket. He held his cowboy hat in his hand and beamed at her.

"How do you manage to look prettier every time I see you?" he asked huskily as he stepped into the living room. "Especially since you started out way ahead of any other woman I've ever known."

"Thank you. You're not so bad yourself," she told him. "Don't think I missed the envious glances I got from the ladies at the movie theater. Speaking of which, how's your beautiful little daughter?"

Hank laughed. "Crystal's just fine. When she found out I had a date with you tonight, she wanted to come along."

"You should have brought her."

His laughter stilled. "And have her parked between us all evening? No way. I hired a baby-sitter."

There it was again, that magnetism that shimmered between them every time they were together. Even the most innocent banter took on a heated meaning.

"I—I've made fresh coffee if you'd like a cup before we leave," she stammered.

"You bet," he said, and began unbuttoning his jacket.

They sat at the kitchen table, and Hank looked around. "You've sure made this place homey. I'll bet those ruffled curtains didn't come with the furnished apartment."

"You're right, I made them and the slipcover on the couch. I'm going to refinish the coffee and lamp tables when it gets warmer so I can work outside."

"Hey, I can do that for you. Woodworking's my hobby. I have all the tools and a workshop in my basement."

"Well...thank you," she said hesitantly, "but I'm afraid I can't afford to have them done professionally."

Hank frowned. "I wasn't intending to charge you, but if you'd prefer, you can bring the tables over and work on them there. I'd like to help...unless you'd rather I didn't...."

She could see that she'd hurt him. Reaching out, she put her hand over his where it lay on the table. "I'm sorry, Hank. I didn't mean to be rude. I just assumed...I mean, in the city where I was raised, nobody does anything like that for free."

He turned his hand over and grasped hers. "Tell me about your life in Los Angeles. Are your parents still there? Do you have brothers and sisters? What does your dad do for a living?"

Briana felt caught. He'd asked her these questions before, and she'd managed to evade them, but this time she had to answer. There was no way she could gracefully avoid it.

"I have four brothers and two sisters. Seven of us altogether. One brother is older than I, and the rest of them are younger. My dad died eight years ago, and Mother works as a waitress in a restaurant in Hollywood."

Hank's expression softened, and he squeezed her hand gently. "I'm sorry about your father. What happened?"

Briana took a deep breath. "It was a viral infection of his heart."

He shook his head. "That's rough. He must have been fairly young."

She took a swallow of hot coffee. "He was forty," she said sadly. "My youngest brother doesn't even remember him."

Hank opened his mouth to comment, but Briana didn't want to go any more deeply into her family's problems.

She withdrew her hand from his and changed the subject. "If the offer's still open, I'd love to work with you on refinishing my tables. I can do the work, and you can tell me how."

She saw the look of understanding in his eyes, and he followed her lead. "Great. Next week I have a Scout meeting on Monday night and a tutoring session on Wednesday, but we could get started on either Tuesday or Thursday, whichever is best for you."

Briana had heard that he was Scout leader for one of the town's two Boy Scout troops, but tutoring?

"Whom do you tutor?" she asked.

He looked a little embarrassed. "Oh, I have a group of seventh- and eighth-grade students who need help with math. I was always pretty good in it, so I have them over to the house once a week and give them some individual instruction."

She smiled and caught his furtive glance. "You should have studied to be a teacher. You obviously like children."

He grinned. "I do, and I do have teaching credentials. At college, I majored in education and minored in business."

Briana was amazed. Hank didn't look or act like any teacher she'd ever known. He was so obviously the outdoor type, big and strong and burning with energy.

"You do? Then why aren't you teaching full-time?"

"I hope to, someday." His tone held a note of wistfulness. "That's why I went for the credentials, but I've always known that my parents expected me to be a partner in the family business, and that has to come first. They're in their sixties and are talking about taking their motor home to Tucson next winter, where my sister lives, and spending the coldest months there."

He drank the rest of his coffee. "I suspect that will be the first step toward retirement, so I'll be needed full-time at the store for several more years, but eventually, I'd like to hire a manager and take up teaching."

He had an animated look on his face as he spoke that told her better than words that this was his dream. A dream he'd willingly postpone for many years in order to fulfill what he considered his obligation to the dream of his parents.

Briana felt a lump in her throat, and silly tears of admiration burned at the back of her eyes for this gentle powerhouse of a man who saw nothing unusual about his selflessness.

She cleared her throat and again put her hand over his. "You're a very nice person, Hank Robinson," she said huskily.

A faint flush of red brushed his cheeks as he brought her hand to his lips and kissed the palm. "We'd better get out of here before I start telling you what a sweetheart you are." His tone was thick with emotion. "If we get started on that, it just might lead to something we're not ready for."

His confession that he was as vitally aware of the attraction between them as she was sent a shiver of exhilaration through her. He was admitting that he wanted her, but he was holding back, unwilling to rush her into anything more intimate before she was ready.

Briana hadn't known many truly honorable men. What a contrast Hank was to Quentin York. If only Elly could have fallen in love with someone like him, but unfortunately, men like Hank Robinson were rare.

He let go of her and stood. "Come on, lady, get a move on. We've got some serious dancing to do."

The weekly workshops, held in the elementary school auditorium, provided a chance for the caller and dancers to try out new calls and learn new steps. Briana was welcomed enthusiastically and invited to join the group. She accepted and was having a wonderful time until Quentin and Janelle York arrived.

Briana had met the couple at the square-dance party last week, but they'd been something of a blur among all the strangers she'd been introduced to. Now she watched them closely. Quentin was nice-looking. Not exactly handsome, but he had a wide smile and the open, winning personality of a successful salesman.

It wasn't hard to believe that a trusting woman like Elly would succumb if he turned on the full force of his charm.

Janelle seemed nothing like Elly's description of her. She was approximately the same age as her husband, but plain and shy. Her brown hair was clean, but dull and too long for her round face and short neck. Her waist had thickened with childbearing, making her appear matronly in her billowing skirt and petticoat.

She looked more like a tired housewife and mother than the bitch Elly claimed she was.

It was also evident that she was in love with her husband, and he was attentive, called her "honey" and seemed content to be with her.

What was going on here, anyway? Was it possible that Elly was kidding herself? Imagining a relationship where none existed?

But there wouldn't be any point in that. She wasn't making herself happy, but miserable, and besides, Elly wasn't a dreamer, she was a doer.

No, if she said Quentin York was coming on to her, then he was. She wouldn't fantasize something like that, but he was doing a remarkable job of hiding it from his wife and the community.

Although the thermometer hovered at near zero outside, dancing was strenuous exercise and body temperatures soared. During one of the breaks, Hank took Briana out in the hall where there was a vending machine and bought her an ice-cold cola.

She drank it gratefully. "Oh, that tastes good. I was thirsty."

He took a swig of his. "Why didn't you say something? I would have gotten you one sooner."

She laughed. "I could have bought my own, but I didn't know the machine was here." A shiver ran through her as the cold from the chilly hall finally penetrated.

Hank put his arm around her and pulled her close as several other couples came out looking for soft drinks.

"You're going to catch cold," he told her, and led her around the corner out of sight of the others.

They stopped and leaned against the wall as he circled her waist with both arms and rubbed his cheek against hers. It was smooth, fresh shaven, and the faint fragrance of shaving lotion, musky and male, was tantalizingly exciting.

"Ah, that's better," he said. "I've been wanting to just stand still and hold you all evening. Are you having fun?"

She snuggled against him. "I'm having a marvelous time," she assured him as her body reacted in strange and wonderful ways to the strength and the warmth of his. "Everyone is so friendly. I suppose most of the families in town have lived here for generations."

He nibbled at her earlobe, sending tremors down her spine. "Yeah, they have," he murmured. "Although with each generation, we lose more of our young people to the cities. Many of those who go off to college never return."

Briana had trouble keeping her mind on what he was saying as his hands roamed lightly over her back.

"But new families move in," she reminded him dreamily. "People get assigned to jobs here—forest rangers and conservationists and teachers...."

Teachers. Now that she'd inadvertently brought that subject up, it was time to come out of the web of magic he was weaving around them and ask some questions. If only she didn't have to break the spell to do it.

His palms were coming closer to the sides of her breasts, and much as she longed for his touch, she had to stop him. It was too soon. She wasn't going to rush headlong into a relationship with any man, certainly not one she'd only known a couple of weeks. She knew she wouldn't be able to resist this one for long if she let him too close.

She shifted slightly so that his hand was on the middle of her back as she forced her mind away from the pleasure he was giving her. "I understand Quentin and Janelle York are quite new in town," she said unsteadily. "Do you know them well?"

Hank seemed to understand that she was asking him to back off a little. Although he still held her close, his wandering hands settled on the broad part of her back, and he raised his head so that his cheek no longer rested on hers. She felt both relieved and forsaken.

"Pretty well," he said. "I'm a member of the school board that hired Quent. He came to us from a high school in Casper. We've had a few meals together, and I was the one who invited them to join the square-dance club. Their son is in my Boy Scout troop."

"You're a member of the school board, too?" Briana was too amazed to be tactful. "For heaven's sake, how do you find time to work?"

Hank chuckled, but his voice was husky. "I like to keep busy. I was married for seven years, and I got used to having someone else around. After DeeDee left, I was lonely. I had Crystal, and she's always been a joy, but she's a little young for profound conversations...."

The music started up again just then and snapped him out of his reverie. He released her, but then reached for her hand. "Sounds like they're ready to dance again," he said with a gaiety that sounded forced. "We'd better get back into the auditorium."

Briana smiled so he wouldn't see how disappointed she was. He'd just started opening up to her. She wondered if she'd ever be able to coax him into doing it again.

She wanted to know everything about Hank Robinson. His joy and his pain. His successes and his failures. And most of all, she wanted to know about his marriage and how badly the divorce had damaged him.

The workshop lasted from eight o'clock to eleven, and as it was breaking up, Quentin and Janelle invited Hank and Briana to stop by their home, where they would be serving refreshments to several of the couples. Briana would have preferred to take Hank back to her apartment where they could be alone together, but the very potency of that desire warned her it would be a dangerous move.

"It's sort of an informal custom," Hank informed her in the truck as they drove to the Yorks' home. "Those of us who want to, take turns acting as hosts and invite three or four couples over after the workshop for a little get-together. There's not much time for visiting when we're dancing.''

"It sounds like fun," Briana said, but she was thinking that this was a great opportunity to get to know Quentin and Janelle better. Her gut feeling told her that he was a womanizer who was playing with Elly, but who would never leave his wife and family. Still, she couldn't be sure. He didn't fit the usual profile of such a man.

As they parked in front of a turn-of-the-century-style, two-story house, Briana vowed to herself that she was going to find out what kind of man Quentin York really was.

There was ice under the snow and Hank put his arm around her after he helped her from the car. "Be careful that you don't slip," he said, and hugged her closer as they climbed the numerous steps that led to the wraparound porch.

The outside light was on, but there was only a faint illumination from inside the house. Apparently the children were asleep, and the baby-sitter was either watching television or reading. Obviously Hank and Briana were the first to arrive.

When they got to the door, he didn't immediately release her or push the bell, but turned her so that she stood full length against him. Their heavy coats made for an embrace that was more frustrating than intimate. He brushed the fingers of his other hand through her hair as his gaze locked with hers, then slid to her slightly parted lips.

"I want to kiss you." His tone was ragged with longing. "I don't think I've ever wanted to kiss a woman as badly as I want to kiss you."

She knew the feeling. She was quite sure that if he didn't stop talking and take her mouth right now, she was going to die of wanting. "Then why don't you?" she asked softly.

He cradled the back of her head as he lowered his face until their lips almost touched. "With the light on?"

The cold steams of their breaths mingled visibly in the freezing air, and she wouldn't have cared if someone had turned a spotlight on them. "Yes." It was barely more than a whisper, but he understood.

His arm tightened around her, and his mouth finally covered hers. His lips were cold, their texture rough, but his kiss was warm and tender. A tentative beginning to the promise of paradise.

The promise was never fulfilled as the screech of tires on the slippery street and the sound of a car braking in the driveway shattered the enchantment and pulled them apart.

Hank muttered an explicit oath, then looked at her and grinned. "Sorry, I meant to say *shoot.*"

"Of course, you did," she acknowledged with a teasing giggle as they turned to greet their host and hostess, but her heart was pounding. If that sample was a preview of Hank's lovemaking technique, she wanted more. But more of that could lead to a repeat of a mistake she'd already made once.

A mistake so grave that she'd carry the emotional carnage with her for the rest of her life.

Hank clenched his gloved fists into his coat pockets to ensure that he wouldn't reach for Briana again. Lord, he'd barely touched his lips to hers, but the sweetness and pleasure were so great that when the noise of the car had startled them into jumping apart, it was an actual physical shock. His heart was racing, and his nerves felt raw.

This whole thing was getting out of hand. He'd known it would from the first time he'd seen her, so why hadn't he stayed away from her?

He shook his head to clear it. He'd intended to put her out of his mind and ignore her, was even doing a pretty good job of it until she showed up at the square-dance party. The minute he'd put his arms around her, he'd been a goner. She had him so befuddled that he'd asked her out before he was thinking straight again.

Thinking straight, hell! He hadn't been able to do that where she was concerned since she stroked his cheek that first day and made him forget all about his toothache.

Chapter Four

The interlude at the York home was great fun. Briana
had learned in Denver that square dancers were about the
friendliest people in the world, and the ones in Whispering Pines were no different. She'd made several new
friends tonight, Quentin and Janelle York among them,
and if Quentin was cheating on his wife, Briana was quite
sure Janelle didn't know it.

Briana didn't have a chance to talk to Quentin alone
until just before she left, when Hank had gone with Janelle to get their coats. She'd been thanking Quentin for
inviting her over, and during a rather awkward pause, she
decided to do a little probing. "I understand you've only
lived in Whispering Pines for a few months. How do you
like such a small town? It must seem pretty dull after
Casper."

He stiffened, and she felt the chill of his displeasure as
his smile disappeared and his expression became inscru-

table. "Not as dull as it must seem to you after living and working in Denver," he snapped.

Briana was caught off guard by his quickness to take offense at her innocuous question. So much for her efforts at discreet inquiry. "Touché," she said in admission of her prying. "But I don't find it dull at all. I hope you like it as much as I do."

He nodded. "I'm sure I do," he said, and walked away.

Well, she'd probably asked for that rebuff, but why was he so thin-skinned? There was no reason for him to take offense at her question. He must have heard it many times before.

It was only natural that people would wonder why he'd left a more prestigious and considerably higher paying position with the school district in Casper, a town of over forty thousand people, to accept the same position with much lower pay and prestige in a village of less than four thousand.

Later, on the way home, Hank seemed preoccupied, and Briana was wrestling with her own uncertainties. Should she invite him in when they got to her apartment?

It wasn't yet midnight, but it was reaching a bit to ask him in for coffee when they'd already had all they could drink. Would he take it as a come-on? On the other hand, they'd never really been alone together for any length of time. They shared this powerful physical attraction, but knew so little about each other....

Before she got her thoughts sorted out, they were stopped in front of her building. Hank went in and up the stairs with her. As she unlocked her door, she spoke before she could change her mind. "Would you like to come in for a while?"

Hank took her by the shoulders and turned her to him. He looked troubled. "I'd love to, but I can't." He spoke softly, and his restless fingers pressed through her coat. "The baby-sitter has a curfew."

His hands moved upward to cup the sides of her head and tip her face up to his. He kissed the tip of her nose. "Thanks for making this a wonderful evening," he said, and brushed his lips lightly across her forehead. "You're a very special lady, and I—I..."

He didn't finish the sentence but lowered his head and took her mouth, gently, but with a hunger that fueled an answering yearning in her. She reached up and wrapped her hands around his wrists as his tongue rimmed her lips. She opened to him and allowed him the intimacy he desired.

He tasted of coffee and chocolate and a nectar that was his alone—male and musky. Briana felt as though she were drowning in a sea of swirling emotions and clasped his wrists even tighter to keep from sinking.

She wanted to press her body against his, but their coats were in the way. If they'd put their arms around each other, they could get closer, but he was actually holding her away with his hands on either side of her head.

He withdrew his tongue and sucked on her lower lip, sending waves of excitement buffeting through her. She wanted to respond, to pleasure him as much as he was pleasuring her, but except for digging her fingers into his wrists, she didn't know how.

Again he covered her mouth with his in a series of short, intense kisses that coaxed a low moan from deep in her throat. It was then that he slowly released her lips and raised his head.

"Good night, Briana," he murmured huskily. "I—I'll call you."

For a moment his hands remained in place as their gazes clung, then he removed them and hurried down the stairs and out the front door.

Briana leaned against the wall and let the ethereal enchantment swirl around her. She felt light-headed and shivery inside, and her mist-shrouded mind refused to let Hank go. It kept replaying that fantastic kiss—so sweet, so compelling, so fraught with yearning.

Oh, Hank, what are you doing to me? I don't trust men, not even you, and with good reason. I let down my guard for a minute, and you stole my heart. It's not a whole heart, it's been broken and only partially mended. I want you to let it go before it gets shattered beyond repair.

Hank climbed into the truck, started the engine and pulled away from the curb. He tried to keep his mind on his driving, but he was still reeling from the cauldron of emotions his brief contact with Briana had stirred in him.

One kiss! Just one short buss on that soft, sweet mouth and he was reduced to jelly, with one vital exception. That part of him that was hard and throbbing even though he'd held her away so they'd have no body contact below the shoulders.

Damn! At least he'd known better than to go into the apartment with her. If he had, they'd have spent the night making love, and that was a certainty, not just a hope.

Not that he suspected Briana of being easy. He knew she wasn't. Nor was he supremely confident of his sexual prowess. He'd been turned down at times, mostly by his wife. DeeDee had been a willing lover before he married her, but once the vows had been spoken, she'd cooled off quickly.

No, he knew Briana wouldn't hold out if he tried to seduce her. The chemistry between them was too strong to be one-sided. She felt it, too. He read it in her eyes and felt it in her reaction to his touch.

She vibrated every time he put his arms around her. So did he. He lit up inside like a light bulb when they made physical contact. She turned him on as no other woman ever had, but that wasn't the real problem.

He could control his sexual urges. It was the deep-seated need he felt to merge their souls as well as their bodies that scared him.

DeeDee had taught him that women couldn't be trusted. Being publicly cuckolded made a skeptic of any man, and Hank wasn't about to give another woman a crack at him.

On the other hand, he wanted a strong family life like the one he'd been raised in. He also hoped to have more children, so he'd probably marry someday, if he could find someone who loved Crystal and would be a good mother.

When the time came, he'd choose a second wife carefully. Never again would he marry for love!

Briana spent a restless night haunted by conflicting desires: the longing Hank inspired and the urgent need to protect herself from another wrenching upheaval such as the one Scott had subjected her to. She couldn't have it both ways.

If she got more deeply involved with Hank, she'd have to tell him about her past, and every instinct told her that he wouldn't understand.

By morning she was so overwrought from the agonizing memories her retrospection had released that she knew what her course of action had to be. When Hank called her, she'd tell him she wouldn't see him again, that she preferred to play the field rather than become involved with one man exclusively.

But he didn't call. Not Saturday and not Sunday.

Monday was Presidents Day, a holiday, and the schools, offices and shops were all closed. Briana didn't have to work, but neither did she want to spend another day at home listening for the phone to ring. The suspense was driving her crazy.

The longer she waited, the less certain she was that breaking up with Hank was what she wanted to do. Not that two dates and a chance encounter could be considered a relationship, but she felt as if it were. That goodnight kiss had led her to believe that their feelings for each other went far deeper than a casual friendship.

Had she been wrong in thinking her ardor was reciprocated? Was Hank Robinson just a shallow flirt who came on to every attractive woman who crossed his path, then lost interest when the next one came along?

No. She didn't believe that for a minute. She had probably misunderstood his promise to call her. She'd assumed he meant in the next few hours, when he obviously was talking about sometime in the next few days.

Briana dressed in jeans and a salmon-colored sweatshirt, and was searching for her tennis shoes when the telephone rang. She jumped and hastily backed out of the closet, then took a deep breath. She'd had several calls over the weekend, but none of them had been from Hank. There was no reason to think this one was, either.

She forced herself to walk sedately to the phone and answer with a businesslike "hello."

The sound of the voice that answered tied her stomach in knots. "Hello, Briana, this is Hank."

After three days of waiting for him to call, she didn't want to talk to him after all. If she did, she'd have to tell him she didn't want to go out with him again, and she wasn't sure she'd be able to tell a lie of that magnitude.

Her first impulse was to hang up, but that was childish. Maybe it wouldn't hurt to wait awhile before making such an important decision. Maybe when she knew him better, the attraction would wear off and they'd just be friends after all. Maybe... Maybe... Maybe...

"Briana, are you there?" Hank sounded disturbed. Apparently she'd hesitated too long and had alarmed him.

"I'm here, Hank," she assured him. "I was just...just trying to remember where I put my other shoe. How are you?"

"Fine. Look, I—I need to talk to you. Do you mind if I come over?"

It was a simple request, but he seemed to be having trouble making it.

This was the time to tell him no, that she couldn't see him, that she was going out with someone else.

But it seemed so cruel to do it on the telephone. The least she could do was let him come over and listen to what he had to say, then tell him in person of her decision.

"Please do," she said.

"Would you... That is, would you mind if I bring Crystal with me?"

Crystal? His little daughter?

"No, of course, I don't mind," she said, trying to keep her surprise out of her tone. "I'd love to see her again."

"Okay, thanks. We'll be there in about twenty minutes."

It was only fifteen minutes later when Briana saw Hank's Silverado stop in front of her apartment building. During that time she'd brushed her heavy black hair until it shone, applied a light coat of lipstick and found her shoes.

She stood at the picture window, watching as Hank lifted Crystal out of the vehicle and carried her to the porch. The sunshine bounced off the white snow and sparkled so brightly that it hurt her eyes.

Briana opened her door when she heard Crystal's small feet bounding up the stairs, with her daddy's heavy tread just behind her. With childish glee, the little girl threw out her arms and ran straight to Briana, nearly knocking her down.

Briana wrapped her arms around the child in an effort to keep her balance, and received a warm hug in response. She looked up to see Hank standing directly behind his daughter with laughter brimming in his eyes.

"I seem to be in line," he said lightly. "Do I get one of those, too?"

It didn't even occur to Briana to refuse as Crystal went into the living room and she moved into Hank's arms.

They closed around her in a hard embrace, and his mouth claimed hers for a quick, probing kiss before he released her and followed Crystal into the apartment.

"We're going to see Grandma and Grandpa Perkins," Crystal announced as Hank shut the door behind him. "They've got lot's 'n' lots of chickens, and a cow that goes 'mooo.'"

Hank's unexpected hug and kiss had almost overwhelmed Briana, and she struggled to pay attention to what the child was saying. "They do?" she asked somewhat vaguely. "I'll bet that's a fun place to go. Do they let you gather eggs?"

Crystal's little brow puckered. "No," she said uncertainly, then beamed. "But Grandma lets me take the eggs out of the nests and put them in her basket. I have to be really, really careful.''

Her enthusiasm was catching, and Briana laughed. "That's right, you wouldn't want to break any of them. Do you milk the cow, too?"

The little girl's expressive mouth turned down. "No, Grandpa does that, but he lets me give some of the milk to Sleepy and Sneezy."

Briana's eyes widened. "Oh, and who are Sleepy and Sneezy?"

Crystal giggled. "They're the kitties."

Briana managed an exaggerated gasp. "They've got kitties, too?" Her voice rang with feigned surprise. "You're sure lucky to have such a great place to visit."

"Yeah," Crystal agreed. "You can come with us. Maybe Grandpa will let you milk Betsy—"

That's when Hank intervened. "Whoa, there, Cinderella. Slow down and give someone else a chance to talk."

He hunkered before her and unzipped the jacket of her snowsuit.

"I'm not Cinderella," she protested. "I'm Dopey."

Both Hank and Briana laughed, and Hank pulled off her stocking cap and ruffled her hair. "You got that right, kid," he said lovingly, and slid her arms out of her jacket. "If you're good, maybe Briana will let you watch cartoons on her television." He looked at Briana hopefully.

She got the message. "Sure you can. First we'll fix some hot chocolate, and then we'll put up a TV tray in my bedroom. You can take the chocolate and some cookies in there and sit on my bed while you watch television."

Crystal wiggled with excitement as Hank pulled her heavy snow pants off. "Can I have marshmallows, too?"

Briana took her by the hand and led her toward the kitchen. "Of course. Whoever heard of hot chocolate without marshmallows?"

Briana made coffee, as well, and when the chocolate milk was warm, she poured it into a plastic glass she'd bought at a take-out restaurant. It had a top that snapped on with a hole in the middle just big enough for a straw.

"I don't know about this," Hank said as she put the cup and a plate of Girl Scout cookies on a TV tray in the bedroom. "She's apt to spill something."

"I doubt it, but it won't matter if she does," Briana assured him. "Everything in here is washable."

A few minutes later, they left Crystal curled up on the bed, contentedly sipping hot chocolate, eating cookies and watching the Disney Channel.

They stopped in the kitchen, and Briana arranged more cookies on another plate, while Hank poured their steaming coffee into thick mugs. "You're awfully good with Crystal," he said thoughtfully. "You must have had a lot of experience with children."

Not nearly as much as I'd like to have had, she thought, then quickly erased it. "Crystal is an easy youngster to relate to," she said instead, "but I helped raise my brothers and sisters. Mom had to work because Dad was sick, so it was up to me to look after the kids and fix dinner when I got home from school. You're right—I have had a lot of hands-on practice."

They took their coffee and cookies into the living room and put them on the low table. Briana sat down on the sofa, and Hank settled there, too, but at the other end, a foot or more away from her. When he spoke again, it was on the same subject.

"Having all that responsibility must have been rough. You couldn't have been more than a kid yourself. I'll bet you resented it—I know I would have."

Briana had the feeling that her answers to his questions were important to him, but she couldn't imagine why.

She shrugged. "You do what you have to," she said philosophically. "They were good kids, and Dad was home to reinforce my authority if they gave me a hard time." She looked down at her hands. "No, I didn't resent it, but, of course, there were times when I'd rather have been hanging out with my friends."

Hank shifted in his seat and reached for his coffee. Briana wondered at his tenseness. Except for the hug and kiss he'd given her when he arrived, he'd seemed strangely elusive, troubled. He'd been uncharacteristically silent, leaving her to respond to Crystal's chatter while he stood back and observed.

When he'd phoned, he'd said he wanted to talk to her, but so far she'd done most of the talking. Something was bothering him, and she suspected that when he got around to telling her what it was, it was going to upset her, too.

The seconds ticked by in silence, and her uneasiness increased. He had his face turned away from her, and when he finally spoke, she started.

"Briana, I—I've been doing some soul searching, and...well, since it concerns you... That is, I've come to a decision and...."

She caught her breath and tensed as her stomach muscles knotted into a ball of nausea. She fought the urge to clap her hands to her ears, to shut out the admission that was costing him so dearly. Dear Lord, surely she'd suffered enough from the slashing words men didn't want to say but said anyway.

Instead she sat a little straighter and came to his rescue. Better to get it out in the open. "What decision have you come to, Hank? How does it concern me?"

He still wouldn't look at her. "I'm really sorry, but I'm not going to ask you to go out with me anymore." The words were almost run together in his nervousness.

The nausea spread, and she swallowed it back, all the while wondering why it mattered so much to her when he was only doing what she'd intended to do to him, breaking off their burgeoning relationship.

"Oh." It came out with a swoosh, as if she'd been hit.

He finally turned and looked at her. "It's not because I don't want you," he hurried to add. "It's because I want you too much...."

With a muttered curse, he jumped to his feet and grabbed the back of his neck with his hand in a gesture of frustration. "Oh, hell, I'm screwing this up like a tongue-tied teenager."

He looked down at her and made no attempt to hide the anguish this was costing him. "Briana, what I'm trying to tell you is that I'm strongly attracted to you, and I can't afford to—to get involved with any woman at this time. That's why I'm going to stop seeing you before this goes any further."

She blinked. "I—I don't understand," she blurted out before she could stop herself. "Are you having financial problems?"

He looked puzzled. "Financial? Oh, no, nothing like that. I'm not strapped financially, but emotionally, I'm bankrupt. I can't afford the emotional damage that gambling on a new love affair could cause."

He was saying the same things she'd planned to say to him, and now she knew how shattering his divorce had been for him. No wonder there was a seductive allurement that vibrated between them; they were kindred spirits, only in this instance, a kindred spirit was the last thing either of them needed.

"I'm sure you're aware of the... the compelling attraction between us," he continued.

There was no point in denying it. "Yes," she said, and she looked away from him. "I'm aware of it."

"Then you know what's going to happen if we keep on seeing each other."

Oh, yes, she knew what he was talking about, but... "M-maybe not," she stammered without conviction.

"Briana, you know better than that." His tone was soft but determined. "I don't have that kind of self-control, and I don't think you do, either. If we keep dating, we're going to end up in bed. I'm not even going to call it making love, because that's not what it would be for me."

He sat down beside her and put his fingers under her chin, tipping it up so that her eyes were gazing directly into his. His expression was one of uncertainty. "God knows I want you, and if you're willing to settle for that, I'm not going to refuse, but I'll never fall deeply in love again. Even if it were possible, and I don't think it is, I wouldn't let it happen. I'll never trust another woman enough to give her that much power over me." There was a throb of pain in his voice.

Briana was appalled to realize that she was tempted by his proposition. She was lonely, and she wanted him almost enough to take him on his limited terms. The lure of the single, career-oriented life-style had always eluded her. She wanted the same things that Hank had wanted in his marriage: a loving partner, a home and children.

She was as emotionally bankrupt as he claimed to be, and it didn't take much soul-searching to realize that coming to him with no hope of marriage and knowing he didn't love her would eventually destroy her.

She closed her eyes and shook her head. "I've only had one lover," she told him, "and he turned out to be a world-class bastard, so I'm just as unwilling to trust men as you are to trust women. I couldn't manage a short-term relationship, but if I could, it would be with you."

He leaned forward and kissed her lightly on the mouth, then stood and walked over to look out the window with his back to her. "I'd like to get my hands on the son of a bitch who hurt you so badly." He sounded murderous.

She chuckled dryly. "I was having the same thoughts about your wife. I can't imagine how she could have left you and Crystal."

"It wasn't hard." He spoke without turning around. "I'll tell you about it if you want me to. I owe you that much."

She wished he hadn't put it that way. "You don't owe me anything, Hank. You didn't lead me on or try to seduce me. I've been as bewitched as you by the...the pull...that vibrates between us, but if you want to talk about it, I'm a good listener."

This time he did turn around. "I don't doubt that for a minute," he said as he walked over to pick up his mug and sit down, this time at the far end of the sofa again.

He settled back, but it was several minutes before he started his story. When he did, he didn't look directly at her, but stared off into space as though watching the drama unfold.

"My ex-wife's name was Darlene Perkins, but she insisted on being called DeeDee. Her parents have a small dairy farm outside of town, and we went to school together although she was a couple of years behind me. She was a cute kid, but too young for me to notice until the year I was a senior and had the lead part in the school play. She was the female lead, and it didn't take me long to discover that she'd grown up.''

He chuckled mirthlessly. ''I guess 'ripened' would be a more apt description. Her mind hadn't matured much, but her body sure had. She was all breasts and butt with a tiny waist in between, and at seventeen, my thinking was dominated by rampant hormones.''

For a moment they made eye contact. ''I'd forgotten how urgent and compelling that particular drive can be until you came along and reminded me all over again,'' he said grimly.

Chapter Five

Briana could feel the warm flush Hank's words induced, but along with it was a tingle of exultation at knowing she could affect him so strongly.

Once more he was the first to look away. "Sorry, I didn't mean to embarrass you," he murmured, having apparently seen her blush.

"You didn't," she hastened to assure him. "Actually I—I'm flattered."

He shook his head as if baffled. "Yeah? Well, I guess baiting the male is the way some women get their kicks," he said bitterly.

Her eyes widened with dismay. "Oh, Hank, that's not at all what I meant." She clasped her hands in her lap and wished she'd thought before she'd spoken. "It was a stupid thing to say, but I was only trying to tell you that I... Oh, damn! I don't know how to explain—"

She was cut off by the sound of tiny footsteps running across the kitchen toward them. "Daddy," Crystal called when she spotted them. "Something's wrong with the television."

Hank stood and swung his daughter up into his arms as he headed for the bedroom, with Briana right behind them.

The screen was blank, but then a message flashed on explaining that this was a temporary interruption. Within a few minutes, the program resumed, and Crystal was once more content.

Hank and Briana returned to the living room and their seats. "Look, honey, I didn't mean to snap at you," Hank apologized. "I had no business taking out my animosity toward DeeDee on you."

Briana breathed a sigh of relief. "Why don't you just go on with your story? I'm wondering what she did to you to deserve your resentment."

"In all honesty, I'll have to admit that she wasn't entirely to blame," he said. "It takes two to break up a marriage, and I made lots of mistakes.

"She was sexy as hell, but, contradictory as it sounds, there was a helpless-little-girl quality about her that appealed to me. She had a driver's license, but always wanted me to do the driving—she never did get the knack of pumping gas—and anything mechanical or mathematical was beyond her.

"I was always a sucker for children and vulnerable females, and I got a kick out of taking care of her. We started going steady during rehearsals for the play and continued until I left for the university the following September. By then, I was hooked."

He seemed to be making an effort to stay detached from the story by reciting it in a monotone with no emotion, and she was almost certain he'd never spoken of this before. "For the next four years we dated others while I was away at school, but we kept in touch through letters and phone calls, and got together again during the summers when I was home."

"Did DeeDee go to college?" Briana asked.

Hank shook his head. "No. Her parents didn't have the money to pay for it, and her grades weren't good enough for scholarships. She got a job as a checker at the supermarket and dreamed of being an actress."

Briana had forgotten Hank had told her before that his ex-wife was in Hollywood. "She must have had a lot of talent," she commented.

Hank shrugged. "Not really. She was a dreamer, always projecting herself into the movies she saw and the books she read, but that was part of the child in her that captivated me. Mostly, she wanted to get out of Whispering Pines, but she had no skills to support herself in a city."

"I knew a girl like that in high school," Briana told him. "She wanted to be a 'star,' but without the hard work of learning to act. She went to all the premieres and awards ceremonies hoping a talent scout would see her and be so struck by her beauty that he'd immediately sign her up."

Briana couldn't help but chuckle. "Actually, she wasn't even all that pretty, but I'll bet she's still hanging around with the crowd of other wannabe's, waiting to be discovered."

"Sounds a lot like DeeDee," he agreed, "excepting that in the whole history of Whispering Pines, no talent agent or movie producer has ever come looking for talent here.

"Anyway, we were married shortly after I graduated. I had visions of settling down in Whispering Pines with my sweetly dependent wife and a houseful of kids, but she wanted me to find a teaching position in Los Angeles so she could get on with her acting career.''

He paused, and an expression of self-disgust twisted his features. "Can you believe that we'd never discussed our goals for the future until after we were married? I can't imagine how we could have been so starry-eyed and naive. All those years that I'd assumed we'd settle down in this small, backwoods town and she'd spend her life content to bear and raise my children, she'd been counting on me to be her ticket to the big city and stardom."

Briana had no problem at all believing Hank. Something like that had happened to her during her first and only love affair, only she, trusting teenage innocent that she was, had been deliberately misled.

"Refusing to acknowledge obvious stumbling blocks is due to the blindnesses of love," she said sadly. "I assume you resolved it since you stayed married for seven years."

He ran his fingers through his hair and sighed. "You could say that. In my shortsighted, chauvinist way, I laid down the law. I was so sure I knew what was best for both of us, and I had no intentions of moving to a big city. Whispering Pines was our home, and that's where we were going to live. As my wife, DeeDee was expected to conform to my decision."

Briana didn't believe that for a minute. Hank was exaggerating. He'd never treat a woman that way.

"Aren't you being a little hard on yourself?" she asked with a touch of humor. "I mean, I really don't see you as the caveman type, and I sincerely doubt that DeeDee was immediately overcome by the wisdom of your utterances and hastened to obey."

He looked up and the corners of his mouth twitched. "You can say that again. She wasn't and didn't. We quarreled for months, and she gave as well as she got, but in the end, she submitted.

"I'm ashamed to say I didn't try very hard to see her side of it." Once more his tone was heavy with regret. "I loved her. I would have given her anything she wanted within reason, but moving away from our home, our families, our friends, even the business that was our livelihood, in order for her to chase an impossible dream didn't seem reasonable to me at the time."

"Does it seem reasonable to you now?" Briana asked quietly.

It took him a moment to respond, and when he did, he shook his head. "No," he admitted, "it doesn't, but I like to think I'd handle it differently now. Since it meant so much to her, I should have given it a try. I wouldn't have lost anything if I'd taken a year or two out of my life to see if we'd be happy living in Los Angeles. Maybe everything would have worked out the way she hoped, but I was too damn stubborn to see that then.

"DeeDee was a child in a woman's body. I don't mean she wasn't bright, because she was, but when she wanted something, she felt entitled to it and never looked ahead to what might happen if she got it. I tended to treat her like a rebellious daughter instead of a wife with equal rights."

"Sometimes people like that have to be watched over for their own good," Briana observed. "I'm sure you were doing what you thought was right."

Hank rubbed his face with both hands. "I was. I honestly thought I was making the right decisions, but I was wrong for being so inflexible, and she got back at me by refusing to give me the children I wanted."

Briana's eyes flew open in surprise. "But you have Crystal...."

Hank nodded. "Yes, thank God, but she was the result of a contraceptive failure, not an eagerly planned pregnancy."

He pounded the arm of the sofa with his fist. "Dammit, having babies was one thing we had talked about before we got married, and she seemed as enthusiastic as I was. She'd agreed to have children, she knew how much it meant to me, but she kept resisting my pleas that we get started on our family, and she was furious when she found out she was pregnant."

Even after all this time, Briana could see that just the memory of his wife's duplicity upset him, and she cringed inwardly. Hank was strongly paternal by nature. The male version of the earth mother, and anything that thwarted that drive was a threat to his well-being.

As a woman, she could understand that, but she hadn't known that some men had a compulsive hunger for children, too. She was pretty sure there weren't many men like him, so why, oh why, did she have to fall in love with one of the few?

A man who, because of his very nature, would never be able to forgive her mistakes.

She was snapped out of her pondering by Hank's voice, sharp with anxiety. "Briana? Did I say something to make you mad?"

She blinked and focused her thoughts back on the present. "No, of course, you didn't," she said softly. "I just didn't realize that some men had strong—" she groped for the right word "—strong nesting instincts... too. It's been my experience that most are more or less led into being fathers because their wives wanted a baby or it was expected of them."

Hank's expression lost some of its grimness. "Aren't you being a little hard on the male sex? I suppose I do have pretty old-fashioned values, but I think most of us plan to have at least one child to carry on the family genes. Your dad fathered seven children. Surely they weren't all accidents."

Briana shook her head. "'Accidents' isn't exactly the right word, but my parents were raised in a religion that endorsed only the most rudimentary birth control, and it wasn't very effective. They loved all of us kids, but after Dad got sick and couldn't work, each new pregnancy was a cause for concern."

She remembered that even as a child she'd been aware of the worry and tension that had accompanied the births of her last three siblings. Her mother had worked up to the last minute, and her father had sunk deeper into the depression he'd tried to hide from them.

Hank reached across the space between them and ran his hand down the length of Briana's dark hair. "I gather they didn't believe in abortion, either."

She shook her head. "No."

He wrapped a strand of hair around his fingers. "Well, DeeDee did, and I pleaded with her for weeks before she agreed to have the baby." His face had a tired, pinched look, and he sounded weary as he dropped his hand and leaned his head back.

"Maybe I was wrong. I should have stayed out of it and let her make her own decision, but I wanted that baby so bad...."

His voice broke and, for a moment, he didn't try to go on.

"It—it was your child, too." Briana couldn't keep the compassion she felt for him out of her tone. "Surely you had a right to ask—"

"You don't understand," he interrupted. "DeeDee knew herself better than I knew her. Some women aren't cut out to be mothers, and she was one of them. She had the baby because I wanted it, but she resented Crystal right from the start. She hated all the mess and being tied down so much. Of course, she blamed me, and we quarreled most of the time.''

The anguish in Hank's voice was almost more than Briana could bear, and she had to force herself to sit still and not move across the space between them to put her arms around him.

She couldn't help thinking of how unfair fate could sometimes be. Everything would have worked out beautifully if, in the early course of their lives, she had been paired with Hank, and DeeDee with Scott Upton. They'd all probably have lived happily ever after. Instead, the incompatible pairings had left scars on the psyches of four people who would never fully recover from the invisible wounds.

Hank seemed reluctant to continue probing the painful memories of his marriage as he sat hunched over and silent, lost in the hell of shattered dreams. Briana had no desire to put him through any more. It really wasn't any of her business. He was only doing it because he wanted her to understand why he wasn't willing to let her into his life, but she already understood far better than he could ever imagine.

She stood and gathered up the empty mugs to take to the kitchen, but her movements jolted Hank back to the present. "What are you doing?" he asked.

"I—I was just straightening up," she said, putting the mugs back on the table. "Hank, I know that reliving this is difficult for you. There's no need for you to continue. I don't blame you for not wanting a relationship. I'm not ready for that type of thing, either. To tell you the truth, I was going to break it off myself. You just beat me to it."

Her voice shook, and she knew she was rambling. He probably figured she was trying to salvage her pride, and maybe she was, but the thought of never again feeling his arms around her, his mouth on hers, his strong body pressed against her own, was almost devastating.

He reached out and captured her hand. "Honey, please, I've never discussed this with anyone before, but I'd like you to hear it all."

He tugged her gently, and she sat down beside him. She understood that he really needed to talk about this, and it comforted her to know that she was the one with whom he wanted to talk about it. In the future they wouldn't be lovers, and they couldn't be friends without becoming lovers, but for right now, he was willing to share with her the most painful episode of his life, one he'd never spoken with anyone else about, and she felt both honored and needed.

"To make a long story short," he continued, "the summer that Crystal was one year old, one of the hotels near the entrance of Yellowstone Park hired a country-western singer to put on nightly shows in their cocktail lounge. He was young, good-looking, and wrote some of his own songs. Made quite a hit with the ladies, and several couples, including us, went up there a few times to hear him."

Hank shifted restlessly, then stood up. "DeeDee and her friends made a big fuss over him, but I was used to her enthusiasm for entertainers, so I shrugged it off as another passing thing."

He jammed his hands into his pockets and walked away. "God, I still don't believe I could have been so blind. I swear I didn't have the faintest inkling of what she was up to. Summer is our busy time at the lumber yard, and we have to make enough profit to take up the slack during the slow winter months. I was working long hours and had a lot on my mind, but still..."

His voice had become ragged, and his movements jerky. Briana could feel the force of his agony, and she would have gladly taken part of it upon herself if that were possible.

What had that woman done to punish him so?

As if in answer to her question, he turned and faced her. "When the season ended, that smooth-talking bastard left for parts unknown and took my wife with him."

For a long time the silence in the room was total except for the faint, indistinguishable sounds coming from the television in the bedroom. Briana had expected something like that, but hearing Hank spell it out was shocking. She didn't have to wonder how deeply DeeDee's treachery had hurt him, it was all there, written on his face, reflected by the defeat in his posture and heard in the bitter rage of his tone.

A wave of compassion for the man who became dearer to her every passing day swept through Briana. "Oh, Hank, I'm so sorry...."

His expression turned mutinous. "Don't you dare pity me," he grated. "I've had enough of that to last a lifetime. It was only after she left that I learned what the whole town had been gossiping about all summer." He shuddered. "She'd been sleeping with that son of a bitch for weeks, and everybody knew it but me."

The brutal implication of his revelation hit Briana like a blow to the heart. Not only had Hank had to face the fact of his wife's adulterous behavior, but he had to live with the knowledge that all his family and friends, people he'd been close to all his life, had known and talked about it behind his back for weeks before he'd found out.

For a proud, virile man like Hank, that would be untenable!

Briana had questions. How did "the whole town" know for a fact that DeeDee and the singer were sleeping together? Also, what happened at the time they left town? Did DeeDee tell Hank she was leaving, or did she just write him a note and sneak out? What about Crystal? Did her mother just leave her behind, too, or did Hank refuse to let his daughter be taken away? He'd said he had full custody, but did that mean DeeDee hadn't wanted her or that Hank had battled in court and won?

So much was left unsaid, but Briana wasn't going to question him. For now, he'd had about all the reminiscing he could take.

She reached out to him, but drew her hand back when he didn't notice. He didn't want her pity, but neither did he want sympathy or compassion. He'd been smothered with them at the time and had found the experience humiliating and shameful.

What was it about men that made them think it was unmanly to need the comfort of being held and soothed in a woman's arms?

"I'm not offering pity, Hank. I'd say if anyone needed pity, it's DeeDee for being so confused and immature that she'd leave a husband as generous and loving and responsible as you."

This time he reached out to her and took her hand. "It's kind of you to say that, but you've never lived with me. I've got plenty of faults."

Her fingers squeezed his. "So have I, and so has everyone I've ever known. None of us are paragons, Hank. We're all just human beings bumbling through life as best we can. That ex-wife of yours made a big mistake, and if she hasn't realized it yet, she will."

Hank released Briana's hand and straightened. "She made a fatal error, all right, but it wasn't leaving me." His tone was as brittle as his expression. "I could have forgiven her for wanting another man, but she walked away and abandoned her one-year-old daughter, who needed her worse than any man ever could."

His hands that just moments before had caressed hers so tenderly, now knotted into fists. "What kind of woman would do a thing like that? Even the most vicious female animal nourishes her young until they're old enough to survive on their own. Actually, I hope that singer is keeping her satisfied, because I don't ever want to see her around here again."

He stood and strode across the room to take Crystal's coat and leggings from the back of the chair where he'd tossed them.

"I have nothing but contempt for a parent, man or woman, who would walk off and leave his or her own child." His tone was chilling in its intensity. "It's the one thing I can never forgive, so don't talk to me about pitying DeeDee. She can rot in hell for all I care."

With long, quick strides, he headed toward the bedroom to help Crystal put on her outdoor wraps. He'd been so immersed in his renewed rage that he hadn't noticed the terrifying effect his tirade was having on Briana.

She sat frozen in place and tried not to cringe as his words ripped open deep and painful wounds that had taken her four long years to close.

Wrapping her arms tightly around herself, she buried her face in the thick upholstery of the sofa back and stifled a sob that tore at her chest and throat.

Dear Lord, what would Hank think if he knew I'd never even held my baby before I relinquished it to the mercy of strangers?

Chapter Six

March in the Rocky Mountains of Wyoming blustered in like the proverbial lion with high winds, zero-degree weather and snow. On the first day of spring, the temperature was twelve degrees, but the gale-force winds made the outside air feel as if it were below zero.

Early in the month, Elly, whose lingering cough and chest congestion had not responded to antibiotics, was bundled off to spend the rest of the winter with relatives in the warm, dry climate of New Mexico, and Briana worried about her friend.

Could Elly's health problems be complicated by her unhappiness? Elly had been reluctant to discuss her relationship with Quentin York after her initial confession, and because she was ill, Briana hadn't wanted to press the subject the few times Elly had felt well enough to visit.

By the first week in April, the lion had yielded to the lamb in the weather department. The winds had subsided, the sun was back in all its bright splendor, and buds began to appear on the branches of the trees even as their trunks were still rooted in snow.

Briana had hoped that once the gray clouds and biting cold had been replaced by warming sunshine, she'd also be freed of the suffocating melancholy that had plagued her since that Monday six weeks ago when Hank had bundled up his little daughter and walked out of her apartment and out of her life.

At first she'd been too numb to feel much of anything. Then the numbness wore off and allowed the pain to overtake her. She wasn't a stranger to pain. It had wracked her five years ago after Scott's rejection, but familiarity didn't make it any easier to bear.

Her only consolation was that this time all she'd shared with Hank were a few kisses and caresses. She didn't have to deal with splintered dreams. At least she'd learned her lesson last time. She knew better than to build unrealistic castles in the air or plan for a happy ever after.

But there was one thing she hadn't expected, and that was the chilling loneliness. The aching need for Hank. The desire to see him, hold him, to have his arms around her, his mouth hungrily covering hers, his hands seeking to know her more intimately.

Five years ago, Scott Upton had earned her searing contempt. She'd felt no grief for him when he walked away from her. She hadn't had time. She'd been too busy picking up the pieces of her present and frantically seeking to secure a future for herself and her unborn child.

Briana had seen Hank several times since that day in mid-February. In a close-knit, self-contained village the size of Whispering Pines, it was impossible not to run into each other once in a while, but they'd managed to avoid being in the same social groups or business situations.

He'd canceled his appointment to have his teeth cleaned, and anything she may have needed from his lumber, feed and hardware store she bought elsewhere. She also resigned from the square-dance club, using the manufactured excuse of an old knee injury that acted up after too much dancing.

It was on Thursday, April 5, that Briana was jolted out of her doldrums. In her apathetic state, she hadn't been paying much attention to the names in her appointment book lately, only the work that needed to be done. It had been a busy day, and she was tired as she washed her hands and went to the waiting room to get her last patient.

She'd barely appeared in the doorway when a high-pitched, childish voice called her name and a small figure flung itself across the room and hugged her around the hips. She crouched down and put her arms around the eager child. "Crystal! What are you doing here? Does one of your teeth hurt?"

The little girl laughed. "Not me—Grandma." She squirmed away from Briana and ran back to a woman standing by a chair.

Briana stood up as the woman spoke. "I'm Gertrude Robinson, Crystal's grandmother."

Of course. Briana had seen the name on the schedule, but hadn't connected it with Hank. This woman was his mother.

Now that she was paying attention, she could see the resemblance. Gertrude Robinson was tall, at least five-ten and lanky in a loose-jointed way with big hands and feet. She had a darker version of her son's wheat-colored hair, but hers was sprinkled with white, and she wore it cropped short and straight, parted on the right and held in place by a gold-colored barrette.

She wasn't a pretty woman. Her features were plain and her weathered skin was wrinkled as often happens to the complexion of both men and women who live in the dry, thin air of the high mountain regions. She wore a brown, midcalf-length wool skirt and a shapeless hip-length, multicolored pullover sweater. Her long, narrow feet were encased in low-heeled black boots, and her only jewelry was a round watch with a wide leather band.

Briana smiled and put out her hand. "I'm pleased to meet you, Mrs. Robinson. I'm Briana Innes, the dental hygienist. You were told that I'm the one who will be cleaning your teeth, weren't you?"

"Oh, yes, but I'd have known it anyway." Her voice was low, and Briana noticed the Western twang that was fairly common in this part of the country. "Guess you know you've been thoroughly discussed since you've been here. Call me Gert. Everybody does."

She sounded neither friendly nor unfriendly, just matter-of-fact, but her pronouncement made Briana uneasy. Did Hank's mother know that he and Briana had dated a few times?

Briana chuckled nervously. "Thanks, Gert, I will. I hope the talk going around about me hasn't been too critical."

Gert shrugged. "Never heard anything but good. They say you're friendly, efficient and the prettiest thing that's come to town in a long time. Haven't found any reason to disagree."

"Briana gave me cocoa and cookies," Crystal chimed in, "and Daddy kissed her."

A hot wave of embarrassment flooded Briana, and she knew her cheeks were glowing pink. "I—I... Please, come with me." She turned and hurried ahead of them down the hall.

In the operatory, Gert settled Crystal on a low stool with a coloring book and crayons, then turned to Briana. "Don't pay any mind to the child. She just reports what she sees. She doesn't make any judgments."

Briana was still nonplussed. "I—I'm sure she doesn't, but do you?"

"Sometimes," Gert admitted. "But I haven't made any about you yet. Do I have reason to?"

Since everyone in town seemed to know Briana's business, she might as well give them the straight story. "No, you don't. Hank and I have done nothing that couldn't be done with his daughter watching, and we're not even doing that anymore. We...we're no longer seeing each other."

Gert nodded and sat down in the dental chair. "I know. Hank's been as grouchy as a grizzly with a thorn in its paw. You two going to patch things up pretty soon before he drives all our customers away?"

Briana couldn't believe she was having this conversation with a woman she'd never laid eyes on until ten minutes ago—and Hank's mother to boot. "No, you don't understand," she said reluctantly as she fastened a paper bib around the woman's neck and adjusted the chair. "We didn't quarrel. It was a mutual decision. Neither of us was ready for a—a serious relationship."

Gert grunted. "Serious relationship? Don't young people ever get married anymore?"

"Mrs. Robinson...!"

"Gert. Sorry if I rankled you, but in my day, we called it like it is. We either fooled around or we got married. Don't remember anybody having a 'serious relationship,' or a 'significant other.'"

Briana wished she could sink through the floor. What did this woman want of her? Was she being sarcastic, or was she just being friendly in her folksy way?

Whichever, she was definitely prying, and Briana put a mouth mirror and an explorer in her mouth to keep her quiet.

Forty minutes later, when Gert's teeth were bright and shiny, Briana unfastened the bib and let her up. "Now you're all set for at least six months," she announced cheerfully. "You have strong, healthy teeth, Gert."

"Always took care of 'em, that's why," Gert answered in her sparse style as she gathered up her purse and Crystal's book and crayons. "Come over for supper tonight, we're having chicken and dumplings. Six-thirty'll be fine."

Briana blinked. "But I—"

"No need to worry about running into Hank. He went to Cheyenne yesterday. Won't be back till tomorrow afternoon. Crystal's staying with us." She took the child's hand and headed for the hall. "Don't be late," she called over her shoulder. "Gotta eat the dumplings while they're light and fluffy."

Briana stared after the retreating backs of the tall woman and the small child, and wondered how on earth she'd managed to become involved with Hank Robinson's family without even being given a chance to resist.

Hank shoved back his chair and stood up, livid. "Dammit, Frank, if the schools in Whispering Pines lose their state subsidy for the hot-lunch program, there're going to be kids going hungry." He glared at the man sitting behind the desk. "We elected you to represent us. Why in hell aren't you doing it?"

A flash of anger twisted Congressman Frank Andrews's handsome features before he brought it under control. "I am representing you, Hank, but there's only so much money to go around. All the school districts are being hit. It's either let the lunches go or start cutting staff."

Hank leaned down and hit the desk with his fist. "That's a lot of bull. There's enough money wasted on frills and junkets and hoopla in this government to feed every kid in the state three times a day, and you know it. The kids get shafted because they don't vote."

He picked up his Stetson and jammed it on his head. "Just remember this, Mr. Representative. The students have parents who *do* vote, and they're going to be madder'n hell if you guys start making cuts in the school budgets."

He turned and stalked out of the office and down several flights of stairs before he ran out of steam.

Outside the capitol building, he stopped and slumped against the statue of Esther Hobart Morris, an early-day proponent of equal rights for women. Now he'd done it. He'd been sent here by the school board to plead their case and he'd screwed up. Once more he'd let his temper run away with his mouth and lost any hope of winning his argument. Nobody talked to a politician like he had and got away with it.

He straightened and walked toward his truck. What was the matter with him lately? He'd always prided himself on his ability to rein in his own impatience and see the other fellow's side of things. All except with DeeDee, he amended. He'd never understand how she could have walked away and left her own child, but he wasn't dealing with his ex-wife now.

Still, lately he'd growled and snapped at anyone who crossed him. Even his dad had told him in no uncertain terms that he'd better calm down and stop alienating the customers before they started going to Cody for their building supplies.

Hank knew his dad was right. He'd been behaving like a jerk, but he couldn't seem to help himself. It'd be easier if he could get more sleep. It seemed as though he was always tired, but after he'd been asleep for two or three hours, he kept waking up, then tossing and turning for the rest of the night.

He rounded a corner and caught a glimpse of a pretty, black-haired woman walking toward him. For a moment his heart sped up and a wave of joyful anticipation washed over him. Then he came to his senses with a sickening thud.

Damn it to hell, wasn't he ever going to be able to squash the instinctive urge to search for Briana in every dark-haired woman he saw? He'd made his decision where she was concerned and it was the right one, so why couldn't he get her out of his mind as easily as he'd put her out of his life? Why did he feel so desolate all the time?

Maybe he just needed a woman, period. He knew several here in Cheyenne who, after dinner in a fancy restaurant and dancing at a country-western bar, would satisfy his physical needs without expecting a commitment. Hell, why not? Maybe then he could sleep.

That thought jarred him. His inability to sleep through the night had nothing to do with Briana. No way. He wasn't that far gone on her.... Well, sure, he thought of her a lot while he was lying awake, but...

He looked around and realized that he'd walked blocks past his car. Oh, boy, he really was going to have to pull himself together. Now he'd have to hike all the way back to the capitol building.

With a sigh of resignation, he turned around. While he was there, he might as well go back in and apologize to

Frank for his childish display of temper and try to make amends.

Maybe if he groveled a little, he could salvage some of the damage he'd done to his credibility.

Briana was sure that if she just had a little more time, she could come up with an acceptable excuse for canceling dinner at the Robinsons', but when she finished her shower and still hadn't found one, she gave up and started dressing. After she'd carefully applied makeup, put on her most expensive lace-trimmed underwear and a green silk dress, then blow-dried her long, black hair into its most becoming style, she realized that she looked as though she was getting ready for a date with a man she loved instead of just going to dinner at the home of a patient.

Was she subconsciously hoping Hank would be there, even though she knew he was out of town? That was nonsense. She'd never get over him if she acted like a teenager with a king-size infatuation.

Quickly she took off the dress and substituted a black skirt and a white, long-sleeved blouse. She liked to think it looked more dignified and professional.

Briana had never been to the senior Robinsons' home, but it wasn't hard to find. It was in an older section of town with big turn-of-the-century-style houses and well-kept lawns and gardens. She was admitted by an exuberant Crystal accompanied by Gert and a man whom Gert introduced as Joe, her husband and Hank's father.

"Glad to meet you at last," he said as he took Briana's hand in his calloused palm. "Been hearin' a lot about you. Hank says you're from Los Angeles. Whispering Pines must seem awful dull, but we're all hopin' you'll settle in and stay awhile."

Joseph Robinson was Jeff to Gert's Mutt. Nearly a head shorter than his wife, he was husky with broad shoulders and chest, and had a pot belly that hung over the belt of his low-riding jeans. The top of his head was bald, but framed on the sides and back by a narrow fringe of brown hair, and he had a smile that started from deep within and lit up his whole being.

Briana smiled back. "I'm pleased to meet you, too, Joe, and I certainly do intend to stay in Whispering Pines." She glanced around the large entryway and to the rooms beyond. "You have a nice home. It's so big."

"Put your coat on that rack by the door, and Crystal and I'll give you a tour while Gert puts supper on the table."

Briana looked at Gert as she unbuttoned her coat. "Oh, but can't I help you?" she asked.

"Nope, got everything under control," Gert answered. "You can help clean up afterwards."

It was the kind of old-fashioned, two-story house Briana had always dreamed of living in. The rooms were large with high ceilings, multipaned bay windows and polished hardwood floors only partially covered with patterned rugs. Downstairs was a living room, dining room, a kitchen big enough to hold a round oak table and six chairs, a bedroom, office and bathroom. Upstairs were three more bedrooms and two baths.

The home was furnished with authentic furniture of a bygone era, all solid wood, some with marble tops and others with heavy concave glass doors. There was a six-foot-tall antique grandfather clock that chimed on the hour and the half hour, a rolltop desk with dozens of pigeonholes, and gold leaf ceiling light fixtures that would cost a fortune on today's market.

Later, over dinner in the dining room, Briana commented on what she'd seen. "You're so fortunate to have such a spacious home. I wonder if your son and daughter know how lucky they were to have their own rooms when they were growing up." Her tone had a wistful quality.

"Didn't seem so roomy then," Gert said. "Seemed like we had hordes of kids running in and out all the time. Some of 'em were always coming for dinner or spending the night." She looked up and caught Joe's glance across the table. "Gets kind'a lonesome sometimes now with them gone, doesn't it, Dad?"

Joe's expression softened, and he smiled. "Sure does, Ma, but we got Crystal to keep us company part of the time." He reached out and squeezed his little granddaughter's hand. "We have two other grandchildren, but they live in Arizona and we don't see much of 'em."

Briana could understand why Hank was so fond of youngsters. His parents were the nurturing types, too.

"That must be difficult," she said, and felt again the suffocating guilt that periodically overcame her because her own mother never had, and never would, see her first grandchild. A fact that had nearly broken her mother's heart.

"Yeah, it is," Joe admitted, "but they're happy, healthy kids, so we can't complain. Do you have brothers and sisters?"

"Six of them, and we sure could have used a house this size. Things got pretty crowded in our little three-bedroom-one-bath place."

"Bet it did," Joe said sympathetically. "Real estate's so much more expensive in the big cities. This home has been in the family for three generations. It was built by my grandfather and passed down to my father and then to me. We'd hoped to turn it over to Hank and his family when we retired, but..." He shrugged. "Well, Hank's got his own little house, and this one is way too big for just him and Crystal, so we'll probably sell..."

His voice trailed off, and Briana could tell how much the thought of letting the family home go upset him.

"Oh, that would be a shame," she blurted before she remembered that it was none of her business one way or the other.

But darn it, it would be a shame. Hank wanted a big family, and his parents were prepared to pass this huge old home down to him, but because his ex-wife had left him, he apparently wasn't ever going to have either.

Briana realized what she was doing and cut off that line of thought. It wasn't up to her to pass judgment on DeeDee. She'd only heard Hank's side of the story. Maybe DeeDee could rationalize her behavior if given the chance. God knew Briana's own past actions would seem unforgivable to Hank, but at the time, she'd done the only thing she could do.

By the time they'd finished dinner and cleared away the dishes, it was time for Crystal to go to bed. "I want Briana to give me my bath," she announced.

Gert looked at Briana, and Briana nodded. "Sure. I'd love to. Come on, poppet," she said as she took the child's hand and led her toward the stairway.

"What's a poppet?" Crystal asked.

Briana laughed as they followed Gert up the steps. "Darned if I know. It's what my dad used to call me."

"Do you have a daddy?"

Briana's laughter was silenced. "I used to, but he died," she answered wistfully.

"Petey died," Crystal said. "I was sad. Were you?"

Briana figured it was safe to assume that Petey was a pet. "Very sad," she answered over the lump in her throat.

"Daddy said I shouldn't cry because Petey's soul had gone to a better place. Maybe your daddy's soul is there, too."

Briana had thought she'd come to terms with her father's death, but hearing such a simple statement of absolute faith from the lips of this little girl was nearly her undoing.

They'd reached the top of the stairs, and Briana knelt and took Hank's daughter in her arms. "Oh, yes, darling." She paused to swallow a sob. "I'm sure of it."

Crystal threw her arms around Briana's neck, and for a minute, they hugged each other. When Briana finally looked up, she saw Gert standing a few feet away watching them with an odd look of satisfaction that puzzled Briana.

Gert supplied Briana with a towel, washcloth and Crystal's pajamas, then left. Briana added bubble bath to the water, and she and Crystal sang songs from the Disney movies while Briana bathed her.

After she'd been washed, dried, dressed in her pajamas and had brushed her teeth, Crystal held back when Briana tried to put her to bed. "I have to say my prayers," she explained.

Again Briana was touched. "Of course, you do. How could I have forgotten?"

Crystal knelt beside the twin-size bed, and Briana knelt with her while the child recited a well-known children's prayer. When she'd finished it, she took a breath and added, "And please take good care of Briana's daddy. Amen."

That time Briana couldn't stop the sob, but managed to smother it against the mattress.

Crystal climbed into the bed, then bounced up and down in the center of it. When Briana finally got her to lie down and pulled the covers over her, Crystal held up her little arms. "Don't forget to kiss me good-night."

Still fighting tears, Briana leaned over and took the warm, moist little body in her arms. "Oh, Crystal," she said in a tremulous whisper. "You're so sweet. If only..."

Another sob shook her, but this time it wasn't for her father, as two little arms again clasped her around the neck. "I love you," Crystal murmured sleepily, and planted a big, wet kiss on Briana's cheek.

Briana managed to get out of the bedroom and into the bathroom before she broke down. It took her fifteen minutes to pull herself together and repair as best she could the damage the flood of tears had done to her face and eyes.

When Briana finally went back downstairs, she found Gert sitting in the living room, knitting. A fire crackled in the big stone fireplace, and the room was warm and cozy.

"Come on in and sit down," Gert greeted. "Joe had some paperwork to do in the office, but he'll come in and have coffee and coconut-cream pie with us later. Have any trouble getting Crystal to bed?"

Briana knew that Gert hadn't missed seeing her red eyes and puffy cheeks, and she was grateful to the other woman for not asking questions about them.

"Not a bit," she said. "That little girl is a delight, even if she did splash water all over me and the bathroom floor."

They both laughed, but then Briana sobered. "Seriously though, you and Hank have done a marvelous job of raising her."

Gert looked pleased but wouldn't take credit. "It's Hank who's raising her, I just baby-sit when he's at work."

"I'm not surprised," Briana said softly. "He's not the type to turn his responsibilities over to someone else, and he adores his little daughter. She's his whole life."

Gert continued to knit. "You know my son pretty well."

Briana looked at her hands. "He's an easy man to know." It was barely more than a whisper.

"No, he's not," Gert said gently. "He's friendly and open on the surface, but there's a part of him that's closed off. Few people are privileged to share his private pain."

Briana raised her head and opened her mouth, then closed it.

"He's shared it with you, hasn't he?" Gert said. It was a statement, not a question.

Briana had no intention of breaching Hank's confidence, but it was evident that his mother was a perceptive woman who wanted a full and productive life for her only son. Since that's what Briana also wished for Hank, it wouldn't be intruding if she listened to what Gert had to say.

"We've talked about the breakup of his marriage, yes," she admitted, "but mostly he only told me what everybody else in town already knows, and then only because he felt he owed me an explanation for not taking me out anymore."

Gert sighed. "That's what I figured. He's woman shy since Darlene broke his heart and made him a cuckold."

Briana's eyes widened with shock at the ugly term. Gert's plain talk was going to take some getting used to. "A proud, high-principled man like Hank would find that pretty hard to take."

"Darn right," Gert said vehemently, "but it shouldn't ruin his whole life. Darlene had him bewitched from the time they were in high school. He couldn't see that she was just using him to better herself. Her parents barely eke out a living with their dairy farm, and they couldn't afford to give her all the things she wanted."

Gert's knitting needles clacked noisily as her agitation increased. "Hank could and did. He was a star athlete in both high school and college, and so his steady girl was sort of a celebrity, too. Darlene loved the spotlight."

"Look, I wasn't here so I don't have all the facts," Briana acknowledged, "but wasn't it possible that DeeDee loved Hank as well as the spotlight? Hank is awfully easy to love."

The words were hardly out before she realized that she'd exposed her deepest feelings, and she blushed under Gert's penetrating gaze. "That is . . . I mean . . ." Oh, great! The runaway thoughts that had spilled over and betrayed her had now gone dry.

"I know what you mean," Gert said as she returned her attention to her knitting, "and I'm pretty sure Hank feels the same way about you. He's been testy ever since you two broke up, but to answer your question, the only one Darlene ever loved was herself. Her parents spoiled her rotten. They never disciplined her, and she grew up to be a willful, selfish brat."

Briana's first instinct was to protest Gert's conclusion that she was in love with Hank, but before she could get a word in edgewise, she realized that it would be both useless and untrue. She did love Hank. She loved him very much, but that love had been doomed before it was ever born.

If he knew the truth about her, he'd hate her almost as much as he hated his ex-wife.

"Darlene was all cow eyed and clinging with Hank when he was home," Gert continued, "but when he was away at college, she ran around with any man who could afford to bring her presents and take her out."

"But Hank has admitted that they both dated others while he was at college," Briana protested.

Gert's mouth set in a hard line. "Oh, sure, they weren't actually engaged until Hank's senior year, but she wasn't just dating every guy who came along. She was acting like a tramp, if you know what I mean."

Briana found the cultural differences between L.A. and Whispering Pines difficult to decipher. In L.A., a woman didn't qualify as a tramp unless she went to bed with two or more men at the same time, but Briana was pretty sure that most of the women in Whispering Pines had never heard of a ménage à trois or any of the other more erotic pleasures of the sophisticated city "tramp."

"I know what you mean, Gert," she said, and her agitation was evident in her tone, "but what I don't understand is how 'everyone in town' knows without a doubt when an unmarried couple is making love. Do they sell tickets, for God's sake?"

This time it was Gert who turned red. Her mouth dropped open and her fingers slackened on the knitting.

Briana was immediately contrite. She shouldn't have snapped at Gert, who was only parroting what other people were saying. Besides, Gert had a right to be vindictive. DeeDee had done a terrible thing to Gert's son and granddaughter by running off with another man.

Briana got up and went over to sit down beside the other woman on the couch. "Gert, please, I'm sorry." Her voice shook, and she took a deep breath. "I didn't mean to sound so judgmental, but Hank said something about 'everyone' knowing that DeeDee was sleeping with the singer before they left together, and you indicated that she was going to bed with everyone she dated. I can't help but wonder if the woman was ever given a chance to defend herself, or if it was all just vicious gossip that drove her away."

For a long time Gert didn't answer. The pendulum on the old grandfather clock ticked away the seconds, and the sound seemed magnified in the total silence of the room. Briana's nerves grew tighter and tighter as the relentless *tick-tock* seemed to batter their raw endings.

Now she'd really done it. If she'd deliberately set out to alienate Hank and his family, she couldn't have done a better job of it. After tonight none of them would ever speak to her again since she'd inadvertently accused Gert of being a vicious gossip.

Slowly Gert retrieved her knitting and picked up a dropped stitch with one needle. "Well," she said gruffly. "You really know how to tell it like it is, don't you?"

By this time Briana was actually wringing her hands. "Honestly, I didn't mean—"

"Yes, you did," Gert interrupted, "and you're partly right. We gossip in Whispering Pines. There's not a whole lot else to do here, but we try not to be vicious."

"Look, please, I—"

"Now you had your say, let me have mine. It's true that no one ever saw Darlene in bed with a man. Not even with her husband, as far as I know, but she was indiscreet enough to set tongues wagging during the time Hank was in college, and she admitted to adultery in the divorce proceedings."

Now Briana really felt dreadful. She should have known Hank and Gert wouldn't say things about Crystal's mother unless they could prove them.

"Is that why she lost custody of Crystal?"

Gert shook her head. "No, she didn't ask for either full or partial custody of her daughter. She didn't show up for the court hearing. She signed a paper relinquishing Crystal to Hank without even asking for visitation rights, and we haven't seen or heard from her since. She doesn't even acknowledge her own child's birthdays."

Gert looked straight at Briana. "If you think we're being too harsh about Darlene, then that's your right, but Joe and I agree with Hank. A woman who would abandon her own baby without even a backward glance has no right to call herself a mother."

Chapter Seven

During her short time in Whispering Pines, Briana had observed that a good share of the population regularly attended the four churches that served the spiritual needs of the community.

The winters in the mountains of northern Wyoming were long and cold, with raging blizzards that often clogged the roads with snow and isolated the far-flung villages for days or weeks at a time. Because of this, the people in these small towns learned to be self-sufficient, and the churches became their social centers. Town meetings, potluck dinners, game parties and other get-togethers drew crowds of all ages, and most of them returned to the denomination of their choice for worship on Sunday mornings.

On this Sunday, three days after her dinner with the Robinsons, Briana had chosen to attend the eleven o'clock service, and since it was such a bright, sunshiny day, she decided to walk, even though Church of the Holy Family was on the other side of town from where she lived.

The invigorating crisp morning air helped to lighten the gloom and guilt she'd been battling ever since she'd left the Robinsons' home Thursday night. Her behavior had been inexcusable. Joe and Gert were just being friendly, and she'd accused them of maligning their ex-daughter-in-law, whom Briana had never met and had no reason to defend.

From then on, it had all been downhill. Gert had changed the subject, and they'd cautiously picked their way through a minefield of innocuous topics until Joe had joined them for dessert. Briana left as soon as they'd finished their pie and coffee, and there'd been no open invitation to "come again anytime" as was usually the custom.

At the beginning of the evening, she'd had the impression that Hank's parents approved of her and would have welcomed her into the family, but with her usual impetuousness, she'd smashed any chance of that. Oh, well, it had to happen sooner or later, and in this case, sooner was better. There was no future for her with Hank or his parents.

By the time the service was over, the sun had disappeared and its warmth was replaced by a chilly breeze. Briana burrowed her chin into the faux fur collar of her heavy red coat and was glad that she'd worn her white wool knitted tam. It would keep her hair in place and her head warm.

After a moment's hesitation, she decided to take the shortcut home. It was a route she seldom used because it involved cutting across a couple of empty lots and down an alley or two, but the temperature was falling fast and the Wyoming wind was a biting one.

She'd gone several blocks and was approaching the First Methodist Church when, as if on cue, the doors opened and people began filing out. Even from a distance she felt Hank's presence before she actually saw him stop to shake hands and exchange a few words with the minister.

Briana shivered, but not from the cold. It was uncanny the way they seemed to be on each other's wavelength, and she wasn't surprised when he looked right at her as if he'd known she was there.

She couldn't control her hungry gaze as it roamed over him, from his cream-colored Stetson, down the blue tweed topcoat she'd never seen him wear before, to the legs of his slate blue wool trousers and the highly polished reptile-skin boots. He had the rugged good looks that made the Marlborough Man a sex symbol, and she had to stop and plant her feet firmly on the cement to keep from running into his arms. Except that his arms weren't opened to her, and neither was his expression.

Hank scowled as he hurried down the steps of the ancient white clapboard building, and stood waiting for her on the sidewalk. "Briana, what are you doing way over here?"

His tone was almost as chilly as the wind, and she realized that he was angry.

They were still several feet apart, but neither of them made a move to close the distance. "I—I've been to church," Briana said haltingly. "I attend Holy Family."

A group of parishioners jolted Hank as they tried to get around him, and he took a few steps down the sidewalk closer to Briana in order to get out of the way of those leaving. "How come I've never seen you here after church on Sundays before?"

She blinked. What had happened to make him so mad at her? "I usually take a different route."

His eyes flashed. "And today you just *happened* to be walking by here at the exact moment the service was letting out?"

"Well, yes, as a matter of fact, I was." She put out her hand toward him. "Hank, what—"

Before she could touch him, he grasped her arm and propelled her along as he started to walk. "Come with me. I need to talk to you."

Briana was too startled by his attitude to resist, and she had to run to keep up with his long strides while he led her to his truck, which was parked a block away. She protested as he opened the door and helped her into the cab, then slammed the door shut and got in on the other side.

"Hank, what are you doing?" she demanded as he started the engine. "Aren't you forgetting Crystal? Where is she?"

"I never forget about my daughter," he snapped as he steered the truck away from the curb. "She's going home with Dad and Mom. We're having dinner with them."

He drove the rest of the way in silence, and since it was obvious that he was taking her to her apartment, Briana said no more, either. Apparently he would tell her in his own good time what had upset him. Trying to pry the information out of him would only make him more stubborn.

Briana had never seen this side of Hank before. He'd always seemed so patient and easygoing. Now she knew he had a temper, but what had she done to set it off?

They pulled up in front of her apartment, and Hank let the engine idle. She turned to him, unsure of what he expected.

"Would you like to come in?" she asked.

He shook his head. "No. What I have to say won't take long. We'll talk right here—it's warm in the cab."

Briana settled back, but it was impossible for her to relax. "All right. Now suppose you tell me what I've done to rile you." She sounded calm, but her nerves were screaming.

Hank didn't even try to appear nonchalant. "Crystal tells me you had dinner at my parents' home while I was gone."

Briana stole a glance at him out of the corner of her eyes. Is that what was bothering him?

"Yes, I did," she said. "Thursday night. It was—"

"How did you get them to invite you?" His tone was harsh.

"How did I...?" She couldn't believe she'd heard him right. "Hank, I don't understand...."

"Then I'll make it plainer," he said. "How did you manage to ingratiate yourself with Mom and Dad and get them to invite you to the house? As far as I know, they hadn't even met you up to the time I left for Cheyenne."

Briana still didn't understand, but her mind had cleared enough to know when she was being insulted.

"I beg your pardon?" she said, her tone heating up with every word. "Just what are you accusing me of? I cleaned Gert's teeth Thursday afternoon, and she invited me—"

"And it also just happened that you came to dinner when I was out of town and Crystal was staying there," he interrupted without waiting for her to finish explaining. "I understand you were a big hit with her. She chatters constantly about how you gave her a bath, heard her prayers and kissed her good-night."

His face twisted in an expression of disgust. "That's really low, Briana, using my own child to get to me. It's been tried before, but I never thought that you—"

Briana felt the blow as if he'd delivered it physically. "Now just a damn minute." Her voice was taut with a mixture of disbelief and anger. "Is that what Gert told you?"

For a moment he looked surprised. "I haven't talked to Mom about it. It's Crystal who thinks you're the next best thing to her mother."

Briana was greatly relieved to know that Gert hadn't been giving Hank a slanted version of what happened that evening. "It's true that I put her to bed," Briana said, "and we sang and laughed and had a good time, but where did you get the monumental conceit to imagine that I was doing it to impress you?"

Briana's own temper was steaming, but Hank merely looked at her and raised an imperious eyebrow. "Oh? And I suppose you didn't deliberately arrange to be in front of the church back there when you knew the chance of bumping into me was good?"

She was dumbfounded. "You think I was loitering there waiting for you to come out?"

"Don't act so innocent," he raged. "That accidental-meeting bit is a ploy the high school girls use. Why were you being so coy, Briana? What did you expect to gain? I've explained why I'm not willing to marry again, and you don't want a casual relationship. There's little chance that either of us will change our mind, so why did you have to involve my parents and Crystal?"

He stared straight ahead out the windshield, and for a moment, he looked weary and unutterably sad. "I'd almost convinced myself that you were the one woman I could trust. That you really did care for me and for Crystal."

His expression hardened again, and he turned his head to look at her. "Well, understand one thing, lady." His voice was like a whip. *"No one uses my daughter for bait."*

Briana stared in shocked incredulity as Hank continued. "She's suffered enough. She cried for weeks after DeeDee deserted her, and nothing we could do would comfort her. Even now she sometimes asks when her mommy is coming back. I swore that no one would ever hurt her that way again, and I intend to keep my vow. We don't come as a package deal. Any dalliance I may have with a woman now or in the future won't affect Crystal one way or the other because I won't allow her to get close to my daughter."

For a moment Briana was speechless. How could Hank think she'd use Crystal or any child in such a callous way? Didn't he really know her any better than that? Or had he been so hurt and humiliated by his ex-wife that, as a form of self-preservation, he'd strike out at any woman he was attracted to?

Not that it mattered. He'd obviously jumped to conclusions about her and wasn't going to change his mind. It wouldn't do any good to try to explain. She'd just break down and cry, and he'd think she was using tears as a weapon.

She reached out and opened the door, then turned to face him. She had to make this quick.

"I'm sorry you feel this way, Hank," she said in a voice that quavered with pain. "For your own peace of mind, I suggest that you ask your mother about the evening I spent with them, but you needn't worry. There's not a chance in hell that I'd ever come to you for anything."

She jumped out of the car and slammed the door behind her just as the sobs that had been clawing to get out exploded from her, and she ran into the house.

The following day was a busy one at the office, for which Briana was grateful. It kept her too occupied to think. They had several emergencies, which necessitated the whole staff working well past normal closing time. When Briana finally arrived home that evening, the phone was ringing, but she was hungry and exhausted and if it was Hank, she was in no mood to deal with him. She unplugged it, heated a TV dinner in the microwave, took a hot shower and went to bed.

The night before, she'd tossed and turned for hours while the scene with Hank replayed endlessly in her thoughts and dreams, but now she fell asleep almost immediately and slept soundly until the alarm rang.

At midmorning on Tuesday, while she was busy with a patient, Paula, the receptionist, handed her a message saying that Hank Robinson wanted her to call him back as soon as possible. She crumpled it and threw it in the wastebasket.

Later that afternoon, Paula handed her the same message again. This time it had "urgent" added. Again she threw it away.

"But Briana," Paula wailed. "He said it's vitally important that he talk to you. What'll I say if he calls again?"

Briana had no intention of giving Hank another crack at her, although she suspected that he'd talked to his mother and was calling to apologize. Gert was a straightforward woman, and Briana was almost sure she'd tell her impetuous son she'd been the one to insist that Briana come for dinner and not the other way around.

Even so, the last thing Briana wanted was an apology, or anything else, from Hank. She still burned with humiliation and outrage at the things he'd accused her of, and from now on, she intended to steer clear of him.

She'd worked too hard to rise above the poverty she'd been raised in and the treachery of the man she'd once loved to allow anyone, man or woman, to abuse her. She'd learned to take care of herself, and that's what she intended to do.

"If he calls again, just take another message," she told Paula. "There's no need for you to tell him anything."

Later that evening Briana dressed for her date with Luke Odell. Her social life had been practically nil since she and Hank were no longer seeing each other, and she'd searched for an excuse when Luke had asked her a few days ago to go to the movie with him tonight. It was one she wanted to see, though, and he'd seemed offended when she'd started to turn him down, so she changed her mind and agreed.

Now she wished she hadn't. She'd even considered calling him to cancel, but she knew that shutting herself away alone with her pain was no way to get on with her life.

In the end, that reasoning had won out, and she was dressed in gray wool slacks and a pink sweater when he arrived. The light in his eyes told her that he liked what he saw, and she invited him in. They'd just settled down on the couch with a glass of beer for him and a cola for her when there was a knock on the door.

Luke looked at her. "Are you expecting someone?"

Briana stood. "No, I can't imagine who it is. Excuse me."

The knock sounded again before she reached the door and opened it. The sight of the man standing there caused her to gasp. "Hank!" For some reason she hadn't expected him to come to the apartment looking for her.

He was holding his Stetson in his hand, and his gold-brown hair was slightly mussed. "Hello, Briana." His tone was soft, and she detected a note of contrition. "You must know that I've been trying to get in touch with you. Don't you answer your phone or reply to messages?"

Her eyes widened. "The phone? Oh, for heaven's sake, I disconnected it several days ago and forgot to plug it back in." She continued to clutch the doorknob and block the entrance. "Look, I doubt that you have anything to say that I want to hear, and I have a date. We're just getting ready to go out, so..."

He looked shaken but determined. "Please, Briana, I've got to talk to you. Can't you spare just a few minutes? I've been trying to get in touch with you all day to set up a...an appointment, but you wouldn't take my calls."

Briana sighed. Dammit, what was that force between them that wouldn't be denied? She'd found it easy to hold on to her righteous indignation when apart from him, but when he showed up at her door, hat in hand, anguish in his eyes and pleading in his tone, she was helpless to resist.

She might as well hear what he had to say.

"Wait there, I'll be out in a minute," she said curtly, and closed the door on him.

She turned to look at Luke. "It's Hank Robinson," she said. "There's some...some personal business we need to discuss. He tried to get in touch with me earlier today, but we didn't make contact. Look, Luke, I know it's rude, and if you'd rather I didn't talk to him now I'll understand, but it won't take but a few minutes and I—I'd like to get it over with."

Luke frowned and stood up. "Do you want me to leave?" he asked reluctantly.

"Oh, no, of course not," she assured him. "I'll just step out in the hall. Make yourself comfortable. It won't take but a minute," she repeated as she stepped out and closed the door behind her.

Hank was standing with his back to her, looking out the picture window above the wide landing at the top of the stairs. It provided natural illumination for the area during the day, but the April twilight cast the hallway into shadows. Briana walked past a light switch but didn't flip it on as she joined him and stood looking out at the big old elm trees that lined the street and were now bare of both snow and buds.

She could feel his heat even though they weren't touching, and the tangy scent of his after-shave lotion reminded her of the night he'd kissed her so lingeringly here in the hall. It sharpened all her senses and magnified the tension that radiated between them as he shifted restlessly from one foot to the other. Why was he hesitating? He'd sure been vocal enough the other day.

Finally she broke the silence. "Look, Hank, I have a date. Will you please just get on with whatever it is you want to talk to me about?"

He turned his head and looked at her. "Sorry. I—I didn't expect to find Odell here. Do you go out with him often?"

A twinge of resentment stabbed her. "What difference does that make to you? You want nothing to do with me. Luke does, so if you'll excuse me, it's nearly time for the movie to begin."

She started to move away, but Hank caught her by the arm, gently but firmly. "Briana, I talked to Mom. She...she told me that she practically forced you to come to dinner, and that it was Crystal who insisted that you put her to bed. Mom said you even defended DeeDee when you thought she had been accused on hearsay rather than fact."

He released her and ran his fingers through his hair. "Oh, damn, I feel like a thick-headed jackass. Why didn't you tell me what really happened? Why did you let me rant on without even trying to defend yourself?"

Even in the dim light, Briana could see the torment in his expression and hear the remorse in his tone. It would be so easy to reach out to him, to put her arms around him and tell him it was all right, that she forgave him.

She had no doubt but that he'd respond, quickly and urgently. They'd make love, and it would be wonderful until the next time she did something to displease him. Then she'd be just another cheating woman in his eyes until she could prove to him that she was innocent.

No, she couldn't live like that. Wouldn't live like that.

She stiffened her spine, both literally and figuratively, and looked at him. "Would it have made any difference if I had? Would you have believed me?"

He opened his mouth, then closed it and shook his head slowly. "No, I probably wouldn't have," he admitted ruefully. "I was too worked up to listen to anything but my own prejudices."

He reached out and put his hands on either side of her waist, sending a shiver of exultation up and down her spine. She'd been so hungry for his touch, for his tenderness.

"Honey, I'm sorry." His voice was unsteady. "If it's any comfort, you're not the only one who's been on the receiving end of my nasty disposition lately. I've growled at everybody. I know that's no excuse, but I've been so damned miserable...."

A shudder shook him, and he put his arms around her and held her close against him while he buried his face in her hair. She knew she should pull away, but she didn't have the strength. Surely just a few minutes in his embrace wouldn't hurt anything. It felt so good, and his apology was obviously heartfelt. Besides, his sheepskin-lined coat prevented any intimate contact.

Her cheek and the palms of her hands lay against the brushed leather of the outside of the garment, and it had a soft, sensual texture that made her senses swim. "Why are you miserable?" she murmured.

"Because not being able to see or touch you is just plain hell." His tone was somber, and she snuggled closer, her caution overcome by her need to be held and to comfort and be comforted.

"I—I find that hard to believe," she said haltingly. She didn't want to seem petty, but she had to know why he had acted the way he did. "You say you were hurting, but apparently you didn't trust me enough to come to me and put a stop to the pain."

She felt him tense as he raised his head and rested his chin on her crown. "It's not that simple. If I'd had only myself to think about, I'd have done just that. You can't know how bad I wanted to, but I have Crystal to consider. I can't gamble with her happiness."

Briana winced and pulled away from him. "You still think I'd do something to hurt her."

Hank groaned and clutched at the back of his neck with his hand. "I don't know. That's what's tearing me apart. I don't think you'd do it deliberately, but Crystal could be severely damaged by losing another mother whom she'd grown to love. Because of that, I'm not willing to marry again, at least not until she's older, and even then, not just to relieve an inconvenient lust—"

A cry of protest was wrested from Briana as his last word flogged her vulnerable psyche. Both hands flew to cover her cheeks as the hot flush of denial left her reeling.

"Is that all you feel for me?" she demanded.

Hank's eyes opened wide with shock. "Briana, I was speaking hypothetically!" he roared. "You must know that what I feel for you is a whole lot deeper—"

Just then the door to her apartment opened and Luke came storming out. "What in hell's going on out here?" he demanded as he looked from Briana to Hank. "Damn you, if you're mistreating her I'll—"

Briana didn't hear any more. She ran into the apartment and slammed the door as the two men continued to shout.

Nine hours later, at 4:30 a.m. early Wednesday morning, Hank sat in front of the television in his dark living room, wearing a royal blue velour robe over his briefs and sipping from a can of beer while munching potato chips. Not the best way to fall back to sleep, but that was a lost cause anyway, so he might as well indulge himself until Crystal got up.

He was tired, and his head ached, and the movie on the screen was so bad that it should have been trashed years ago.

If only he could sleep. His eyelids felt gritty, his temper was short, and the only times he'd eaten anything nourishing lately were when he had dinner or supper with his parents. His mom fed Crystal three meals a day during the week, so he didn't have to cook if he didn't want to.

The cowboys on the screen were singing up a storm as they chased cattle rustlers across the prairie, and Hank's beleaguered mind wandered back to the scene with Briana earlier last evening.

When was he going to learn to keep his big mouth shut? Every time he opened it around her, he put his size-twelve foot in it. He'd been telling himself that it was only lust he felt for her, that it would wear off or go away or even better, that any woman would do.

He muttered a coarse expletive. All three excuses had proved to be crazy. It hadn't worn off or gone away, and when he'd had the perfect opportunity last Friday to fulfill all his male fantasies with a woman in Cheyenne, he couldn't even get aroused.

That had never happened to him before. Never!

He'd tried to call Briana several times since he'd stormed out of her apartment house after engaging in a childish shouting match with Luke Odell, but either she wasn't home or she wasn't answering her phone again. Just the thought of Luke raised Hank's hackles. Briana had been with him at the square dance party the night Hank had asked her for their first date. . . .

The muscles in his belly clenched at the thought of her in the other man's arms, and for a minute, he was afraid he was going to lose the beer and chips he'd just consumed.

When the wave of nausea passed, he looked at his watch. Almost six o'clock. She'd probably be waking up about this time, maybe he should try again to get her.

He reached for the cordless phone on the lamp table, but then drew his hand back. What could he say to her if she answered?

I'm sorry? He'd already said that.

I love you, and want to marry you? No, he wasn't ready to make that kind of commitment, and he wasn't sure he'd ever be. His first responsibility was to Crystal.

I want a sexual relationship with you? He could handle that, but Briana couldn't. They'd already discussed and discounted it.

So what was left? An on-and-off platonic friendship that left them frustrated and eventually bitter?

Neither of them could survive that for long. No, he was going to have to pull himself together and quit acting like a teenager having a temper tantrum. He was a grown man and a father; he couldn't afford to fly off the handle every time something didn't go his way. Starting today he was going to put Briana Innes out of his mind and get on with his life.

He yawned and rubbed his face with his hands. It'd be a hell of a lot easier if he could banish her from his dreams and sleep through the night.

For the next week and a half, the sun shone bright and warm. By the last Friday in April, although the mountaintops were still white, the snow around Whispering Pines had melted and the citizenry had exchanged their heavy winter clothing for lighter weight sportswear.

Briana welcomed the change, but Dr. Wainwright sounded a note of caution. "Don't pack away your warm woolens just yet," he warned her. "The weather can change any day. It's not unheard of to have snow in May."

"Is that why Elly is still in Arizona?" Briana asked hesitantly. Lately she'd been uneasy about her friend. Elly had been gone so long.

"Her congestion's all cleared up," Dr. Wainwright said, "but the doctor down there says she should stay in the dry climate until we're sure the snow's gone for the summer. Don't want to take the chance of a setback."

"I agree," Briana said. She had lots of friends, but Elly was more like a sister, and Briana needed someone close to talk to.

She hadn't seen or heard from Hank since that fiasco when he came to apologize and left in a huff. Not that she'd expected to, but it would be easier if Elly were here to confide in.

Elly would understand. She was in the throes of a forbidden love affair, too, although she hadn't mentioned it since. That's what was really bothering Briana. Was it possible that Elly had been evading the truth when she said she and Quentin hadn't been sleeping together? Could she have gone away because she was pregnant? Dear God, Briana hoped not.

It was almost noon, and Briana was just finishing with a patient and looking forward to the lunch break when she heard the fire alarm, a loud, raucous noise that called the town's volunteer fire-fighting force together. It was a familiar sound, and, except for wondering where the fire was, she paid little attention.

Since the office was closed daily from noon until one-thirty, Briana usually went home, where she could relax while she ate. As she strolled down Main Street, she reveled in the warm sunshine.

When she neared her apartment house, Mr. Stillwell, her landlord, a retired man who lived with his wife in one of the first-floor apartments, came flying out the front door, still pulling on his jacket. She'd never seen him move so fast before, and she waved and called, "Hey, where are you going in such a hurry?"

He stopped and turned toward her. "Goin' to help search for the little girl who's missing. If they don't locate her quick, they may never find her in that forest."

Briana stopped short. "What little girl? What are you talking about?"

"The child who wandered away from the Perkins place and apparently got lost in the woods back of it. They called out the fire department to help look for her. Didn't you hear the siren?"

Oh, no! Briana had heard stories of small children who wandered away from their homes or campsites in the heavy mountain forests. Their bodies weren't found for months. "Whose child was it? Do you know?"

The man finally got his jacket on and zipped it up. "Yeah, it's that little girl of Hank Robinson's. Crystal, I think they call her."

Chapter Eight

The horror of Mr. Stillwell's words staggered Briana, and she swayed as the light around her turned gray.

No! Please God, not Crystal.

Her knees buckled, and she felt herself sinking into the mist when two hands supported her, and a voice, fraught with concern, snapped her back to her feet. "What's the matter, girl?"

Mr. Stillwell put his arm around her waist and supported her as he slowly led her toward the house. "You're white as a ghost. Sit down here on the step and put your head between your knees."

She did, and gradually, the world stopped spinning. "You sit right here," he ordered. "I'll get Olivette—"

Briana sat up. "No, please, Mr. Stillwell, I'll be all right. Don't call your wife. It was just the shock.... I'm very fond of Crystal Robinson and her family. Where did you say it is that they're looking for her?"

Briana had to go to Hank. He must be suffering the torment of the damned. Crystal was his life. If he lost her...

Oh, dear Lord, I've been through that blazing hell. Don't let Hank suffer it, too!

She couldn't shop shivering as her landlord answered her question. "The Perkins dairy farm out west of town. They're her mother's parents, you know. The place is surrounded by trees, and since they've searched the house and grounds, the forest is all that's left." He looked at her sharply. "You sure you're gonna be okay?"

Briana nodded. "I'm fine. You go ahead. I'm coming, too, just as soon as I change my clothes. Can you tell me how to get there?"

Twenty minutes later, Briana was driving along the narrow back road that led to the Perkins home. Mr. Stillwell had been right about it being in the middle of a forest. The area was thick with trees, both large and small, and underbrush heavy enough to obscure the ground in places.

She shuddered with foreboding. This was no place for a four-year-old child to be wandering alone. She sped up as she spotted a clearing ahead with several buildings.

Before starting out Briana had changed into jeans, boots and a heavy sweatshirt. She had left a message on the answering machine at the office that she was going to join the search for Crystal and to cancel the rest of her appointments, then stopped at the bakery to buy out their supply of doughnuts and Danish. The searchers would appreciate something to eat.

As she turned into the barnyard of the rundown old farm, she saw several automobiles behind her. She'd heard about the way people turned out in a small town to help in an emergency, and it hadn't been an exaggeration.

There were vehicles all over the place, as well as the fire truck and the town's seldom-used ambulance.

She found a place to park beside the weather-beaten barn, and as she stepped from the car, Hank came out of the back door of the house. He was accompanied by two other men and seemed to be giving them instructions as they walked toward a metal toolshed several yards to the right of where she stood.

They hadn't seen her standing among the parked cars, and she watched as Hank suddenly veered in the opposite direction from her as the other two continued on to the toolshed.

Briana started to run. She couldn't let him get away without his knowing she was here; that Crystal was precious to her, too.

His long strides were lengthening the distance between them, and she called to him. He didn't hear her and hurried on as she called again, this time louder.

He stopped, and she called his name a third time. He turned to watch her tearing across the flat, empty space between them. The brim of his hat shadowed his face, so she couldn't see his expression, but after a second, his arms came up and out, welcoming her as she stumbled breathlessly into them.

He clasped her to him in the hard, rough grip of a powerful man who is momentarily unaware of the intensity of his strength. She didn't care about the discomfort. She wasn't looking for tenderness as she threw her arms around his neck and buried her face in his shoulder.

He was trembling, and she was aware that this was the first time he'd held her when there weren't several inches of sheepskin and leather between them. Today he wore only jeans and a sweatshirt, and she could feel his shoulder bones beneath her face and the hard muscles of his chest and arms against her breasts and back.

For a long while they just stood there, clinging to each other. It wasn't a sexually arousing embrace. They were both too upset about Crystal for that. This union was more intimate than physical; it was the coming together of two people who needed each other to be complete.

Finally Hank loosened his hold on her slightly and nuzzled the side of her neck. "Briana," he murmured brokenly, "how did you know how bad I needed you?"

"I didn't," she said breathlessly, "but I knew how desperately I needed to be with you. I came as soon as I heard...." Her voice broke on a sob. "Oh, Hank, will she be all right?"

He raised his head and caressed her back. "Yes. She has to be. You will stay, won't you?" He sounded anxious.

"Of course. I'm going to help you search."

He jerked upright even as his arms tightened around her. "No! You're not to go into those woods. You don't know your way around them, and they're treacherous. Promise me you'll stay in the house."

The terror in his tone was real, and Briana wasn't going to add to his torment. "If you want me to, I will," she assured him. "I'll do anything I can to make this easier for you."

He relaxed a little. "Having you here, warm and soft in my arms, has already done that, but now I've got to get back out there. It would be a real help if you could keep Margaret from falling apart."

Briana looked at him. "Margaret?"

"Margaret Perkins, she's DeeDee's mother, Crystal's other grandmother. She blames herself for Crystal getting lost. She was taking care of her at the time."

Briana felt a wave of sympathy for the woman. "I'll do the best I can," she assured Hank. "Is there anything else you want me to do?"

He leaned down and kissed her gently on the mouth. "Yes. Pray," he said, and turned to walk quickly away.

Briana carried the three large, flat boxes of pastry to the house. She went in by the door Hank had come out of and found herself in the big, roomy kitchen. Several women were bustling about, and the rich smell of freshly brewed coffee wafted on the air.

Since she didn't know any of the women, she introduced herself and asked to be put to work. "Just stack those boxes on the counter by the coffee maker," said the one who gave her name as Jenny and seemed to be in charge. "Take the lid off the top one and those eating will work their way down. Someone went to town for bread and lunch meat—you could help us make sandwiches when they get back."

"I'll do that," Briana said. "Is Gertrude Robinson here? I'd like to see her."

"Oh, Gert's out there searching with the men. She knows these woods. There was no holding her back when she found out her granddaughter was missing."

Determined, just like her son, Briana thought. Stubbornness like that could be a fault, but it could also be an advantage. She knew that as long as Crystal was missing, neither Hank nor Gert would give up looking for her, even if the time came when there was no hope of finding her alive.

Briana's throat ached with pent-up sobs, and she quickly changed the subject. "Hank suggested that I talk to Margaret Perkins. He says she's awfully upset."

Jenny brightened. "That's a good idea. Margaret's in the bedroom, and I'm afraid all the sympathy she's getting is just making things worse. You go on and see what you can do."

The kitchen opened onto a dining room, and the dining room onto the parlor. They were all large rooms, sparsely furnished with neat but old and worn furniture. The floors were bare except for an occasional throw rug, and the formerly white curtains at the windows had yellowed with age.

Gert had intimated that DeeDee's family was hard-pressed financially. Apparently small dairy farms weren't a very lucrative business in the area.

There were numerous people milling around. Briana was greeted by several that she knew, and found it difficult to break away. Finally she asked, "Can you tell me where I can find Margaret Perkins?"

"First bedroom on the right at the top of the stairs," said the woman who worked as checker at the supermarket. "Poor thing's in bad shape. I offered her one of my tranquilizers, but she wouldn't take it."

Briana frowned. "It can be dangerous to give medication to someone it wasn't prescribed for. You should at least check with the doctor first."

"I tried," the other woman said, "but Doc was called to Cody because of an emergency with one of his patients in the hospital there and couldn't be reached."

That bit of news was doubly disturbing to Briana. What if Crystal were seriously injured? With Whispering Pines's only doctor out of town, medical treatment could be delayed when they found her. The fire department had oxygen, and a couple of the fire fighters were trained as paramedics, but they were limited in what they could do.

Upstairs, the door to the bedroom was open and there were several more women hovering around the old-fashioned iron bed, all talking at once.

Briana knocked loudly on the doorjamb, and the one closest to her turned around. "Excuse me. I'm Briana Innes, a friend of the Robinson family. I—I came up to tell you that there's coffee and sweet rolls in the kitchen if you'd like to take a break," she improvised. "I'll stay with Margaret."

The ladies turned around and moved apart, giving Briana a view of a figure stretched out on the bed and covered with a worn blanket. The women all started talking at once, thanking Briana for spelling them as they filed out of the room.

The woman on the bed didn't move or speak as Briana approached her. She wondered what she could possibly say to this brokenhearted grandmother.

Reaching down, she touched her gently on the shoulder. "Mrs. Perkins, I'm Briana Innes. I'm—"

"I know who you are," said the thin voice. "Crystal talks about you a lot. Oh, God, forgive me. I'm so sorry...." The wail was high-pitched and bordering on hysteria.

Briana decided to ignore the fact that she was a stranger and to act like a friend. She sat down on the side of the bed and carefully brushed a tangle of gray-streaked brown hair back off the pale, ravaged face.

"Margaret, I'm not a nurse, but I have had some medical training. Enough to know that you'll feel better if you get up and move around."

"I don't want to feel better. I just want to die."

Briana knew she was out of her area of expertise, but someone had to do something, and she was probably better qualified than anyone else immediately available.

"You mustn't talk like that," she said, her tone kind but firm. "It doesn't help anything and just upsets those who care about you. There are a lot of people downstairs who have come to help out, and they're worried about you. I'm sure you don't want that, so let me help you get out of bed and to freshen up a little."

She folded the blanket down and supported the dazed woman as she sat up and swung her legs over the side of the mattress. Margaret was short with a matronly build, and she was wearing worn jeans and a faded blue sweatshirt. Her shoes had been removed, but her feet were encased in heavy white cotton socks.

Briana spoke soothingly to her as she helped her to her feet and saw her safely down the hall to the bathroom. "Wash your face with warm water, then splash it with cold to take down some of the puffiness. I'll go back and find something a little more dressy for you to wear."

When Margaret came back to the bedroom, Briana helped her change into the navy blue slacks and a blue-white-and-red blouse she'd found hanging in the closet.

At first Margaret protested. "There's nothin' for me to get cleaned up for."

"Of course, there is," Briana assured her. "All your friends are here, and you don't want Crystal to see you all red eyed and puffy faced when they bring her back, do you?"

That brought on another onslaught of tears. "They'll never find her. I—I let her get lost. I'll never see her again."

"Now, Margaret, that's not true," Briana said firmly, "and I don't want you to say it again. You didn't go away and leave her here alone, did you?"

Margaret's eyes widened. "Of course not, I'd never do that."

"Where was she when you saw her last?"

Margaret thought for a moment. "She was in the barnyard playing with the puppies, but I could see her from the kitchen window."

"What were you doing?"

"I was washing dishes and watching her."

"Then what happened?"

Margaret wrinkled her brow. "Well, the phone rang. I went into the dining room to answer it, and it was Frank Johnson at the bank." Her voice picked up volume as she continued. "He said our business account was overdrawn. I knew that wasn't true, because I was in there myself on Wednesday and deposited a check for more than enough to cover it."

Carefully, Briana probed further. "Did you tell him that?"

"You bet I did," Margaret said indignantly. "I made him check right then, and he finally found that someone had forgotten to record it. It took him so long that my cookies were just about to burn by the time I got back to the kitchen."

The pattern was becoming clear. "So then you had to attend to the cookies?"

Margaret nodded. "Yes, and when I looked out the window again, Crystal wasn't there. I went out to look for her, but I couldn't find her. She didn't come when I called, so I went to the barn to get Arno, my husband. When neither of us could find her, we called Hank."

Another sob shook Margaret, and Briana quickly distracted her. "Did Crystal know that she wasn't to leave the yard?"

"Oh, my, yes. We did the same with her as we did with Darlene. From the time she was old enough to walk, she was warned never to go out of the barnyard. She knew the danger of getting lost in the forest, and she never disobeyed until today."

A cold chill swept over Briana. Was it possible that Crystal had been abducted?

She didn't want to alarm the other woman any more than she already was. Surely that possibility had been discussed, but until she could get in touch with Hank and find out, there were some questions she had to ask. She found a brush and started brushing Margaret's disheveled hair. Maybe she could disguise her queries so Margaret wouldn't know what she was getting at.

"Then surely you must see that you'd done all you could to protect your little granddaughter," Briana said reasonably. "You'd warned her about going out of the yard, and you watched her closely—"

"But I didn't watch her," Margaret broke in. "I was talking on the phone—"

"That was a business call," Briana reminded her as she continued to stroke the brush through the graying hair. "Everybody knows you run a business from your home. You have to answer the telephone, and you can't be blamed if it's a fairly lengthy conversation. Crystal was playing happily when you took the call. You're only human. You can't be everyplace at once, and you couldn't have known that Crystal would pick this time to wander off. You must stop blaming yourself."

Margaret didn't answer, and Briana took a deep breath and continued. "Was there much traffic by here earlier this morning?"

"No. There never is."

"Did any visitors or customers drop by?"

The woman shook her head. "No. Hank asked that, too, but there wasn't anybody around until after Crystal got lost. I'd have noticed a stranger."

Briana wasn't so sure about that if the stranger didn't want to be seen, but she didn't probe further. She'd discuss it with Hank later.

When she'd finished arranging Margaret's hair and had added a touch of lipstick and blusher to her pale lips and cheeks, the older woman looked, and apparently felt, better.

Downstairs, Briana steered Mrs. Perkins into the kitchen, and they both pitched in to help make sandwiches.

As word filtered out to the searchers that there was coffee and food at the house, they started coming in a few at a time to take a break and eat. Among them were Gert and Joe Robinson. They both hugged Briana and thanked her for coming, then Joe introduced her to Margaret's husband, Arno.

Arno Perkins was a tall, skinny man dressed in overalls and a plaid flannel shirt. A battered old Stetson covered his thinning gray hair. A man of few words, he also thanked Briana for coming, then went looking for his wife.

The comments made by the searchers when the two sets of grandparents were out of earshot were discouraging, and Briana's heart sank. It had been hours since the little girl disappeared, and still there was no trace of her. They were now talking about searching for abandoned wells and mine shafts that a child could have fallen into.

That thought was terrifying!

It was fortunate that the snow had melted and the ground was fairly dry, but why didn't Crystal hear the calls and respond? Although it had been warm during the days lately, the temperature still plummeted at night, and she wasn't dressed for cold weather.

They had to find her before dark!

When it came time for school to let out, most of the women who had been helping with the food left to pick up their children. Briana's apprehension increased as she watched for Hank to come in, but it was late afternoon before he did. She was alone in the kitchen, making another of the numerous pots of coffee that had been consumed during the day, when the door opened and he strode in, his hat in his hand.

She didn't have to ask how the search was going; she could tell it was bad by the slump of his shoulders and the anxiety that twisted his features. Before she could move or speak, Margaret came hurrying into the room. "Oh, Hank," she said as she rushed over to him. "Have you found her yet?"

He put his hand on her arm. "No, Margaret, we haven't," he said gently, and she wilted against him.

He tossed his hat on the countertop and put an arm around her. "We've arranged to have a search-and-rescue dog brought over from the ranger station in Yellowstone. Those dogs are highly trained. It'll find her."

He looked over Margaret's head at Briana, and she saw the doubt and fear in his eyes. She plugged in the coffeemaker, then walked over and took the stricken woman from him.

"Come on, now," she said quietly. "Remember what I told you. The waiting will be easier if you stay busy. Why don't you go out and check on the chickens? They seem to be out of their pen. I guess somebody opened the gate."

Margaret sighed. "Yes. All right. I'll do that." She headed outside, leaving Hank and Briana alone.

He put out his arms and she went into them. "I need another hug," he said as he crushed her against him.

There was a tight line of tension all the way through him, and his face was gray with worry.

"So do I," she answered, and wrapped her arms around his neck. "Oh, darling, I wish there was something I could do."

"Doesn't the fact that you're keeping me sane count for anything?" he murmured in her ear.

She stroked the knotted muscles at his nape. "Am I?" she asked. "I've hardly seen you...."

"Just knowing you're here where I can touch you, hold you when the apprehension becomes intolerable, is keeping me going." He rubbed his cheek in her hair.

"Is it intolerable now?"

He didn't answer, but she felt his throat constrict and his head nod against hers. She brushed his neck with her lips, and asked the question that couldn't be put off. "Hank, have you considered the possibility that Crystal was—" she swallowed the lump in her throat "—was taken away?"

An involuntary shudder shook him. "You mean kidnapped," he said in a strangled tone. "Oh, yes, I notified the police as soon as Margaret called me, and they've put out an A.P.B. on her. They're also looking for her in town."

"Well, at least everything is being done that can be." Briana was trying to reassure herself as well as Hank. Then she changed the subject. "When you get tired of holding me, I'll fix you something to eat."

He groaned softly. "I'll never get enough of holding you, and I couldn't eat. My stomach is too tied up in knots. Besides, I've got to get back out there."

"I know, but not until you've had some nourishment. It'll keep you going, truly. How about a milk shake? It will go down easily and isn't hard to digest. You really need something to fuel that powerful body of yours.

You'll want to be alert and able to function when you do find Crystal."

For a moment he just stood there holding her and letting her massage the kinks out of his upper back. "I guess you're right," he said finally, sounding too tired to argue. "Why don't you fix me a chocolate one while I go wash up?"

Slowly and with obvious reluctance, he put her away from him, then walked out of the room while she headed for the refrigerator.

Briana was waiting for him in the living room when he came out of the bathroom. "Come sit down," she said, patting the sofa cushion beside her. "You look like you haven't slept in a month."

"You've got that right," he said as he picked up his milk shake from the coffee table and sat down. "Actually, it's been closer to two months."

Briana realized that he was serious and a new fear gnawed at her. "Really, Hank? Is something wrong? I mean, are you sick?"

He took a large swallow of the ice-cream mixture. "Yeah, there's been something wrong. Pure damn stubbornness. I've wanted you so bad, I couldn't sleep, but I was too bullheaded to admit it or do anything about it except pace the floor most of the night."

Briana's mouth dropped open. "You wanted me?" Surely that isn't what he said. "But I thought..."

He put his glass down and reached for her. "I know what you thought, sweetheart," he murmured as he cradled her against him. "You thought what I wanted you to think. The problem was that I couldn't convince myself. I kept telling myself that I just wanted you for...you know...sex, but that wasn't it at all. I need you for so much more than that—"

Just then the sounds of a heavy vehicle turning into the barnyard and dogs barking claimed Hank's attention.

"It's the park ranger with the search dog," he said, and jumped to his feet. Turning back, he picked up the glass and emptied it, then leaned down and kissed Briana hard on the mouth. "Promise you won't go away. That you'll stay here until this is over."

She licked at the remnants of the chocolate drink he'd smeared from his lips to hers. "I'm not going anywhere until you come for me," she assured him as he ran out the door.

For the next hour, Briana followed her own advice and stayed busy mixing tuna fish with onions and mayonnaise, and slicing ham for sandwiches, but her thoughts and her prayers were with Hank and Crystal.

Where was the little girl? As time ticked by, it seemed more and more likely that someone had picked her up and taken her away, otherwise she'd surely have been found by now.

That thought was the thing nightmares were made of, and Briana couldn't dislodge it. The Robinson family was comfortably fixed financially, but surely they weren't rich enough to tempt anyone to risk kidnapping Hank's daughter for ransom. Besides, everybody in this town knew everybody else. There'd be no place to hide. Any suspicious actions would be noticed.

Were there any sex offenders in Whispering Pines?

The sharp knife she was slicing ham with jerked and just missed her finger. Oh, God, no! Not that! If there were anyone in town with that type of record, the police would know and he would be the first person they'd investigate. Sex crimes against children happened in the city all the time, but there was no way a practicing pedophile could hide such an aberration in a small town. On the other hand, a drifter...

She shuddered and forced her thoughts back to the mundane subject of food.

When Briana had finished mixing tuna salad and slicing the ham, she cleared the countertop and started making more sandwiches. Tramping through those woods was hard work, and she found it difficult to keep up with the demand for food now that most of her help was gone.

She was spreading butter on slices of bread when the faraway but unmistakable retort of a gunshot split the air. Her knife clattered to the floor. The shot was quickly followed by another, and the relief that pounded through her was almost shattering.

Two gunshots! The signal that Crystal had been found unharmed!

She practically flew out the door, followed by several others who had been in the house. They joined the growing group of searchers already starting to stream out of the woods and into the barnyard.

Everyone had questions, but nobody had answers and wouldn't have until the ones who had found Crystal brought her in. Briana spotted Margaret leaning against a car, crying, this time with joy. She went over and hugged Crystal's grandmother. "You see," Briana said as tears of exhilaration streamed down her own cheeks, "I told you Crystal would be all right."

She silently vowed never to tell Margaret of her own terrifying doubts.

Margaret leaned against Briana and nodded, but was unable to speak through her wracking sobs of thanksgiving.

Briana stood with her arm around the older woman, her attention riveted to the people converging from all sides of the property. Where was Hank? Had he been the one to find his daughter? There was no sign of the ranger or the dog, either.

She shifted impatiently from one foot to the other. How long would it take to bring Crystal in? The two gunshots signaled that she wasn't seriously injured, but she could have something wrong that needed attending to before she could be transported.

Come to think of it, Briana didn't see either of the fire department paramedics in the crowd.

By now, Margaret's elation had given way to apprehension, too. "Where are they?" she asked. "What's taking so long? Maybe Crystal's hurt and can't be moved. Maybe..."

Once again, Briana reined in her own anxiety and forced herself to speak cheerfully. "Margaret, she's been missing for hours. She probably wandered far away. They'll have to carry her, and it may take quite a while to bring her out of that forest. There aren't any roads, are there?"

Margaret shook her head. "No, they couldn't get a vehicle in there, but she's just a baby. How could she go very far?"

Just then Briana spotted Arno Perkins coming toward them, and she raised her arm and waved. "There's Arno," she told Margaret, and pointed. "Maybe he has some information."

Margaret hurried out to meet him, and he put his arms around her as she once more started crying. "It's all over, Maggie, there's no need to cry."

"But where are they?" she wailed.

He patted her. "I don't know. The shots could have been fired from two or three miles away. Don't be so impatient, it's only been about ten minutes. They'll get here as soon as they can."

Briana left the couple and circulated among the waiting people, hoping to pick up some idea of what was going on, but no one seemed to know any more than she did. She spoke with Gert and Joe who, like the Perkinses, were almost incoherent with relief. Gert looked exhausted, and it was only then that Briana remembered that Hank's mother was in her sixties. Although Gert was big and strong looking, she shouldn't have been allowed to tramp for hours in the rugged forest with only one short break.

On the other hand, Briana couldn't imagine that anyone would have been able to restrain Gertrude Robinson from searching for her beloved lost granddaughter.

While they were still talking, someone hollered "Here they come," causing all heads to turn, most of them to the northwest, which had been the area of the most intensive searching. Briana strained to see over all the people until the Robinsons uttered a glad cry and rushed off in the opposite direction.

She whirled around and saw Hank coming across the road at the eastern side of the property with a small figure huddled in his arms. Crystal had her arms around her daddy's neck and her face buried in his shoulder. Behind them came the ranger and his dog and one of the paramedics carrying a half-grown puppy.

As she moved closer, Briana saw tears running down Hank's ravaged face, the first he'd shed all day. Probably the first he'd shed since his own childhood.

His parents reached them first, and he shifted Crystal slightly so that he could put one arm around his mother and hug her while his dad patted him on the back and dried his own tears on his shirtsleeve.

Then they were surrounded by people, all talking at once, asking questions, expressing their happiness that the child had been found. Briana held back, not wanting to push forward and intrude. These people had known the Robinson family all their lives, a lot of them were relatives, whereas she was a newcomer.

When they got to the house, Hank climbed the three steps leading to the front porch, then turned to face the group. He still held Crystal, having refused to release her to anyone else, and she clung to him and wouldn't look up. His gaze searched the crowd until he found Briana, and he smiled at her, then looked away as he started to speak.

"I—I'm in no shape to make a speech right now," he began, "but I know you're all eager to hear what happened. From what we've been able to learn from Crystal, it seems that she was playing with the puppies when one of them ran off. She ran after it and ... well ... once they got deep in the woods, she couldn't find her way out."

Crystal whimpered, and Hank stroked her back. "What threw us off was the fact that she was on the other side of the road. She's been warned never to cross it, and she never has before, so we didn't search that side as thoroughly as we did the area over here."

He paused, and there was some murmuring among the group before he started talking again.

"Let me just say one thing about that. Tomorrow morning, I'm going to come out here bright and early and start putting up a fence around this whole property. It's gonna be high and strong with gates that lock, and I guarantee you no child is ever going to wander into these woods and get lost again."

The people clapped, and he waited until they'd quieted down. "I've just got one more thing to say for now, and I—I don't know how to go about it."

He swallowed and looked around at the upturned faces. "We couldn't have gotten through this without all of you. There . . . there just aren't words for me to tell you how grateful—"

His voice broke, and for a moment he closed his eyes. "Look, let me put it this way. If any of you ever need anything from me, anything at all, all you have to do is ask. You gave me back my daughter. There's no greater act of friendship. . . ."

This time his voice broke on a sob, and he turned and carried Crystal into the house.

Chapter Nine

For a long time after everyone else had left, Briana stood in the waning sunshine. She felt drained. The adrenaline that had kept her in a state of high tension all day was gone and she was bone weary.

Crystal was home and safe, and for that, Briana fervently thanked God and would continue to do so in her prayers. It was unworthy of her to feel left out because Hank was too wrapped up in his daughter right now to single Briana out for special attention. She was sure she'd feel the same way if their positions were reversed, but still, she felt somehow rejected.

She didn't know what he wanted of her. Did he still need her now that his little girl had been found? Or had Briana served her purpose and was expendable?

Hank's feelings for her were so mercurial, hot one minute and cold the next. He hadn't said anything about wanting to start seeing her again once Crystal was found.

He hadn't even said he loved her, only that he wanted her and needed the comfort she was so willing to provide during this terrible experience.

She reached up and brushed a lock of hair away from her eyes. Had she once again misunderstood the attentions of a man who wanted something from her without giving anything in return?

She walked over to the front steps and sat down. Although most of the searchers were gone, there were still a lot of people in the house, relatives and close friends probably, and she could hear the noisy talk and laughter as they were released from the terror that had gripped them and celebrated the return of the lost child.

They had a right, and Hank most of all. She should be in there celebrating with them instead of sulking in self-pity. She had no reason to expect him to seek her out. He had his hands full with a cold and frightened daughter and highly emotional grandparents, to say nothing of his own shattered nerves. It was her place to go to him.

She hadn't even told him yet how happy she was that Crystal had been found.

Leaning her head against one of the posts supporting the railing, she closed her eyes and sighed. She wasn't proud of her reticence, but Hank had told her plainly that he didn't want to get involved with her. He'd been adamant about it, even to the point of being furious when he thought she was trying to get to him through Crystal, so how could she be sure that today he hadn't just been clutching at the solace she so freely offered during a period of great distress?

She wasn't strong enough to risk rejection again.

The sound of heavy footsteps alerted her, and she opened her eyes to see Hank coming around the side of the house.

He saw her at the same time and hurried toward her. "Briana. What are you doing out here all alone? I've looked everywhere for you. I—I was afraid you'd left."

He lowered himself wearily to sit on the step, but didn't touch her. "What's the matter? Why didn't you come in the house? Why...that is..." He looked away. "I thought you'd be glad that we'd found Crystal."

Briana's eyes widened, and the breath seemed forced out of her lungs. Oh, Lord, surely he didn't think she was indifferent....

A massive sob brought her breath back as she lunged toward him, and then she was in his arms, sobbing wildly while her tears dampened the front of his shirt. For a long time, she clung to him, desperate to make him understand how much she loved his little daughter, how much she loved him, but she couldn't speak because of the wracking sobs that shook her.

Hank held her close and rocked her gently back and forth, but didn't attempt to quiet her. He seemed to know that she had to get out all the anguish that was stored up inside her before she could function again. He rubbed her back, trailed little kisses in her hair and cheek, and murmured tender endearments that helped her get her runaway emotions under control.

When her misery was finally spent, her tears wrung dry and the sobs reduced to light hiccups, Hank reached in his back pocket and handed her a red bandanna handkerchief. She mopped up her face, blew her nose, then laid her cheek back on his chest and cuddled against him.

"Okay, sweetheart," he said tenderly as he stroked his fingers through her hair, "now tell me what brought all that on and why you're out here by yourself when you should have been with me in the house."

She rubbed her palm over his orange sweatshirt and again thrilled at the hard muscles of his chest underneath. "Oh, Hank," she said in a voice still rusty from tears. "I couldn't bear to have you think I was unfeeling about Crystal's disappearance. I was terrified from the moment I heard about it. If anything had happened to her, I ..."

A cross between a hiccup and a sob warned her that her control was still precarious, and she didn't try to go on.

He put his fist under her chin and lifted her white face, then lowered his head to kiss her on her still trembling mouth. "Then why didn't you come to be with me when I brought her home?"

There was no recrimination in his tone, but Briana knew he was hurt, and that was even worse. She raised her hand and caressed his face with her palm while she brushed his weather-roughened lips with her thumb. They parted and closed over it, then sucked gently.

Such a small gesture, but at the same time so intimate that she almost started to cry again in gratitude. "I love you, Hank," she said carefully as he caught her thumb between his teeth. "I don't think you want to hear that, but I do."

He released her thumb from the love bite, then caressed it with his tongue, making her vibrate with pleasure. "I fought against loving you," she continued. "When you said you didn't want to get involved, I told myself it was for the best, but then you accused me of using Crystal, and I was crushed."

She pulled her thumb out of his mouth and put her hand back on his chest, then lowered her head beside it. "I don't understand you, Hank. I don't know what you expect of me. You're so inconsistent. You want me one minute and can't stand me the next...." Her voice trailed off.

"I always want you." Hank's tone was ragged, and his arms tightened around her. "There's never a time when I don't want you, and that's what scares me so. I know I've behaved like a bastard, but it's not because I don't care for you. It's because I care too much."

His hand worked its way under her sweatshirt, and his callused palm against the smooth bare flesh of her stomach made her shiver with need. "Don't ever think I don't like for you to say you love me," he murmured as he moved his hand up to cup her lace-covered breast. "I can never get enough of hearing it."

A moan escaped him, and he gently kneaded the high, firm mound. "Oh, Lord, Briana, have you any idea how often I've ached to do this?"

She closed her eyes and gave herself up to the exquisite gratification of his erotic manipulation. "Then why didn't you?" she murmured dreamily.

His thumb brushed back and forth across her nipple. "Because I knew I wouldn't be able to stop. I hardly dared touch you for fear of losing control."

She clutched at his shirt as he continued to stroke her. "Then why are you doing it now?" It was a whisper.

"Because I can't fight it any longer. My need for you is greater than my fear of being betrayed again." He leaned down and kissed her temple. "I'll do anything you want me to if you'll just let me love you."

A tiny doubt rankled her, demanding to be voiced. She raised her head to look at him. "Just how do you mean that?" she asked softly.

"Any way you want to take it," he answered just before his mouth covered hers and she forgot everything but the sweetness of his breath and the musky taste of his tongue as it sought and found hers in a mutual mating dance.

It was Gert's voice that brought them back to earth. "Hank. Hank, where are you?" she called from the barnyard side of the house.

Startled, Hank and Briana jumped apart, and she hastily adjusted her bra while he stood and straightened his sweatshirt. "Here, Mom," he called back. "What's the problem?"

He helped Briana to her feet and muttered a hasty apology for the interruption as he took her arm and they rounded the house to meet his mother coming to find them. "Oh, Hank," Gert said, "Crystal wants you. Margaret gave her a warm bath and dressed her in clean clothes, but then when your daughter couldn't find you, she started to cry again."

Hank squeezed Briana's arm, then let loose. "I'll see what I can do," he said, and took off on a run.

Gert turned to Briana. "I'm sorry," she said. "I didn't realize he was with you, but Crystal is really scared. She was lost and alone for such a long time. I'm afraid it's going to take a while for her to get over it."

A wave of guilt washed over Briana. If she'd gone into the house with everyone else as she should have, Hank wouldn't have had to come looking for her. She should have realized that the child would be terrified and cling to her father for protection.

"Don't apologize, Gert," she said as the two of them started walking toward the door. "It's my fault. I was sort of holding back, and Hank came looking for me."

Gert nodded. "That son of mine has been prickly as a pinecone for weeks. I figured it had something to do with you. Has he been giving you a bad time?"

Briana hesitated, then spoke. "Well, he was pretty mad at me for going to your house for dinner while he was in Cheyenne. We'd...we'd decided not to date anymore, and he thought—"

"Yeah, I know what he thought," Gert interrupted. "That damn wife of his really messed him up, but that's no excuse for him taking it out on you. I told him so, too, but can't say he appreciated my interference."

She looked sideways at Briana. "Didn't look like he was in a fightin' mood just now, though. You two make up?"

Briana could feel herself blush. She probably did show the effects of that explosive kiss. Undoubtedly Hank did, too, which made her blush all the more. "I...yes, I guess you could say that."

They'd reached the door, and Gert pulled it open. "I'm glad. You'll be good for him. Just don't let him get away with any of that I-can't-ever-trust-a-woman-again nonsense. DeeDee hurt him bad, but he doesn't have to give up on marriage just because the first time was a disaster. He needs a wife—he just doesn't know it yet."

Inside, Hank was again carrying Crystal around as he prepared to leave. He'd apparently said his goodbyes and was heading toward the door when Briana and Gert walked in.

He caught Briana around the waist and hugged her against him as he kissed his mother on the cheek. "We're going home," he told Gert. "Crystal needs to be fed. She hasn't eaten since breakfast, and she's also worn out. Dad said he'd handle things at the store tomorrow so I can stay home with her."

With his arm still around Briana, Hank headed out the door.

Crystal whimpered softly as they walked to Hank's truck. When he opened the door on the passenger side, Briana hung back. "I have my car here, Hank."

"Yeah, I know," he said, "but I want you to come home with me, and I'm not taking any chance of you getting away again. I'll bring you out tomorrow to get your car—"

He broke off and looked at her. "That is, unless you don't want to spend the night with me."

She was surprised at the uncertainty in his tone. Couldn't he hear her heart pound and feel her tremor of desire?

She smiled and hugged him around his waist. "Oh, I most certainly do," she murmured, and climbed into the cab.

Crystal refused to be pried away from her daddy, and he finally drove home with one hand while holding her on his lap, still clutching him around the neck. Briana offered to take her, but didn't press it when the child refused.

Hank lived in a three-bedroom home in one of the newer sections of town. It had green siding trimmed in white, and a tile roof with a slant steep enough to discourage snow from piling up on it. Inside, it was spacious, a little cluttered, but clean, and the furniture was top quality and well coordinated. Obviously little had been changed since DeeDee had left.

Hank built a fire in the brick fireplace, then sat in the big leather chair with Crystal again on his lap, while Briana heated homemade soup that she found in the freezer, courtesy of Gert, no doubt. It contained thick chunks of chicken and vegetables, nourishing but not heavy enough to upset already queasy stomachs.

Crystal ate little and said less. It was heartbreaking to see the child, usually so animated and talkative, sitting passively in her chair, pale and silent.

Being lost and alone in the woods had been a terrifying experience for her, and Briana knew that the next few hours were crucial to Crystal's recovery. Either too much or too little attention could fuel her extreme dependence on her father, but how were those who loved her so dearly to know how much was too much and how little was too little?

Finally, Crystal's eyes closed and her head dropped forward. Hank wiped his mouth with his napkin and looked across the table at Briana. "I'm going to put her to bed," he said as he pushed back his chair and stood. "She'll wake up when I get her out of her clothes and put her pajamas on, so I may have to stay with her for a while. I'm sorry. I—"

Briana stood and started toward him. They met in back of Crystal's chair, and he took her in his arms.

"Don't be sorry," she said as she wrapped her arms around his waist. "Your only concern right now should be your daughter. Stay with her as long as she needs you."

He leaned down and kissed her, a sweet kiss filled with gratitude and longing. "I don't like leaving you alone so much. I didn't bring you here to be the cook and maid. Just leave the dishes. I'll clean up in here later."

She squeezed him. "Don't worry about me, Hank. I'd like to help comfort Crystal, but she won't let me, so all I can do is make it easier for you to be with her. Now go along and get her into bed."

He kissed her again, lingeringly and thoroughly, then picked his daughter up and carried her toward the bedrooms.

It was forty-five minutes before he returned to the living room, and in that time, Briana had cleaned up the kitchen and was stretched out on the sofa in front of the fireplace with the television turned to the Denver station. She'd been watching a musical special, but had dozed just enough to hear the music without registering anything else. When the side of the couch sagged under the weight of a heavy body, her eyes flew open.

Hank was sitting there, looking at her, and she smiled and moved over to make room for him. There wasn't enough space for him to stretch out beside her, but he settled his backside more comfortably and leaned down to nuzzle her throat.

His lips moving along the sensitive hollow of her neck made her shiver, and she put her arms around him and held him. "Did you get Crystal to sleep?" she whispered in his ear before drawing the lobe into her mouth.

One of his hands cupped her breast. "Yeah, but it took a while. She wanted me to stay with her. I think she's afraid of being abandoned."

Briana put her hand under the loose neck of his sweatshirt and stroked his bare shoulder. His skin was warm with the consistency of fine leather, and his muscles contracted under her palm. "I know," she said. "You can't blame her. Poor little girl. It may take quite a while before she feels secure again."

Pushing Briana's shirt up, he scooted down the sofa so he could kiss her breasts, and her fingers dug deeper into his shoulder. He caressed the area under her ribs with his thumbs, sending tremors downward to her groin.

When his lips began a trek toward her navel, she put her hands on either side of his head and moaned with pleasure. Immediately he stopped and laid his cheek against her stomach. She assumed he'd misunderstood.

"I wasn't trying to stop you." Her voice was husky with passion.

"I know." He squeezed her waist between his hands before he sat up. "But I've been tramping through the woods all day and I'm not going to go any farther with this until I've had a shower." He smiled down at her. "Would you care to join me?"

Tomorrow morning she probably would, but tonight she was still too shy to be so bold. She'd never even seen him without his shirt, and so far, they hadn't seen or touched each other's bodies below the waist.

She could feel the flush that stained her face. "Would...would you mind if I used the other bathroom instead?" She sounded like a schoolgirl.

He looked at her for a moment, his expression one of uncertainty. When he spoke, his tone was almost harsh. "Briana, have you ever been with a man before?"

She tensed and looked away. "Yes. I'm not a virgin, Hank. Is that important to you?"

He chuckled and reached out to run his finger down her cheek. "Only because I'm not in the habit of deflowering virgins. Your past is none of my business, sweetheart, but I didn't want to hurt you if you were still...uh...intact."

Your past is none of my business. Oh, how blissful ignorance can be, Briana thought. Her past would be very much his business if they should ever marry, and the unsavory details could destroy him, as well as their love.

It was the urgency in his voice that recaptured her attention. "Briana, what's the matter? Did I say something to offend you? You turned so white all of a sudden."

She managed a smile. She wasn't going to let the past intrude on this special night. "I'm all right," she assured him. "I guess the stress of the day is just catching up with me. I'm sorry to be so old maidish, but the idea of taking a shower with you embarrasses me. We...we don't know each other very well.''

This time his laughter was full-blown. "I promise to remedy that as soon as I get out of the shower." He took her hands to help her up. "Come on, you can have the bathroom in the hall, and I'll take the one in the master bedroom."

A few minutes later, he knocked on the bathroom door and handed her a garment. "Here, it's one of my pajama tops—a concession to your modesty. It'll be long enough to cover you. There are new toothbrushes and a clean hairbrush in the top vanity drawer. Help yourself."

Briana opted for a hot, fragrant bubble bath instead of a shower, and it was so relaxing that she actually dozed again in the tub. When she woke, the water was cool and she knew she'd been there far longer than she'd intended. She was surprised that Hank hadn't gotten impatient and come knocking on the door.

Quickly she toweled herself and brushed her teeth and her hair, then put on the oversize gray pajama top that came to her knees. The sleeves covered her hands, and she rolled them back, then picked up her clothes and headed for the master bedroom at the end of the hall.

Only the small lamp atop the bookcase headboard was lighted, casting the room in a soft, romantic light. At a glance, she noticed that it was a thoroughly masculine room decorated in earth tones and with heavy, dark-stained furniture, including a desk instead of a vanity. The closed drapes were only a shade darker than the beige walls, and the only wall hanging was an oil seascape above the bed. This must be the one room in the house that Hank had completely redecorated after DeeDee left him, Briana thought.

When her gaze dropped to the bed, she saw Hank lying on top of the turned back covers, wearing only a pair of skimpy, white briefs, sound asleep. She crossed the room on the thick, soundless carpet to stand beside him. He'd obviously lain down after his shower to wait for her and had gone to sleep.

She couldn't blame him. After all, she'd dozed off in the bathtub and kept him waiting. They were both exhausted after a long day of tension and anxiety, and he'd admitted to not sleeping well for the past few weeks.

She leaned over and carefully brushed a damp lock of hair off his forehead. Dear Lord, the man was gorgeous. A living, breathing Michaelangelo sculpture—big, muscular and symmetrical.

In total relaxation, he looked younger, almost boyish, with his tousled blond hair and long, thick, brown eyelashes. The lines of strain were gone from his smooth, freshly shaven face, and she could smell the tantalizing fragrance of his shaving lotion, musky and expensive. His nose was slightly irregular—it had probably been broken at one time—and she'd have known that his wide, firm mouth was made for kissing even if she hadn't experienced its delights.

Her hands itched to explore his long, brawny body. To tangle her fingers in the thatch of equally blond hair on his broad chest and taste the hard, dark rose nipples that seemed to beckon her.

She felt her own nipples harden and would have welcomed his mouth on them, his tongue caressing them.

She knew she should stop this, that she was intruding on his privacy, but she couldn't keep her gaze from wandering lower, across his flat belly to the tight, white briefs that did little to hide his maleness.

A sharp tug deep in the core of her femininity jolted her, and this time, she tore her gaze away. Good heavens, what was the matter with her? She'd never been this fascinated with a man's body before. What if Hank woke up and caught her violating him?

A tiny smile tipped the sides of her mouth. If she knew Hank, he'd probably violate her right back, and they wouldn't stop until morning.

She wasn't going to wake him. He badly needed his sleep, and there would be lots of other nights. She could bed down on the couch, but it was a little chilly in the house and she didn't want to leave him uncovered. Maybe she could pull the covers out from under his hips and put them up to his shoulders without disturbing him.

She tried sliding them, but he was too heavy. They wouldn't move. Then she pulled, but only made a little headway. Finally, she pulled them down on the other side of the bed and tried moving him over there. That was when his hand clamped unexpectedly around her wrist, throwing her off balance and across him.

He still didn't wake up, but neither did he loosen his grip on her. She tried to pull away, and he muttered almost unintelligibly, "Come to bed."

She knew he wasn't awake. He probably thought he was talking to his wife. She slid back until her feet were on the floor, then tried to pry his fingers loose. This time his muttering was clearer. "Briana, don't leave. Come to bed."

She gave up the struggle and put her mouth close to his exposed ear. "You'll have to let loose of me so I can."

His fingers relaxed, and she stood up and pulled the covers over him, then went around to the other side of the bed and shut off the light before she climbed in beside him. He reached for her and cuddled her against him, then murmured, "Sorry. I'll wake up pretty soon. Stay with me." Then he fell into a deep sleep.

A frightened cry from far off started Briana on the journey up from the depth of heavy sleep. It sounded again, and she fought harder to wake up, but it wasn't until the third time that she identified it. It was Crystal calling "Daddy!" in a chilling wail.

She opened her eyes and tried to sit up, but something was holding her down. She put out her hand and touched warm, bare flesh. Then she remembered. Hank. He was still cradling her in his arms, and as she struggled, they tightened.

He hadn't heard Crystal, and she didn't want to wake him unless she had to. Putting her hand to his cheek, she said softly, "It's all right, darling, I just need to get up for a minute."

She seemed to be able to get through to his subconscious. He released her and didn't protest when she rolled off the bed and headed out of the room.

Crystal was still calling, and Briana shut the bedroom door behind her as she stumbled down the hall toward the frightened voice. She flipped the light switch on the wall as she rushed into the bedroom. She saw Crystal, wearing pink-flowered flannel pajamas, sitting in the middle of the bed, crying out in terror. "Daddy. Daddy. Daddy," she screamed as Briana ran across the room and clasped the child in her arms. "I want my daddy," Crystal sobbed, but she cuddled against Briana.

"It's all right, sweetheart," Briana crooned as she stroked and patted the little girl. "Daddy's asleep, but I'm here. I won't leave you."

"I want my daddy," the child repeated, but more quietly, and she didn't try to pull away from Briana.

"I know you do," she said, "but Daddy's so tired. Why don't we let him sleep, and I'll stay with you?"

"The bear will get me," Crystal sobbed illogically.

"No, it won't." Briana was playing it blindly. "There's no bear here. You're at home in your own bed, and I'm here with you, and Daddy's right next door." She hugged the youngster tighter. "It was just a bad dream. Everything's all right now. You don't have to be afraid."

"The bear will take me away," the little girl insisted, still obviously in the throes of a nightmare.

Briana hugged her tighter. "The bear is gone. She went back in the woods, and she won't ever come after you."

It didn't seem likely that Crystal had actually seen a bear while she was in the forest, but Briana decided to talk to her as if she had. "That was a mama bear who had little baby bears, and she was afraid you might hurt them if you came too near. She'll stay with them in the woods. You're safe here at home with Daddy and me. We won't let you get lost again."

Crystal relaxed against her, and for a while, Briana held her and sang "Rockabye Baby," the only lullaby she knew, as they rocked gently back and forth on the bed. When she thought Crystal was asleep, she started to lay her back down, but the traumatized child clutched at her and cried, "No, the bear will come back and eat me."

Briana sighed. There was only one way to handle this. She switched on the Winnie-the-Pooh nursery lamp that sat on the chest beside the bed. "Do you want me to sleep with you for the rest of the night?"

Crystal nodded.

"All right. You lie down while I go over and turn off the ceiling light. I'll be right back."

Surprisingly, Crystal didn't object when Briana got off the bed and flicked the switch on the wall, leaving only the dim illumination from the lamp. She went back and reached for the lamp switch, but Crystal stopped her.

"I want the light on," the little girl said anxiously.

"Then we'll leave it on," Briana assured her as she crawled into bed beside her. "Now, you go to sleep, and let me worry about the bear," she said, and cradled the little girl's back against her chest.

Crystal snuggled right down and within minutes, was sound asleep. Briana laid her cheek on the moist little golden head and silently mourned for the tiny daughter she'd lost.

Her own baby would now be the same age as the child she held in her arms. She wondered if Hank really understood how lucky he was to be able to raise his daughter.

Chapter Ten

Hank felt the discomfort in his joints and muscles before he was fully aware of it. In a reflex motion, he rolled over onto his back and stretched, then felt better and relaxed into the softness of the mattress.

Something was amiss, but he was too tired to think. He rolled onto his other side and clutched the extra pillow. Pillow? He wasn't supposed to be hugging the pillow.

He was supposed to be making love to Briana!

His eyes flew open and his feet hit the floor at the same time, causing his senses to swim. It was dark, and he sat on the edge of the bed and held his head in his hands until it quit spinning. Good grief! What happened last night? Where was Briana? And why was he waking up with a hangover?

He shook his head and it began to spin again. Even so, it didn't feel like a hangover. There was no pain, just a woozy feeling, a sense of being disoriented and dizzy. As if he'd slept too soundly and then woken up too quick.

He turned on the lamp and looked at his watch. Five o'clock. His mind wandered backward, searching for a memory, and stopped with an image of him in the shower. He'd been exhausted and hoped the hot, stinging water would wake him up. He had felt a little more alert. He remembered drying himself and stepping into a pair of clean briefs, then lying down on the bed to wait for Briana....

He ran his fingers through his hair. After that, everything was blank until just a few minutes ago. He'd obviously gone to sleep, but where was Briana?

The thought brought him to his feet. Dear God, was she all right? Had she ever come out of the other bathroom?

He tore out of the room and down the hall to find the bathroom empty and neat, with everything in place. He couldn't even tell it had been used. Slumping against the doorjamb, he rubbed his hands over his face. She must have finished her bath and come into his bedroom to find him dead to the world.

He slammed his fist against the wall. "Damn it to hell!" This time he'd really done it. How was he going to make her believe that making love to her, having her with him, were the most important things on earth to him now that Crystal was safe?

He might have had a chance if he hadn't so self-righteously announced such a short time ago that he didn't intend to get involved with her under any circumstances. Boy, had he underestimated the depth of his feelings for her!

What a pompous ass he'd been for assuming that he had complete control over his emotions. He couldn't even control his sleep patterns. He'd been totally out of it for over eight hours. It was a good thing Crystal hadn't wakened during the night. . . .

Crystal! Was she all right? He'd been sleeping so soundly that he doubted she could have wakened him if she'd tried.

He lunged across the hall and found the door to her room shut. He hadn't closed it. He never closed either her door or his so he'd be sure to hear her if she called him in the night, but now that he thought of it, his had been closed this morning, too.

He turned the knob and pushed. The lamp was on, and he could see that the bed was occupied. A wave of relief was cut off when he saw that the figure in the bed was too big to be Crystal!

His heart pounded with anxiety as he strode across the room. It wasn't until he got closer that he realized there were two people in the bed, a larger one curled onto her side and holding a small one safe and warm in the arc of her body.

It was Briana, and she and Crystal were sound asleep. A thick lock of ebony hair covered Briana's exposed cheek, then fell over her jaw and rested against her bare throat. Hank had never been so touched by the sight of a woman sleeping, not even DeeDee. Awake, Briana was startling beautiful, but in sleep, she was even more appealing. She looked so young and ethereal with her light, rosy skin in contrast to her shining black hair and deep green eyes, hidden now behind delicate eyelids with long, raven lashes that curled against her cheek.

Her delicate features were peaceful in repose, as untouched by life as Crystal's. They looked like big and little sisters sharing the same bed, and Hank was reminded of every one of his thirty-two-and-a-half years. He was so much older than Briana, not only in years, but in experience. He'd already been married, divorced and was a father, whereas she was still trying her wings.

If he were half as honorable as he should be, he'd get out of her life and give her a chance to fly, to go places and see things and find a man nearer her own age, one who hadn't yet become disillusioned and jaded. But he was through being honorable. It hurt too much and he couldn't bear the pain any longer. Briana was old enough to know what she wanted, and he was going to take what she offered and hope for the best.

If she, too, eventually left him, he'd deal with that when it happened. He'd try to protect Crystal, but it was already too late for him. His defenses had crumbled and there was no chance of reconstructing them.

He walked around the bed quietly and stood behind her. Leaning down, he touched her shoulder and whispered her name. Her shoulder twitched, but she slept on.

He touched her again, and this time shook her lightly as he murmured, "Briana, wake up."

"Wh-what?" she stammered, trying to turn onto her back, but her movement was restricted by Crystal.

Hank hunkered down by the bed and blew gently on her neck. "Hey, sleepyhead, wake up," he whispered. "What are you doing in here?"

She twisted her head to look at him and smiled. "Hank." Her voice was fuzzy with sleep. "I might ask you the same question."

Carefully, she pulled her arm out from under Crystal and rolled over into his eager embrace. She was warm and moist and soft, and he shivered as she put her arms around his neck and cuddled against him. "What are you doing in here?" he asked again. "I woke up and thought you'd gone home. What happened last night? I don't remember a thing after I got out of the shower and laid down on the bed." He spoke in low tones so as not to wake Crystal.

"When I got to the bedroom after my bath, you were sound asleep," Briana explained, also keeping her voice low. "You were so exhausted, I decided to sleep on the couch, but you grabbed me when I tried to cover you and told me to come to bed, so I did."

"But you weren't there when I woke up just now," he pointed out. "I... Oh, God, Briana, I was half-crazy for fear you were offended because I'd gone to sleep."

She moved her lips against his bare chest, stirring up hormones all through him. "How could I be angry? You looked so peaceful stretched out on the bed, wearing nothing but your undershorts."

He nibbled on her ear. "If you'll come back to bed with me, I'll be happy to take them off. Let's go before we wake up Crystal."

He started to pull back the covers, but Briana stopped him. "Hank, I don't think I should...."

He felt as if a lead weight had just been dropped in his stomach. It served him right for conking out on her and giving her time to have second thoughts about getting intimately involved with a man like him, who couldn't even make up his mind about what he wanted from her.

"I mean, Crystal had a nightmare," she continued, "and I had to promise to stay with her before she could go back to sleep. I don't want her to wake up and find me gone. She might be frightened and think she can't trust me to keep my word."

He was forced to admit that she had a point, but his aching groin wasn't willing to concede. "We can leave the light on, and it'll be daylight soon," he reminded her. "It's not as if she'd wake up in the dark again."

She stroked the back of his head, and he didn't think he could bear to let her go now that he had her in his arms again. "I—I don't know," she said. "You know your daughter better than I do. Maybe she wouldn't mind, but she was so upset . . ."

Hank knew he was being not only selfish, but childish. Briana was right. Crystal's well-being was a hell of a lot more important than his own. He remembered the sense of panic he'd felt when he'd wakened in bed alone, knowing Briana was supposed to be there. He wasn't going to take the chance of his little daughter being frightened when she awakened, too.

He swallowed his disappointment and tried not to let it come through in his voice. "You're right, honey. I'm afraid she needs you right now even worse than I do, although I'm not sure that's possible. Go back to sleep, and thank you for taking such good care of my little girl."

He kissed her, long and lingeringly, then again and again until it was all he could do to tear himself away from her warm and willing arms instead of picking her up and carrying her off with him.

Afterward, he headed for the bathroom and a long, cold shower.

It was eight o'clock before Crystal woke up. After Hank left, Briana had slept fitfully, too aroused to totally relax, but enjoying the sensations induced by the memory of his roaming hands and his hungry mouth on her sensitized body. She was delighted to know that he wanted her so badly, and sorry that she couldn't be with him.

She was dozing when she felt Crystal stir, then sit up beside her in the bed. "Good morning," Briana said as the child looked at her with surprise. "Didn't you remember that I was sleeping with you?"

The little girl rubbed one blue eye with her small fist. "You chased the bear away."

Briana smiled. "That's right. Are you hungry? What do you want for breakfast?"

"Sugar Krispies," Crystal answered without hesitation.

Briana winced at the thought of all that sugar. "Is that what you eat for breakfast?"

"No. Grandma and Daddy say it will make my teeth hurt, but I like it."

Briana chuckled. "Your daddy and grandma are right, but I'm sure we can find something that you'll like almost as much." She threw back the covers and got out of bed. "Why don't you go to the bathroom and brush your teeth while I get dressed, then we'll go see what we can find to eat?"

Crystal looked around the room. "Where are your clothes? Why are you wearing the top to Daddy's pajamas?"

That stopped Briana cold. There were times when she'd had to explain unorthodox behavior to her mother, but never to a four-year-old child.

"My...my clothes are in..." She paused. She couldn't tell Hank's little daughter that her clothes were in her daddy's bedroom. "In another room," she finished lamely. "And your daddy loaned me his pajama top because I—I didn't have a nightgown here...."

"Oh," Crystal said as though the explanation was perfectly clear, then she hopped out of bed and scurried away, leaving Briana gaping after her.

As Briana stepped out of the room, she encountered Hank coming down the hall. He was dressed in his usual jeans and a black-plaid Western-style shirt. He stopped a few inches away to let his gaze roam over her from her tousled hair, over the too-big pajama top that had some-how come unbuttoned nearly to the waist, and down to where it ended at midthigh, then skim her bare legs to her equally bare feet.

He groaned audibly and ploughed his hand through his hair. "I'm not even going to touch you until you put some clothes on," he said, his voice raspy. "I've been suffering the frustration of the damned from tangling with you earlier. I'm not going to put myself through that again."

He couldn't seem to tear his glance away from the hem of the pajama top that left her decently covered—but just barely. "Are you wearing anything under that?" His voice was hoarse.

She smiled seductively. "No."

He looked around. "Where's Crystal?"

"She's in the bathroom."

He glanced at the closed bathroom door, then with a muttered curse, picked Briana up and carried her into his bedroom. He closed the door and leaned against it, then lowered her slowly between his legs until she fit into his pelvis, and he held her there with his hands moving over her bare derriere.

He was rigid with barely controlled desire, and she trembled from her own need to accommodate him. His breathing was ragged, and his heart pounded against her breast as he lowered his head and devoured her mouth with moist, open kisses.

She clutched him around the neck and in a desperate effort to assuage their mutual urgency, moved her hips back and forth to rub against him. Shock waves of pleasure rocked her, and Hank's cry was one of actual pain.

"Briana, enough!" He was shivering as he lowered her feet to the floor and disengaged himself from her. "I can't take any more of that. Please, get dressed while I see to Crystal." His voice was low and unsteady.

He put his hands on her shoulders and kissed her, hard and hungrily, but without any other bodily contact. "This is going to be a long day," he muttered before opening the door and stepping in to the hall.

The night's sleep and her naturally sunny disposition had done much to restore Crystal's animation, and she chattered happily through breakfast. She was still reluctant to let Hank out of her sight, however, and followed him around like a puppy.

While they ate, Hank told Briana of his plans for the day. "I wish we could spend it together," he said, "but today and tomorrow are the only days I have to put up that fence around the Perkins's property. I'm not going to take any chances of either Crystal or another child wandering into those woods again. I lined up a couple of guys yesterday who are going to help, so I'll go pick up the material and you can ride out to the farm with me to get your car."

He reached across the table and covered her hand with his. "I'm sorry, honey. Sorrier than I can say, but this is something that can't be put off any longer. You're welcome to stay there with us if you want to, but I won't be at the house and I don't want you to feel that you have to look after Crystal. Margaret will do that. I'm quite sure she'll never let the child out of her sight again."

Briana brushed aside her disappointment. She remembered now hearing him tell the crowd that he was going to start putting up a fence today, and she was touched by his concern that she might think he wanted her to baby-sit.

Turning her hand up, she squeezed his and smiled. "Of course, you have to do it. I understand, but I can't stay. I have a lot of things to do around the apartment."

"You will come back here for dinner, won't you?" He sounded anxious, as though she might refuse. "I'd take you out, but I don't think I can leave Crystal with a sitter just yet."

"I'd love to come," she assured him. "Can I bring anything?"

"Just bring yourself." His eyes brimmed with anticipation. "I'll take care of everything else."

By the time Briana got back to her apartment, it was early afternoon. Margaret had insisted that she stay for lunch, and Briana couldn't refuse without hurting her feelings.

The phone started ringing as she was unlocking her door, and she rushed inside to answer it. "Briana, it's Mother," said the voice at the other end.

Something about her mother's voice made Briana's heart jump alarmingly. "Mother? How are you? I—I was planning to call you tomorrow," she said, referring to the telephone call she placed to Los Angeles every Sunday so that her mother wouldn't have to pay the cost of a long-distance call to Whispering Pines out of her meager waitress's salary.

"I know, dear, but something's come up and...well...I thought you should know as soon as possible."

Briana's nerves screamed. "What's the matter? Are you all right? Is it one of the kids...?"

"No, no we're okay," Kathleen Innes assured her, "but night before last, I had a call from Scott Upton—"

Briana gasped. "*Scott* called you?"

"Yes," Kathleen said. "He wanted to know how you are and where you're living."

Briana was trembling with a combination of rage, indignation and more than a touch of apprehension. "That bastard! He's about five years late with his concern. You didn't tell him, did you?''

"No. Of course not. He...he also asked about the baby." Kathleen's voice was low and barely audible.

Briana felt the shock all the way to her toes, and she gripped the phone until her knuckles were white. "Oh, my God," she moaned. "You didn't—"

"You're darn right I didn't," Kathleen said angrily. "I told him the baby was none of his business, and if he ever called here again, I'd have him arrested for making obscene phone calls."

Briana almost smiled in spite of her outrage. Her mother was nothing if not inventive. "What did he say then?"

"He just hung up, but..." Kathleen's voice trailed off, and Briana's nerves again went on alert.

"But what, Mother?"

"Oh, honey, Paddy just told me this morning that he ran into Scott on his way home from school yesterday."

Paddy was Briana's ten-year-old brother, Patrick. "You mean Scott's in L.A.?"

"Yes, he bought Paddy a malted milk at that ice-cream place where the kids hang out. He—he asked Paddy how you were and if you were married and had any children—"

"That bastard! Taking advantage of a little boy." Her bitter exclamation slipped out before Briana could stop it. "I'm sorry, Mom, go on."

"Well, Paddy said no, and then he asked where you were living. Oh, Bree," her mother wailed, using the nickname the family had given her. "Paddy didn't know any better. He told Scott that you were living in Whispering Pines, Wyoming."

For a moment, Briana just stared into the phone, too dumbfounded to speak. If that sleaze showed up around here, she'd strangle him with her bare hands, and no jury made up of women would convict her. Where had he been when she needed him? And why was he asking about her now?

A racket nearby brought her back to the present, and she realized that it was her mother hollering into the phone. "Briana! Briana, are you there?"

She put the receiver back to her ear. "I'm here, Mother," she managed to say in a half whisper.

"You're not mad at Paddy, are you?" Kathleen sounded panicky. "He doesn't know anything about—"

"No, I'm not mad at Patrick," she assured her mother. "But tell him not to ever talk to Scott again."

"Don't worry, I already have." Kathleen paused. "Bree, what do you think Scott will do?"

Briana swallowed the bile that rose in her throat. "I don't know, but don't worry, I can take care of myself."

She laughed, and there was a touch of hysteria in it. "Hell, I won't even have to strangle him. I'll just threaten to tell my story to the news media, and he'll never bother me again. He can't afford that kind of publicity."

There was a gasp on the other end of the line. "Briana, what are you talking about? Surely you wouldn't do that? What would all our friends and the people at church say?"

Briana slumped forward and closed her eyes. Would she never get used to the fact that her devout mother had always been more concerned with what other people would think of her daughter's sin than she was about what Briana may have suffered or wanted? Briana had always been taught that giving was the highest form of love, so how could giving love be a sin? And unwise though it turned out to be, she had loved Scott.

"No, Mother, I wouldn't do that," she said sadly. *Not unless he forces me to,* she added silently. "Thanks for telling me about this. At least I'll be forewarned if he tries to get in touch with me. Tell all the kids hi, and I'll talk to you again next week. Bye."

She hung up and tried to sort out her chaotic thoughts.

The second call came later that afternoon. She answered it and was greeted by another familiar voice, this one bubbling over with excitement. "Hi, it's me, Elly."

Briana's spirits rose at the exuberance in her friend's voice. "Elly, you must be a mind reader. Your dad and I were just talking about you yesterday."

Had it really been only yesterday morning that she and Dr. Wainwright had been chatting about Elly, before the peace of the town was shattered by Crystal's disappearance?

"Nothing bad, I hope," Elly said with a laugh.

"Swear on my honor it was all good," Briana assured her. "I asked him when you were coming home. Seems like you've been gone forever."

"Seems that way to me, too, but the doctor down here has finally released me and I'm catching the morning flight tomorrow. However, there's a hitch."

Elly paused to catch her breath, and Briana sagged with relief. If Elly was coming home, then she obviously wasn't pregnant.

"The flight to Cody would mean a long layover in Denver, so I decided to fly into Billings," Elly continued. "I assumed Dad could pick me up there, but he's committed to giving a speech at a dental-society conference in Sheridan tomorrow. It's too late for him to back out, and

Mom's not strong enough to drive that far. Is there any chance that you could meet me?''

Billings, Montana, was approximately two hundred miles to the north. Briana was delighted that Elly was coming home, and she would enjoy meeting her in Billings, but what about Hank? Did he expect her to spend tomorrow with him? Or would he still be working on putting up the fence? He hadn't mentioned any plans he might have for Sunday.

Elly's voice interrupted her thoughts. "Briana? Isn't it convenient for you to meet me?''

"Of course, it is, and I'd love to," Briana assured her friend. Just because she'd slipped up and fallen in love with Hank Robinson didn't mean she had to put her life on hold for him. If he wanted her with him, he'd have to schedule it in advance or take his chances that she'd be busy. "Tell me what time, and I'll be there.''

Briana dressed with great care for her dinner date with Hank and Crystal that evening. After a warm, invigorating shower, she put on her best underwear—a lacy mauve bra and panty set—then donned a loose-fitting, black cotton fiesta dress trimmed with big, bold, hand-embroidered, abstract swirls in bright colors across the front. She'd bought it last year for half-price at a designer boutique in Denver.

Shunning panty hose, she slipped her bare feet into purple flats made of soft leather, then applied blusher, lipstick and a touch of eye shadow that highlighted the green of her eyes. She brushed her hair, separated out the wispy bangs and let the rest fall free to below her shoulders.

She arrived at Hank's house on the stroke of six, the time he had set, and Crystal opened the door for her.

"We're having barbecue," she gushed. "Daddy's out on the deck. Come on, I'll show you." Before Briana could respond, Crystal grabbed her hand and led her across the dining room and through the sliding glass doors onto the redwood deck.

"Daddy, Briana's here," she announced as Hank turned to see for himself.

He was wearing beige cotton dress slacks and a chocolate brown shirt open at the throat. It was the first time Briana had ever seen him in anything but Western attire, and he looked smashing.

His equally admiring gaze roamed over her for a moment before he put his hand at the back of her neck and brought her face close enough to kiss. Their lips barely touched, but the magnetism between them sizzled.

"Hello, sweetheart," he murmured, and he rubbed his forehead against hers. "God, I thought six o'clock would never come."

"Me, too," she whispered as their lips touched again and clung.

"We got corn on the cob," Crystal said, still pulling on Briana's hand, "and potatoes, too. It's in the fire, see."

With a sigh, Hank and Briana moved apart, and Briana went with Crystal to look at the foil-wrapped vegetables in the hot coals.

Evenings in the high mountain area of Yellowstone Park were still too chilly for eating outside, so Hank served their dinner in the dining room. The steaks were thick, juicy and tender, the vegetables soft and steaming, and the salad was tossed with a dressing Hank said was an old family recipe of his mother's that was so secret, she wouldn't even give it to him.

"She makes it for me a quart at a time," he said, and Briana could understand why Gert didn't want to share the recipe. It was delicious.

During the meal, Hank told her that he had at least another day's work putting up the fence. "There's over an acre there to be closed in," he said. "If we don't finish tomorrow, I'll let Bud and Dusty finish up by themselves."

Briana talked about Elly's phone call. "I'm meeting her plane in Billings at two o'clock tomorrow. I'll sure be glad to have her back, not only as a friend, but that temporary chairside we hired from the agency in Cody is more of a pain than a help."

When it came time to clear the table for dessert, Crystal insisted on helping. "We got choc'lat pie," she said excitedly. "Daddy bought it at the bakery."

"You got a big mouth, kid," Hank muttered good-naturedly as he reached down and mussed her hair. "Jeez, try to keep a secret around this house."

After the first bite, Briana assured him that while he may have bought it at the bakery, it was definitely home-made and better than any she'd tasted that had come from the specialty pie shops in Denver or Los Angeles.

After dinner, Hank and Briana teamed up to do the dishes, and then it was time to put Crystal to bed. She was the I-can-do-it-by-myself type of child who insisted on undressing and putting on her own pajamas. After she'd brushed her teeth and climbed into her bed, Briana gave her a good-night hug and kiss while Hank found the book she wanted him to read to her.

"Are you going to sleep with me again tonight?" Crystal asked Briana, momentarily throwing her off balance.

Hank had made it plain this morning that he wanted her to go to bed with him tonight, but did he expect her to stay all night? Or was she supposed to go home after they'd made love?

She watched him out of the corner of her eyes as she answered, "Not tonight, honey. I have to go home and sleep in my own bed."

For just a moment, she thought she saw relief in Hank's face, but it was gone so quickly that she couldn't be sure.

She went into the living room to wait while he read his daughter a bedtime story. Settling herself comfortably on the couch in front of the crackling fire in the fireplace, she pondered Hank's reaction. She'd expected him to be disappointed, or at least neutral when she'd said she wouldn't be sleeping here, but she wasn't prepared for the flash of relief.

Actually, she'd come prepared to stay, but had left the small suitcase with a change of clothes and her makeup in the trunk of her car. There was one indispensable item that she carried in her purse, a box of condoms.

She was afraid Hank would expect her to be on the pill, but until now, her only lover had been Scott, and he'd assured her that he had been taking precautions. She'd been too naive to know that some of the time he hadn't acted quickly enough to protect her.

She had no intentions of letting that happen again, so she had stopped at the drugstore on her way over earlier.

Briana squirmed uncomfortably. There was something awfully premeditated about calculating the act of making love this way. Like analyzing a miracle.

Chapter Eleven

The sound of footsteps announced Hank's approach, and Briana looked up as he came across the room toward her.

"Sorry to keep you waiting," he said. "I cut the story as short as I could, but she knows it by heart, so she caught me when I tried to skip parts."

He sat down on the couch beside Briana and took her in his arms. "Sometimes being a single father has its disadvantages," he murmured as he snuggled his face in the curve of her neck, sending tickles through her. "It was all I could do to keep my hands off you during that interminable meal."

She tipped her head to give him easier access. "That was a delicious dinner," she said softly. "I enjoyed every mouthful."

He nibbled on her earlobe. "Weren't you even once tempted to put your hand on my leg under the table?"

She almost purred with contentment. "You mean like this?" she said, caressing his thigh.

Beneath her palm his muscles twitched. "Oh, yes, just like that...and that...and...don't stop now," he moaned as her hand moved slowly higher and higher until it nestled chastely in the crease between the top of his leg and his groin.

She was enjoying it as much as he was, but she knew if she continued higher, they'd never make it to the bedroom. Not that she'd mind making love on the thick carpet in front of the fire, but they weren't alone in the house. There was always a chance that Crystal might wake up and come wandering out.

"I think we'd better cool it a little," she murmured, and moved her hand downward to the middle of his thigh. "There's no hurry. We have all night."

"Speak for yourself, love." His voice was raspy as he found her knee under her skirt and fondled it. "I've just about run out of control. It seems like I've been in a permanent state of arousal ever since you appeared in the doorway at the dentist's office and beckoned so enticingly for me to follow you."

He released her knee and stroked the inside of her thigh as his fingers inched toward her throbbing heat, scattering her thoughts and giving her a taste of her own teasing.

"I—I didn't entice you," she stammered.

"You may not have meant to," he said as his fingers continued their upward spiral, "but you did, and I haven't been the same cool, patient and sensible man since."

His words blurred as his escalating touch drove her wild. "Now I'm hot, impatient and unable to concentrate on anything but how much I want you."

His seeking fingers found their goal, and she stiffened and gasped as her whole body was wracked with tremors.

Hank tore himself away from her, then stood and swept her up into his arms. "We've just ran out of time," he muttered as he headed for the hall.

She was as hot and impatient as he, but retained just enough of her wits to remember one vital necessity. "My...my purse." It came out a whisper, and she cleared her throat. "I need protection."

"I'll take care of it," he said as he strode into the bedroom and closed and locked the door behind them. He stood her on the floor beside the bed and then turned on the lamp. Opening the top drawer of the bedside chest, he handed her a small foil package. "Don't worry, sweetheart." His tone was soft. "I won't get you pregnant."

She knew he meant it to be reassuring, but in her blurred state of mind, she felt a jolt of disappointment and wished he'd said, "I want you to marry me and have my baby."

He took the package from her and put it on top of the chest, then pulled the bed covers down and reached for her. She snuggled into his embrace and raised her face to his. His green eyes were dark with wanting, and his heart hammered against her.

When his lips touched hers, it was with an unexpected gentleness, and she knew he was holding back, trying to prolong the experience. His hands skimmed down her back and hips, then under her skirt to settle on her satin-and-lace-covered buttocks. "You fit into my hands just like I knew you would," he whispered raggedly as he held her tight against his pelvis. "After tonight, I don't know how I'm going to keep my hands off you in public."

He was trembling when he finally stepped back and slowly inched her dress up and over her head, leaving her nude except for the bikini panty and abbreviated bra. A wave of shyness made her blush as his gaze drifted over her. "So exquisite and still so sweet," he said, his tone a mixture of admiration and awe.

Reaching out, he cupped the undersides of her breasts while his thumbs rubbed over her hard rosy nipples. For a moment he closed his eyes, and a flicker of intense emotion, almost like pain, crossed his face.

"There have been times when my hands ached so bad to do this that even my fingernails hurt." There was no hint of levity or teasing in his tone. "Especially when you wore those low-cut square-dance dresses that fit tight across the breasts."

His words were as arousing as his hands, and her voice quavered as she spoke. "Does it feel as good as you thought it would?"

"Even better." His voice wasn't steady, either, as he lowered his head and kissed her on first one breast and then the other while unfastening the bra and sliding it off her shoulders.

She stepped out of her panties while he pulled off his shirt, then reached for his belt buckle.

Briana put her hands over his. "Wait," she said, not wanting to be left out. "It's my turn. Let me do that."

He sucked in his breath and raised her hands to his mouth to kiss the back of each before releasing them. "All right, but be careful. If you touch me, I'm not sure I can control my response."

She fumbled with his buckle. "I've already seen you without your clothes on," she said, hoping to distract him for a moment until she got his pants off. "Last night, when I came into this room, you stretched out on the bed sound asleep in nothing but your briefs. I had time to study you."

She found the metal pull and started lowering his zipper, careful to keep her eager hands from brushing him.

His fists knotted at his sides. "Did...did you like what you saw?" His words were slightly slurred.

She smiled up at him as she worked. "Oh, my, yes. You have a magnificent body. I hated to pull the covers over it."

She finally got his slacks open and hooked her fingers under the waistbands of both his slacks and his shorts to push them down at the same time. He took over and removed his clothes, then stood before her without a trace of shyness. Not that he had any reason to be embarrassed.

He put his arms around her and pulled her against him. "Feel free to study me anytime you like," he said huskily, "but right now, there are better things for us to do."

He lowered her onto the bed, then followed to lie partially over her with his groin against her hip and his knee between her legs. He was a big man, and heavy, but somehow he managed to hold her so that he wasn't putting his full weight on her, and she reveled in the feel of his bare flesh.

He lowered his head and took one of her nipples in his mouth, creating sparks in her that threatened to burst into a conflagration. She arched against him and ran her palms over the thick skin of his back. His powerful muscles rippled at her touch, and his belly knotted against her hip as he fought for control.

She shifted so that she was totally under him and dug her fingers into his shoulders. Later they could take the time to savor their lovemaking, but not now. They'd denied themselves for too long, and she had a raging need to be one with him, to come together in the soul-searing flame that would meld them in a union that could never be ripped apart.

She could feel his chest heave in short, irregular gasps as she twined her legs with his. "Hank, please." Her tone was a cross between a moan and a plea. "I want you now."

He raised his head and looked at her with passion-glazed eyes, then reached behind him for the package. A moment later, his eager mouth devoured hers. Their bodies joined, and the whole world exploded.

The mind-boggling gratification seemed to go on forever as they hovered on the brink of paradise. Briana felt like a harp string strung so tightly that, once set in motion, it couldn't stop quivering. She was floating, and each time it seemed she'd reached a pinnacle, the explosion would come again, rocketing her even higher.

A long time later, she was aware of Hank moving off of her and holding her close against his sweat-dampened body. His chest hair was rough under her cheek, and she turned her head just enough to kiss the dark nipple and caress it with her tongue. It tasted salty.

"Are you all right?" he asked, and rubbed his face against the top of her head. "I was getting a little concerned."

"I'm fine," she said on a sigh of contentment. "It's just that I've never experienced anything like that before."

He stroked his fingers through her hair. "Neither have I."

Her eyes widened, and she raised her head to look at him. "Really?"

He smiled and kissed her forehead. "Really."

"But . . . but you've been married. . . ."

"That was never like this." His eyes half closed as his arms tightened around her.

She nestled her face back into his chest. "I thought I was going to touch heaven. Oh, Hank, I love you so."

Again he stroked her hair and the back of her neck. "I suspect we both came as close to touching heaven as mortals ever get," he said softly. "Now rest for a while."

She did better than that; she went to sleep.

It was dark in the room when she was wakened by Hank pulling away from her, and then she heard Crystal's shrill cry. "Daddy! Daddy, the bear's going to get me!"

Hank turned on the lamp and was scrambling into his pants when Briana came fully awake and sat up. "It—It's Crystal," she muttered in confusion.

"I know," he said as he closed his zipper. "She's having another nightmare. Stay here, I'll take care of her." He tore from the room as his daughter's terrified cry sounded again.

Briana threw back the covers to go with him, but then realized that she didn't have a stitch on. She pulled the sheet up around her neck and looked at her watch. It was two-thirty.

She could hear Crystal crying with terror and Hank trying to soothe her. The poor little girl. Was she going to have to endure recurring nightmares? Briana'd had good luck calming her the night before, maybe she could do it again.

She got out of bed and started to dress, but as she pulled on her underwear, she remembered that she wasn't expected to spend the night. Actually, she and Hank hadn't discussed it after she told Crystal she had to go home, but Briana couldn't dismiss the look of relief that had so briefly crossed his face. If he'd wanted her to stay, he'd surely have said so, if not in front of Crystal, at least the next time they were alone.

But he hadn't. He'd never referred to the subject again, and she certainly wasn't going to stick around and make him have to send her away. Or worse, let her stay out of politeness when he didn't want her there.

By the time she'd put on her dress and shoes, repaired her lipstick and combed her hair, Crystal's screams had subsided to subdued sobs as Hank spoke to her, too softly for Briana to make out the words. She straightened the disheveled bed and then went next door to Crystal's room.

The door was open, and Hank was sitting on the bed, cradling his little daughter on his lap and talking to her quietly. He looked up and saw Briana standing in the doorway and put out his hand in a beckoning gesture. "Look, honey," he said to Crystal. "Here's Briana. She'll tell you there's no bear here."

Briana went in and knelt on the floor beside them. "That's right, sweetheart," she said, reaching out to take the little girl's hand. "Remember, I told you last night that the mama bear had babies in the woods who needed her. She'll stay there with them. She won't come into town."

"But I saw her," Crystal sobbed. "She was going to get me."

"That was just a dream. Daddy wouldn't let her get you."

"Of course not," Hank said. "Now, why don't you lie back down, and I'll stay with you until you go to sleep?"

Crystal clung to him. "No! I want to sleep in your bed!"

Hank looked at Briana, and she could have laughed at his frustrated expression if it hadn't been such a serious moment. The poor man was trapped between his girl-friend and his daughter in a no-win situation.

She stepped in to rescue him. "It's all right, Hank, I have to leave now. I just came in to say goodbye."

"Briana, please..." She heard the torment in his voice. He was an honorable man, and she knew he was worried that she would feel used and then abandoned.

She was ashamed to realize that to a small extent, she did feel that way, and she quickly pushed the thought aside. She'd known when she went to bed with him that his first duty was to his traumatized child.

If only she could put her arms around him and snuggle close, showing as well as telling him that he was forgiven. But she couldn't because Crystal was there between them.

Another unworthy thought made her cringe. Hadn't that always been their biggest problem? She'd assumed that it was the hurt his ex-wife had inflicted that made Hank wary of committing himself to her, and to some extent, it probably was, but time was healing that wound.

No, it wasn't DeeDee who dictated what Briana's future with Hank would be, it was his duty to his four-year-old, motherless daughter. Crystal was his sole responsibility, and he had no choice but to put her needs above anyone else's. Even his own.

The following morning Briana went to early service, then left immediately for Montana. Because of the uncertain winter road conditions, she'd seen little outside the area of Whispering Pines and Cody in the four months that she'd been living there, and she'd never been to Billings.

As she drove along the nearly deserted two-lane highway, she was looking forward to the hustle and bustle of a city again, even if this one only boasted a population of about seventy thousand people. After spending most of her life in Los Angeles and the past four years in Denver, a tiny country village like Whispering Pines took some getting used to.

Not that she didn't love it, she did, but she missed the numerous shopping malls, the public transportation that, for a small charge, would take her anywhere she needed to go, and the huge libraries, museums and entertainment centers.

An annoying interference on the car radio intruded on the local station Briana had been listening to, and she turned the dial to the nearest clear one. It was a stronger Billings station featuring country music. Hank's favorite.

Immediately her mind was wiped clear of everything but the magic she and Hank had experienced last night. How could anything reach such mind-blowing ecstasy and then end with a dull thud?

Oh, knock it off and stop feeling sorry for yourself, Bree, she scolded herself mentally. *It was just one of those things that Hank had no control over. He's solely responsible for his daughter's well-being. You should understand that.*

She did understand. She'd even convinced Hank before she left that she wasn't upset. It was just that sneaking out of the house in the middle of the night without even a hug or a good-night kiss was so...so anticlimactic.

You didn't "sneak" out of the house, and what did you expect, anyway? That he'd make mad passionate love to you there on the doorstep with his little girl looking on?

Of course, she hadn't expected passion, but a light kiss and maybe a whispered "I love you" wouldn't have scarred Crystal forever.

So, maybe he's bashful about kissing a woman who's not her mother or his wife in front of her. Don't forget, you didn't used to like for Scott to kiss you in front of your younger brothers.

That was different. Scott didn't have any inhibitions. He was all over her when he kissed her. Actually, in spite of her disappointment, she had to admire Hank for his restraint. If only she could be sure that he'd really wanted to kiss her.

My God, he'd just made love to you like no woman was ever loved before. What more proof do you want?

Briana shook her head. What more, indeed? He'd been alternately loving, passionate, deeply apologetic about having to put his daughter's needs above hers, and he'd promised to call her today. She was being selfish and unrealistic to expect more of him.

So why didn't you stay home and wait for his call instead of leaving town hours before you had to?

Briana knew the answer to that question. She'd left the house early because she didn't want to pace the floor in anticipation of a call that might never come.

Briana was waiting at the airport in Billings when Elly got off the plane, and the two women hugged each other exuberantly, then Briana stepped back to assess her friend. "Elly, you're looking wonderful!" she exclaimed as her gaze moved from the thick mane of shimmering red hair, to the clear shining brown eyes and the golden tan that subdued the sprinkling of freckles across her nose and cheekbones. "You're positively glowing with good health, and you've even put on a little weight."

Elly wrinkled her nose. "Thanks a bunch, friend," she said with mock sarcasm. "It's only ten pounds, and I'll take them off as soon as I start working again."

Briana laughed. "You don't need to take them off. They do wonders for your bosoms and buns."

Elly squealed happily. "Really? In that case, I'll keep them. Hey, you're looking great, too. What have you been doing for fun while I was gone? Are you and Luke still going together? Or what about Hank Robinson? As I remember, you and he were striking sparks off each other about the time I left."

Briana was more interested in Elly's clandestine relationship with Quentin York, but now wasn't the time to start any serious discussions. "We'll talk on the long drive home, but right now, we have to pick up your suitcases," she said as they started walking toward the baggage area. "They should be out any minute."

An hour later, they'd collected Elly's luggage, threaded their way past Northwest College and the new Sheraton hotel on twenty-ninth street to the highway, and had put Billings behind them as they traveled south toward Powell, Cody and then home.

To a background of muted country music from the radio, Elly managed to coax from Briana the story of her on-again/off-again friendship with Hank, up to and including Crystal's disappearance and the search that followed. Briana told of having dinner with Hank and Crystal the past two nights, but let Elly think she'd left early and gone home to fall asleep in her own bed.

The intimate details of her relationship with Hank were something she wasn't inclined to share with anybody.

However, Elly's sharp mind and vivid imagination weren't fooled for a moment. She gave Briana a condescending look and sighed with feigned resignation. "Okay, it's obvious you aren't going to tell me whether or not you're sleeping with him, so I won't ask."

Briana turned to look at her. "Thank you very much," she said sweetly, and grinned. "So, how's your love life?"

"Oh, hell," Elly said, and grinned back. "If I had one, believe me, I'd tell you all about it."

"Sure you would," Briana drawled, then sobered. This was the perfect opening for the question she'd been waiting to ask.

"Look, Elly..." she began hesitantly, "I know you've been dodging the subject of you and Quentin York, but you confided in me once and then just dropped it. I—I'm not being nosey, I'm really concerned about you. Are you two still...you know...keeping in touch?"

Elly's infectious grin had disappeared, and when she spoke, her tone was caustic. "You don't have to worry about my virtue. It's pretty hard to make love with a man who's clear across the country."

Briana winced. She'd hoped Elly had gotten over this dangerous attachment to a married man during their separation. "That's not what I'm asking, and you know it."

Elly leaned back and closed her eyes. "Yes, I know. It's just that I'm not sure myself how I feel. I've only heard from him a couple of times since I've been gone. We couldn't write letters for fear of them being intercepted, and it wasn't safe to call each other because we never knew who might answer the phone.

"Not that Aunt Grace and Uncle Marvin would pry into my private affairs," she hurried to explain, "but they like to tease me about boyfriends, and they might inadvertently have said something to Mom and Dad, who were calling every few days."

She opened her eyes and looked at Briana. "At first the separation was just plain hell, but gradually I got used to it. Now?" She shrugged. "I think I'm over Quentin. I hope so. Believe me, forbidden love loses its allure quickly and becomes a real drag. I hate the secrecy, the sneaking around and the guilt." She shuddered. "The guilt most of all. Even though we haven't been going all the way, it's been a relief not to be tempted."

By unspoken mutual agreement, they changed the subject, and Elly's animation returned as she spent the rest of the trip telling Briana about her two months in New Mexico. When they got to the Wainwright house, Elly's mother had a welcome-home dinner waiting, featuring Elly's favorite foods. Everyone there insisted Briana stay and eat with them, so it was nearly nine o'clock before she got back to her apartment.

As she pulled into the small parking space at the back of the building and turned off the engine, she saw the headlights of another car pull in behind her and stop. A momentary wave of fear washed over her before she remembered that this was rural Wyoming and not Los Angeles or Denver. Rapes and muggings weren't something the people here worried about.

When she opened the door and stepped out of her car, she saw that the vehicle behind hers was a truck. Hank's Silverado, and she collided with him as they hurried toward each other.

She lost her balance, and he caught her in his arms to steady her. She snuggled into the warmth of his massive frame, grateful for his protection from the cold night air.

"You're shivering," he scolded. "Why aren't you wearing a coat instead of that sweater?"

He sounded angry, and she suspected that he was upset because he'd tried to call her as he said he would and she hadn't been home all day. That was rude of her, and she was ashamed. She should have waited for his call or phoned him as soon as she got into town.

"Let's get you inside before you freeze," he muttered, and with one arm still holding her close to his side, he led her around the house to the front door.

Inside her apartment, she turned up the thermostat and Hank took off his hat and leather jacket and tossed them onto a chair. "Why didn't you call me?" he demanded. "You could at least give me a chance to apologize and explain—"

"But, Hank, I just got home," she interrupted. "I told you I was meeting Elly's plane in Billings this afternoon. Besides, you said you'd call me."

He ran his fingers through his hair and turned away. "I did call you. I started at seven-forty-five this morning. Surely you didn't leave before that."

She'd guessed right, he had been trying to get her, and she couldn't blame him for being angry. She should have waited until later to leave.

"Actually, I did," she said regretfully. "I left the apartment at a little after seven-thirty to go to church, and then started out right from there for Billings as soon as the service was over."

He turned again to look at her, and she could see the anxiety in his expression. "Briana, you have good reason to be mad at me. I don't know what I could have done differently, but I admit you were treated pretty shabbily last night. I just wanted to apologize and try to explain my position to you. Why are you punishing me without even giving me a chance to... to tell you my side of the—the misunderstanding?"

She went to him then and put her arms around his waist. His muscles were knotted with tension. "Oh, darling, there was no misunderstanding. You couldn't help what happened last night, and I'm not punishing you. If I've been thoughtless, it was because I was afraid you wouldn't call."

She laid her head against his chest. "I didn't want to pace the floor in front of the phone waiting for it to ring, and then be disappointed."

He put his arms around her, and she felt him relax. "My beautiful little skeptic," he murmured huskily. "Haven't I shown you in every possible way how I feel about you?"

She had to admit that he had. He'd shown her how much he desired her, even how much he needed her. He'd shown her with his kisses how much he enjoyed her response, with his caressing hands how quickly her breasts could arouse him, with his magnificent body how erotically they could soar together into the realm of mind-blowing ecstasy, but it wasn't enough to quiet her cloying fear of rejection.

It wasn't what he *had* done, but what he *hadn't said* that tormented her. Just three words, *I love you,* would have made all the difference, and two more, *marry me,* would have obliterated all her doubts.

She couldn't forget that he hadn't wanted a relationship with her. He'd only given in to his powerful physical attraction for her, not to any deep emotional commitment.

Hank spoke her name, and she realized her pause had been too long. "Briana, answer me. Haven't I shown you how much I want you?"

"Yes, of course, you have," she assured him, but she hadn't missed the fact that he had said *want,* not *love.*

He leaned down and touched her lips with his. "Then what's the problem?" Again his lips brushed hers.

Problem? How could she think of problems when he was scrambling all her circuits?

She raised her hands and put them on either side of his head, then held it still as she captured his mouth with her own. His arms tightened around her as she caught his lower lip between her teeth and gently sucked.

For a long time they stood there, lost in the sweet, inventive kisses that melded them together in a timeless, serene world of their own where nothing mattered but being together in each other's arms. It wasn't until Briana felt Hank unbuttoning the heavy cardigan she wore that she came back down to earth.

She lowered her hands to his chest and pushed herself back. "Hey, come back here," he muttered as he pushed the sweater off her shoulders and let it drop to the floor, then tightened his hold on her.

She deflected another kiss and buried her face in his chest. "Don't you think we should finish our discussion before we go up in smoke?"

"Discussion?" He sounded bewildered. "What were we discussing?"

She couldn't help laughing. Apparently he'd been as bewitched as she. "You asked me why I was still so unsure of your... affection," she finished lamely.

He chuckled. "Honey, affection is what I feel for my sister. I think we can find a stronger word to describe my obsession for you."

Ah, yes, obsession. *That's a powerful word, all right, but* love *would have been so much better.*

Briana shook her head to dislodge the thought and chided herself for being so picky.

"Let's go over and sit on the couch," she said, and stepped out of his embrace. "Would you like a beer? Or a cola?"

She started for the kitchen, but Hank reached out and grabbed her arm. "No, I don't want anything to drink," he said, and led her to the couch. "And stop trying to run away from me."

They sat down, and again he put his arms around her and pulled her close with her back against his chest. "Okay," he said, "now tell me why you thought I might not call you this morning."

His hand resting tantalizingly on her stomach almost caused her to lose her train of thought. "Maybe it would be easier to explain if you would answer a question for me."

"All right. What is it?"

She took a deep breath. "Why were you so relieved last night when I told Crystal I wasn't going to spend the night at your house?"

Chapter Twelve

Hank stiffened. "How did you... I wasn't..."

Briana heard the shock in his tone and turned to look at him. "Yes, you were, Hank. I saw it in your expression for a few seconds before you were able to disguise it."

He slumped and his eyes reflected his remorse as he put his hand to her cheek and cradled her head against his chest. "I'm sorry you saw that and misunderstood, sweetheart," he said tenderly. "It wasn't relief that I felt. There's nothing I'd like more than to spend the entire night with you, to wake up in the morning with you beside me in bed, but...well...it's my duty as a father that I was concerned about. I've never brought a woman to my house before, and—"

Briana raised her head, her eyes wide with surprise. "You mean you haven't had a woman since DeeDee—"

He shook his head. "No, that's not what I'm saying. I haven't been celibate since the divorce, but the few times

I..." His face was flushed with embarrassment. "It always happened somewhere else. I've never brought a woman to my home since DeeDee left."

Some of her misgivings faded, and Briana couldn't hide the smile that played at the corners of her mouth. "Then I'm the first?"

His finger traced her jawline, and there was a soft light in his eyes. "Not just the first, love. The only. I know I'm hopelessly old-fashioned, but I'd never confuse my daughter by including her in numerous encounters with the women I date. You're the only one I've cared enough for and trusted enough to bring into my home, and already I've caused you grief. Crystal's never seen me in bed with anyone but her mother, and I honestly don't know how to handle it.

"And remember—she tells everything she knows. In a small town like this, that could be extremely embarrassing for you. Not to mention tarnishing your reputation."

Briana frowned. "I understand and agree with your concern for Crystal, but why should sleeping with you ruin my reputation? We're both adults."

He put his fingers under her chin and lifted her face for his kiss. "You've lived all your life in big cities where standards are less stringent and people don't pry into each other's business."

He kissed her again and cupped her breast. "I expect that the people in Whispering Pines aren't that much different from city folk, but they're more hypocritical. They play around, but they do it on the sly and pretend that they don't. Anyone who gets caught at it is fair game for the sanctimonious moral outrage of the rest, and I won't have you the butt of their crude jokes and sly remarks."

His fingers were doing exciting things to her nipples. "You learn early to play the game in a small town," he continued. "Everyone knows who everyone else is sleeping with, and as long as they're not caught at it, it's winked at and overlooked. But rub the citizens' noses in it by being publicly indiscreet, and they'll crucify you."

He hugged her close and buried his face in her hair. When he spoke again, his voice was hoarse with anguish. "DeeDee committed a double sin. She was not only indiscreet, she committed adultery, and the town rose up in righteous wrath. Unfortunately they saw me as the poor, simpleminded cuckold who was too much in love with his wife to see what was going on, and they not only didn't tell me, but actually protected me from finding out."

In his agitation, his breathing had become irregular, and unwittingly, his fingers dug painfully into Briana's soft flesh. She shifted slightly, and he loosened his hold. "Sorry," he murmured, and kissed her on the temple. "I didn't mean to hurt you."

"You didn't," she assured him, "and I'm sure that none of the citizens of Whispering Pines thought of you as simpleminded."

He uttered a sharp, bitter oath. "If they didn't, they should have. It wasn't all DeeDee's fault. What they didn't realize was that I didn't know what was going on because I didn't love her enough to notice. If we'd been closer, I'd have recognized her discontent and rectified it."

"Don't beat yourself up over this, Hank," Briana said soothingly as she let her palm roam over his chest and shoulder. "It's true that if all married couples were always in perfect harmony with each other, there'd be no divorce, but unfortunately, it just doesn't work that way. None of us is perfect and we all make mistakes. I read somewhere that most of the problems people have with each other are due to faulty communication."

Hank sighed. "I suppose, but I'm not going to subject you to snickers and double entendres. And that's another thing. We still have the good old double standard around here. You know, boys will be boys, but a woman who does the same thing is a tramp."

Briana's stomach muscles clenched, and she bit back a cry of protest. Just how far removed was he from the chauvinistic standards of the community he'd been raised in? It was true he'd spent four years at the university, but that was ten years ago, and Laramie was a small town of only twenty-five thousand people in a state with less than five hundred thousand population, most of them staid conservatives. In contrast, just the metropolitan area of Los Angeles where she'd been born and raised was populated with over seven million diverse and mostly liberal, freethinking human beings!

No matter how broad-minded he might believe he was, could he ever adjust to and forgive her mistakes of the past? Already they were having differences of interpretation. What he considered "protecting" her was what she would call "sneaking around."

She shrugged out of his embrace and sat up, then moved away from him. "You'll pardon me if I seem a little dense, Hank, but what is it you're trying to say?" Her lips trembled, and she pressed them together in an effort to control them. "Is this your way of telling me that since your sexual needs are now satisfied, you've decided you don't want a relationship with me after all?"

For a moment he looked as if she'd hit him. He neither moved nor uttered a sound, just sat there looking shocked and sick. It was obvious that she'd deeply offended him, but, dammit, what else could he have been leading up to?

When he finally spoke, his voice was low and tightly contained. "What could I possibly have said to make you think that?'' He stood up slowly, as though moving were painful. "Talk about difficulty in communicating. We don't communicate at all. I talk—and you hear something altogether different."

He walked over to the chair and picked up his hat and jacket. "I don't know what I've done to give you such a low opinion of me, but I'm sure that anything else I say will only make it worse."

Still carrying his wraps, he opened the door and walked out, shutting it silently behind him.

For hours, Briana paced the floor, too upset even to cry. She hadn't meant her question to be an attack on Hank's integrity, although the way she'd phrased it made it sound as if she had. In fact, subconsciously, she probably had wanted to revile him a little because he'd hurt her with his intimation that there was something shameful about them making love.

Actually, now that she'd had a chance to think about it, she realized that he wasn't implying that at all. He was too open and honest to make insinuations. He'd meant exactly what he'd said. The town was narrow-minded and hypocritical about sex outside of marriage, and he wanted to protect her—and his little daughter who would hear about it—from the self-righteous scorn of their neighbors.

It wasn't Hank's fault that the people in this rural area were twenty-five years behind the times, and it was admirable of him not to want to expose her to it. The gossip wouldn't hurt him. As he'd pointed out, that sort of thing was not only tolerated, but expected of males; it was the women who wore the scarlet letters.

How could she and Hank hope to make a go of any kind of liaison, even friendship, when their backgrounds were so diverse? It would be best for both of them just to let this unlikely attraction end now and get on with their lives. He had family obligations that didn't include her, and she had a duty to herself. She'd been badly burned once by a man who didn't love her enough, and only a blind fool would deliberately walk on that bed of hot coals again.

That decision sounded so wise and rational. So why couldn't she shake the image of the shock that had contorted Hank's suddenly white face, the dark pain that had looked out of his unusual green eyes and the uncharacteristically slow, halting way he'd moved when he got up and left, as if the blow she'd delivered had crippled him.

A great, tearing sob shook her and drove everything from her mind but her need to apologize to the man who was dearer to her than her own future peace of mind. A glance at her watch alerted her that it was past midnight, much too late to go calling, but she had to see him, to try to ease the pain she'd caused him, to apologize for being so cruel as to mock his concern for her.

The night air was cold, and Briana could see her breath as she started her car's engine and turned on the heater. Not even a moon illuminated the dark backyard of the house, and she could see nothing of what was behind her as she backed out of the parking space and headed toward the poorly lit street.

As she drove toward Hank's house, it occurred to her that he would probably be in bed. What would she do if he were? If she banged on the door or rang the bell loud enough to wake him, she would disturb Crystal, too. In that case, it would all have been in vain, because Hank would have to comfort his still easily frightened daughter.

As Briana approached his house, it seemed to be dark, but when she drove up to the curb, she could see that there was a dim light in the living room. She breathed a sigh of relief, but then pressed her foot lightly on the gas and drove on to the end of the block and around the corner.

She parked several houses down, then got out and walked back. This was a newer section of town and the street lighting was better. She could see enough to get around as she climbed the three steps to the covered porch and knocked lightly on the door.

At first she thought she hadn't been heard and was about to knock again when footsteps in the entryway alerted her that someone was coming. She braced herself as Hank turned on the outside light and opened the door. He was still dressed in his shirt and jeans, but the shirt was pulled out of his pants and unbuttoned, the sleeves turned back, and he was barefoot.

He looked at her with an owlish expression, then blinked and looked again. "Briana!" He hastily unlocked the screen door and pushed it open. "Come in, it's cold out there."

He scanned the street as she scooted inside. "Where's your car?"

"Oh, I parked it around the corner," she told him.

"Around the corner? Why did you do that?" He looked outside again, as if still expecting to find it parked at the curb, then he shut the door.

"Well, you said the neighbors would talk if—"

He uttered a low groan and held up his hand to shush her. "Never mind, I don't want to get into that again," he said tonelessly, then took her arm. "Come on in the living room. I've got a fire and it's warm. Can I get you something to drink?"

She saw the two empty beer cans on the coffee table and shook her head. "No, thank you, but you go ahead if—"

"I've had more than my quota already," he informed her coolly. "I seldom drink when I'm here alone with Crystal, but tonight I made an exception."

She felt the stupid tears that wouldn't come when she was at home alone now burning at the back of her eyes, and she blinked rapidly to keep them from falling. She hated what she'd done to him and couldn't blame him for not being happy to see her, but at least he hadn't turned her away.

They were standing in front of the sofa, and he motioned toward the chair beside the fireplace. "Sit down. Are you staying long enough to take off your wraps?"

She nodded and pulled off her knitted wool hat, then unbuttoned her coat and shrugged out of it. Tossing it across the chair he'd intended for her to sit in, she ran her fingers through her hair to fluff it, then sat down on the sofa. He looked a little disconcerted, but lowered himself beside her.

It was a long couch and there was a wide space between them as he turned to look at her. "All right, now suppose you tell me what you're doing here at this time of night. What is it you want, Briana?"

He wasn't going to make this easy for her, but she hadn't expected him to. "I—I want you." Her voice was low and tremulous, and she knew she was blushing.

Hank caught his breath, and his eyes widened. "Say that again." It was clear that he didn't believe what he'd heard.

She moistened her dry lips with the tip of her tongue and looked directly at him. "I said I want you, Hank. I'd like for us to make love, but if you don't want to, I'll understand. I know you don't want the neighbors to—"

"To hell with the damned neighbors," he roared. "What I want to know is why you've come to me now, when just a few hours ago, you accused me of being a bastard who'd do anything to seduce you for a one-night quickie?''

"Because I was wrong," she answered quickly, anxious to apologize. "I felt diminished . . . I guess *tarnished* is a better word . . . by the idea of having to sneak around to express my feelings for you in a close, intimate way. I'm not promiscuous—''

Hank gasped and storm clouds gathered in his expression. "That's not what—''

"I know," she interrupted. "You weren't intimating that I am, but I—I had a pretty shattering experience with the only other lover I ever had, and it left me supersensitive to slights and rejection. Not from the general public—I learned long ago not to let the opinion of so-called friends bother me—but from any man who claims to care for me.''

She saw he was about to protest, and she hurried on. "I guess I have as much trouble trusting men as you have trusting women." A sob burst through her tenuous control, and she looked away and bit her lower lip.

Hank shifted uncomfortably. "What did he do to you?" His tone was more gentle, less reserved.

Briana hesitated. Now was the time to tell him the whole, uncensored truth if she ever intended to. He'd given her the perfect opening. Confessing everything was the only way she'd ever be free of the heavy burden of her past. Otherwise, she'd always be haunted by the fear that he'd find out from somebody else.

But how could he? The few people who knew what had happened would also be adversely affected if the secret were revealed. They all had compelling personal reasons for keeping the past buried, so what was she afraid of? If she didn't tell him, there was no way he'd find out.

She hated keeping such a vital part of her life hidden from Hank, but if he knew, it would destroy any chance they might have for happiness together. Hadn't she suffered enough? Surely she wasn't meant to spend her whole life in purgatory because of one soul-searing mistake.

With a short, silent prayer for forgiveness, she looked away and reluctantly answered Hank's question with a lie. "He—he married someone else."

Actually, what she said was true, Scott had married recently, it had been in all the papers, but that had nothing to do with the reason he'd walked out on her.

She heard Hank's sharp intake of breath and when she looked up, he reached across the space separating them and took her hand, tugging gently. "Come here."

With a soft cry of relief, she scooted across the empty cushion and into his arms. He cradled her to him and rocked her gently as she snuggled against his bare chest and put her arms around his waist under the open shirt.

His skin was warm, and the hair on his chest was thick but not bristly. She rubbed her cheek in it, making the muscles beneath it contract. He smelled of musky male, and for her, it was more arousing than any expensive cologne, because it was a part of him.

"Do you want to talk about it?" he murmured.

"No." That was the last thing she wanted to do. "It happened a long time ago. I was very young, and I suppose what I felt for him was infatuation rather than love. The hurt was deep and painful, though, and I don't like to relive it."

"Do I remind you of him?"

The idea was so ridiculous that she almost laughed. "Not at all," she hastened to assure him. "He wasn't as big as you are, and he was dark with dark hair and eyes. Also, your personalities are totally different. Scott was vain and selfish, and always needed to be the center of attention."

"His name was Scott?" Hank said it so softly that for an instant, she almost said, "yes, Scott Upton," but she stopped herself just in time.

She hadn't intended to use Scott's name at all. Hank would probably recognize it. She should have been more careful.

"Yes," she admitted. "We were high school sweethearts, and were planning to get married when..."

She let her words trail off and hoped Hank wouldn't question her further.

"It's probably just as well you didn't," he said. "That's the mistake I made, marrying my high school sweetheart. Are you over him now?"

She turned her face into his chest and planted kisses on it. "Oh, yes, but he left me a legacy I can't seem to get rid of, the legacy of distrust. I didn't ever plan to fall in love again."

Hank's hand was caressing her thigh through her lilac-colored cotton slacks. "Neither did I." His voice was so low that she suspected he was talking to himself. "What fools we mortals be."

Hank was still having trouble adjusting to the sudden change of mood, from deep despair to soaring hope. What was it about this woman that kept him in a constant state of turmoil? She was beautiful and sexy, but so were a lot of other women. She was bright and intelligent, but he'd known a lot of bright, intelligent women in college, and none of them had affected him the way she did.

Briana had spelled trouble from the word go. She made him feel things he didn't want to feel, dream things he didn't want to dream.

He should tell her she was forgiven for misjudging him, and then send her home.

Sure he should, but how could he when just the thought of sending her away was like a blow to the gut?

He shivered as the talented little fingers that had been tangling in his chest hair began to move slowly downward, making him even harder than he already was. He gripped her thigh and hung on as her fingers continued inching lower, making him squirm with anticipation, but what he was throbbing for didn't happen. Instead, when she got to the top of his jeans, she slid her hand around under his shirt to his bare back.

He moaned with frustration and fought back the overwhelming urge to take her hand and press it against his fly, but he didn't trust his control that far.

She leaned down and kissed him on the belly just above his pants, and he clutched both hands to her head to keep her soft lips moving tantalizingly against his bare flesh. For a few minutes, she bedeviled him by alternately sucking and nipping until he was nearly wild with desire, but when he moved his hand to unsnap his jeans, she caught it and raised her head.

Her eyes were filmy with passion, and her voice trembled as she spoke. "Wait. We'd better go into the bedroom. Crystal . . ."

He almost cried out with frustration. He'd forgotten all about his daughter. He'd forgotten everything but his flaming need to join body and soul with this raven-haired sorceress who seemed bent on driving him stark raving mad.

"I don't think I can walk," he muttered thickly as she sat up and looked at him.

He felt bereft, as though a vital part of him had been ripped away. He reached out and clasped her in his arms. She came willingly, and he could feel her heart hammering almost as hard as his own as she lay across his chest.

"What kind of spell do you cast when we're together that mesmerizes me and drives everything from my mind but the terrible need to hold you tight and never let you get away from me again?" he asked as he trailed little kisses at the back of her neck. He knew he was making himself vulnerable by telling her how she affected him, but he was unable to hold back.

She angled her head to give his mouth greater access. "I thought you were the one who was casting the spell," she answered dreamily. "Every time you touch me, I melt."

"I'd noticed," he whispered, adding another flame to his already overheated libido.

God, how he'd noticed and reveled in her ardent responses. He loved it when she came to him so willingly, when she trembled under his touch, moaned when his tongue caressed hers, and caught fire along with him when his hands roamed over the rises and curves of her soft, ripe body.

A sharp ache in his groin warned him that he'd better change the direction of his thoughts or he'd never cool down enough to make it to the bedroom.

He pulled her shirttails out of her slacks and put his hand underneath her blouse to unfasten her bra and stroke the sides of her breasts. So firm and full. They just fit in his hands, and he could feel her heart fluttering. He longed to take the nipples in his mouth and feel her shiver when he suckled.

Enough already! Reluctantly, he dragged his hands out from under her blouse and put her away from him, then stood and reached down to help her up. Without speaking, they walked hand in hand to the bedroom and closed and locked the door behind them.

Chapter Thirteen

Briana woke to the all-enveloping scent of pine, and without opening her eyes, she pictured the two-bedroom log cabin near Old Faithful Geyser in Yellowstone Park, where she, Hank and Crystal had been spending the past three nights.

She squinted at her watch. Ten minutes until six. It was cold in the early mornings at this elevation, well over seven thousand feet, and she burrowed under the heavy blankets and snuggled against Hank's wide back to bask in the heat that always radiated from him. Today was the last Monday of May, Memorial Day, and they'd be leaving later this afternoon to return to Whispering Pines, but she was glad she'd wakened early to savor this past weekend spent living openly with Hank and his daughter.

In the month since she and Hank had first made love, they'd never before spent an entire night together. Usually they came back to her apartment after going out to a movie or square dancing, but Hank had to be home by midnight because of his teenage baby-sitter's curfew. The few times Briana had come to his house, she'd left long before Crystal could wake up and find her there.

Dating a single father could be the pits sometimes, and apparently Hank thought so, too. Briana had been flabbergasted when he'd proposed this holiday weekend trip for the three of them. He had been getting dressed to go home after an especially fervent hour of loving when he had sprung it on her.

"As you've probably heard, the park opens next week in time for the Memorial Day holiday," he'd said. "You've never been there. Would you like to go up after work Friday to spend the weekend? Of course, we'd have to take Crystal...."

She'd been too surprised to be tactful. "But I thought you didn't want her to know that we're...uh..."

He'd been sitting on the side of the bed, putting on his boots, and he'd reached for her hand and pulled her down to sit on his lap.

She smiled now as she remembered that she'd been totally nude at the time.

That fact hadn't escaped him, either, and he'd run his palm along her thigh as he spoke. "I know, but dammit, sweetheart, I have rights even if I am a father, and I've had about all I can take of this deceit. We're not doing anything wrong. We have a loving, monogamous relationship, and I'm sick of sneaking out in the middle of the night, or, worse yet, letting you do it."

His hand had began to wander, and he'd been distracted for several minutes by the nearness of her breasts to his mouth. When he'd spoken again, his voice had been gravelly. "After we've made love, I want you in my bed when I fall asleep and again when I wake up. I don't see how that can hurt a four-year-old child. I'm sure it would have been much worse for her to have to listen to her mother and me quarrel all the time, which is how it was for quite a while before DeeDee left.''

After that, they'd both been consumed by the flame they'd rekindled, and once he'd gotten dressed the second time, he'd been late getting the baby-sitter home.

Now they were winding up a wonderful vacation away from prying eyes, and Crystal was having a great time. The child never tired of watching Old Faithful erupt at hourly intervals on the grounds where they were staying, spewing thousands of gallons of steaming water over one hundred feet into the air. The first time it happened, she'd screamed and had flown into her daddy's arms, but once she got used to it, she didn't want to miss it.

Briana was fascinated by the Paintpots, the bubbling springs filled with hot clay in colors of white, pink and black, but her choice for the most spectacular sight was Canyon Junction, the magnificent Grand Canyon of the Yellowstone.

Before she'd graduated from high school, Briana had never been outside the sprawling, smog-choked, traffic-clogged area of Los Angeles, so this twenty-four-mile long, twelve-hundred-foot deep gorge was a visual feast in stunning shades of yellow, with touches of brilliant reds and fiery oranges. Two high waterfalls spilled over the canyon wall, reflecting sunbeams of gold.

Today they planned to stop at Yellowstone Lake on their way out of the park and take one of the scenic cruises, but she was in no hurry to get out of bed. She wanted to savor her last chance to lie beside Hank without having to worry about Crystal waking early and finding her there, or what the neighbors would say if they saw her car parked in his driveway overnight.

She put her arm across his waist and lightly kissed his bare back. Even in his sleep he responded by tucking her arm under his and clasping her hand.

Briana was content. Surely he wouldn't have relaxed his rules against involving Crystal in their relationship if he weren't at least considering the possibility of making it permanent.

He did love her, she was sure of that. He had demonstrated it in every way except by putting it into words. He still couldn't seem to bring himself to say "I love you," but he would. It was just a matter of time, and she could wait.

Hank lay in the bed beside Briana, pretending to be asleep. He didn't want to admit he was awake and be forced to acknowledge that this was the last day of their fantastic three days and nights together. Their pseudo-honeymoon.

He winced as the strange term came unbidden into his mind. Pseudohoneymoon, hell! It sounded cheap and tawdry. Briana deserved better than that, and it was time he faced the fact that he was going to lose her if he didn't stop hiding behind his hurt pride and admit that he was crazy in love with her. He didn't want a *pseudo*honeymoon, he wanted a real one following a wedding in the church with vows repeated before God and all their friends and relatives.

He'd let DeeDee and her adulterous betrayal mess up his life long enough. So she'd mortified him with her behavior. So what? She hadn't permanently damaged anything but his overinflated ego, and that was no loss.

The time had come for him to stop wallowing in self-pity and build a new life with Briana. He'd done her a grave disservice by comparing her to his ex-wife. Briana was nothing like DeeDee. She was loyal and loving and the best thing that had ever happened to him. He knew now that he could trust her, not only with his life, but with his little daughter's well-being.

Briana would never abandon a child who needed her. Never in a million years.

For the first time in years, Hank felt young and carefree and completely happy. He could feel the deep, steady rhythm of her breathing against his back and knew she'd fallen asleep again. That was all right. He loved it when she curled around him this way. It made his heart speed up and his psyche sing with exhilaration.

Later, in the afternoon, when they got back to Whispering Pines, he'd take her home with him and then, after Crystal was in bed, he would tell Briana how deeply he loved her and ask her to marry him.

"Please, Briana, oh, please," Crystal begged. "I want to see the water blow up just once more before we go. Please."

Briana stood in the living room of the cabin, contemplating Hank's irresistible child display her talent for getting what she wanted. She tugged at Briana's hand and jumped up and down as she pleaded. "It won't take long. It's almost time. See, there're lots of people there already, waiting."

Hank was ready to leave, and Briana wasn't going to get in the middle of an argument between father and daughter. She fought the smile that fluttered at the corners of her mouth and managed to look stern. "You'll have to ask your daddy."

Crystal ran over to Hank, who was locking the suitcases, and started her song and dance all over again.

"Please, Daddy, please, please. It's the last time I'll get to see it."

Hank glanced over her head at Briana, and there was an amused twinkle in his eyes. "If you want to go with her, I'll put the luggage in the trunk and then check out."

They'd brought Briana's car because it was roomier and more comfortable for the three of them than Hank's truck.

"Okay, we'll meet you back here when it's over." She took the ecstatic little girl by the hand, and they headed in the direction of the geyser.

As Crystal skipped along happily at her side, Briana noticed that several of the gathering crowd looked at them and smiled, probably thinking they were mother and daughter. Although they didn't actually look alike, their coloring was similar and they were dressed alike in matching royal blue sweatshirts, with YELLOWSTONE PARK emblazoned in white across the front, that Hank had bought for them in the gift shop at the lodge.

The bleachers were all occupied, so Briana and Crystal stood at the back and off to one side. As they waited for the eruption, Briana began to feel uneasy.

She shrugged it off and chatted with Crystal for a few minutes, but the longer she stood there, the more edgy she became. She had the distinct impression that someone was watching her. Not the smiling glances at a cute mother-daughter team, or even admiring ones for her as an attractive woman, but a concentrated stare that made the back of her neck tingle with apprehension.

She looked around, searching the mingling tourists with her gaze, but she saw no one paying special attention to her. Then the geyser spouted and she was busy keeping track of Crystal, who pranced with glee.

When it was over, they hurried back to the cabin. The car was there, but Briana saw no trace of Hank and decided he was probably still at the office.

She and Crystal had just stepped into the small living room when she heard a voice call her name from outside the screen door. Lightning bolts of shock tore through her and brought her to a shuddering halt. It was an unforgettable male voice from her past, one she'd hoped never to hear again.

"Briana, I've been looking for you. I went to your apartment and the manager told me you were up here. We have to talk."

The door opened—and Scott Upton stepped inside.

For a moment she could neither speak nor move. Dear God, what had she done to deserve this? Were the good citizens of Whispering Pines right? Was she being punished for the sin of loving a man as completely as she loved Hank Robinson?

Scott stood still, giving her time to adjust to his unexpected presence. He didn't look much different than he had five years ago when he was nineteen, except that he had filled out. Still, he wasn't as husky as she'd imagined. The few times she'd seen him on television had been on the football field where he wore heavy padding under his uniform.

He shifted his gaze from Briana to Crystal, then back again, and she could see that he was angry.

"Your little brother lied to me." His tone was harsh, accusing. "He said you didn't have any children. Aren't you going to introduce me to my daughter?"

Briana gasped. *His daughter? How had he found out—*

Then it hit her. He thought *Crystal* was her child! Hers and his!

A wave of blinding fury swept over her, and her fists clenched as she finally regained her senses. "You bastard." Her tone was low pitched and filled with scorn. "You haven't changed a bit, have you? Now get out of here before I call the park rangers and have you thrown out."

"Oh, I don't think so." His voice was filled with menace. "You'd better calm down and be nice. I can always claim I just found out about her and file for custody."

He put his hand out to Crystal, who by now was huddled against Briana, frightened by the animosity that permeated the room, even though she probably didn't understand the conversation.

"Come here, little honey," he coaxed, "and let me look at you. You're a beauty just like your mama, aren't you?"

Crystal cringed and clung tighter to Briana, who put her arms around the child and turned so she stood between Crystal and Scott. "She's not your daughter. Leave her alone."

Scott's expression darkened, and he stepped closer and grabbed Crystal's arm.

Before either Crystal or Briana could react, another voice, thick with rage, boomed through the cabin. "Take your hand off my daughter or I'll geld you!"

Stunned with a mixture of relief and horror, Briana looked up to see Hank looming in the bedroom doorway looking like the wrath of God. He filled the small space with his great size, and his face was dark and distorted and dangerous.

Briana's heart and breathing seemed to stop, and her head began to swim. Dear God, he'd been in the bedroom and heard every word Scott had said!

Scott dropped his hand from Crystal's arm and straightened to face Hank. He was only a couple of inches shorter than Hank, but not nearly as imposing. "Who the hell are you, and what do you mean, your daughter?"

His tone was harsh, but Briana detected a note of uncertainty.

If Hank heard it, he ignored it. "I mean exactly what I said, Crystal's *my* daughter, not yours and not Briana's. Now, are you going to leave peacefully, or do you want to take me on?"

Briana cringed. For the first time since she'd known Hank, she was actually afraid of him. He'd shed the gentle teddy-bear image and looked more like a grizzly prepared to attack. She didn't doubt for a minute but that he'd fight like one, too, if he thought his daughter was in danger.

Scott blanched and looked from Hank to Briana. "So she conned you into thinking the kid was yours," he said with a sneer. "Well, get this, buddy, she told me it was mine and I gave her money for an abortion. Looks like she suckered both of us—"

With a sharp, bone-crunching jab, Hank hit him. It happened so suddenly that neither Briana nor Scott saw it coming. One second, Scott was jeering, and the next, he was stumbling backward, crashing against the wall and upsetting a table, chair and lamp in the process.

Just before he sank to the floor, Hank grabbed him with a handful of the heavy sweatshirt Scott wore and hauled him to his feet, then banged him against the wall again. Crystal was screaming, and Briana knelt and wrapped the frightened child in her arms. She pressed the tear-stained little face between her breasts and tried to soothe the child's sobs while she listened to Hank's low but deadly voice.

"Now listen to me, Upton, and listen good, because I'm only going to say it once more. Crystal is my daughter. I can prove it beyond a doubt in any court. Since you've obviously made a mistake, I'm going to give you one more chance to walk out of here under your own steam. If you still need to be persuaded, I'll put you in the hospital, and then I'll have a chat with your father-in-law, the U.S. senator. That's not a threat, it's a promise. So which is it going to be?''

Briana shivered as she huddled with Crystal on the floor. Hank had recognized Scott Upton. That wasn't too surprising considering that Hank was a sports fan and watched the college and professional football games on television. Scott had been a star receiver in college, and was now an up-and-coming rookie with the pros. Most anyone interested in football would probably recognize him, and anyone absorbed in politics would know him as the man who had recently married the daughter of an influential senator who would be standing for reelection soon.

If Scott answered, Briana didn't hear him over Crystal's sobs, but when Hank released him, he staggered out of the cabin, leaving Briana alone to face her share of Hank's wrath.

She buried her face in Crystal's soft hair, unable to face him as she heard his heavy footsteps approaching. What would he do? What would he say? Had Scott just blown her life apart for the second time?

The floor beside her vibrated, and she saw Hank's black boots almost touching her leg as she sat Indian-style with his daughter in her lap. For a moment the only sound in the room was Crystal's diminishing sobs, then he reached down and without touching Briana, put his hands at the child's waist and lifted her up into his arms.

Briana clasped her arms around her own waist and bent over, her eyes downcast and her face only inches from the rough wood of the floor. How could she face him? The things Scott had said about her were true but out of context and twisted to make her sound like a scheming whore.

She couldn't even begin to explain her actions without being defensive and admitting that she'd deliberately set out to deceive Hank. She braced herself for the physical and verbal abuse she feared was coming. She'd often seen men punish women that way in the neighborhood where she'd grown up, and with a lot less provocation than she'd given Hank.

Not that she'd ever thought of him as that type of person, but the barely civilized man who had appeared in the bedroom doorway just minutes ago wasn't the same Henry Robinson she'd known for four months. She had no idea what to expect from this one.

The one thing she hadn't expected was for him to turn and walk silently away from her, but that's what he did. She listened to his footsteps heading for the bathroom, then heard water being run and his soft voice soothing and reassuring his little girl.

After a few minutes, the footsteps started back across the living room, then stopped beside her again. "Get up, Briana," he said, his tone devoid of emotion. "We're leaving."

She knew then that she'd have preferred the tongue-lashing.

Briana got to the car as Hank was strapping Crystal into her safety seat in the back. She climbed into the front and busied herself with fastening her seat belt. When Hank finished with Crystal, he slid behind the wheel, tuned the radio to his favorite country-music station and took off without a word.

Briana felt sick. She had to find a way to confess all the things she should have told him weeks before, but so far he hadn't even acknowledged her presence. He looked straight ahead, his expression hard and set as he steered the car along the road, which was still rough and under construction to repair the winter damage.

Even Crystal was quieter than usual, but at least she'd stopped crying and was playing with a stuffed fawn, a replica of the ones that romped alongside their mothers in the meadows and forests of this huge wildlife sanctuary.

The tension mounted, and finally Briana couldn't stand it any longer. She had to try to make him understand.

"Hank." Her voice sounded rusty, dry, and she swallowed and tried again. "Hank, it's not what you think. I didn't—"

"Not now, Briana," he interrupted. "We can't talk freely in front of Crystal. Wait until we're alone."

She slumped against the back of the seat and rubbed at her temples in an effort to quiet the pounding headache that started at the back of her neck and circled her head like a vise.

When they came to Yellowstone Lake, where they'd planned to take the scenic cruise, Hank didn't even slow down. Crystal saw the water and the boats and reminded him. He told her they couldn't stop now but would come back another time.

For the rest of the trip, Briana huddled against the door and tried to organize her thoughts so that she could tell Hank her side of the distorted accusations Scott had aimed at her and try to salvage as much as she could out of this latest catastrophe in her life.

They arrived in Whispering Pines in midafternoon. Hank drove directly to his parents' home. When Briana questioned him, he merely said, "I'm going to leave Crystal with Mom," then carried the child, who had fallen asleep, into the house, leaving Briana sitting in the car.

He returned alone a few minutes later and they drove in silence to her apartment. She unlocked the door and let them in, then turned up the thermostat and went into the bathroom where she took a couple of aspirin.

As she swallowed the pills with a glass of water, she was appalled at her reflection in the mirror. She looked ghastly. Her hair was disheveled, her face was white and pinched looking, and her eyes, usually a sparkling green, looked dark and bruised.

She pressed a cold, wet washcloth to her face, but it didn't bring back her color. Makeup and a fancy hairdo weren't going to help her now. She might as well do what had to be done and get it over.

Back in the living room, Hank was sitting in the upholstered chair with his elbows on his knees and his face in his hands. He looked utterly defeated. If Briana hadn't been all frozen up inside, she would have cried. All she'd wanted was to make him happy, but she'd handled it so wrong.

She'd always known that she'd done the one thing he'd never be able to understand or forgive, but still, she'd continued to pursue a relationship with him. How could she love him so much and still set him up for this kind of agony?

He looked up when he heard her coming, and for the first time, she got a good look at his face. It was gray and seemed to have aged in just a few hours. There were deep lines at the sides of his mouth and across his forehead, and his warm, green eyes that only this morning had seemed to glow with excitement were now cold and expressionless.

She couldn't stand to see him hurting so much. She had to make one more attempt to reach behind the barrier he'd erected around his shattered emotions.

Walking across the room, she knelt beside his chair and put her hand on his arm. He didn't move, but just looked straight ahead. "Hank," she said softly. "There's one thing you have to know before this goes any further. I have never had an abortion. Nor did I ever consider having one."

He looked at her for a moment, then nodded. She didn't know if he meant he believed her or was just signaling her to continue.

"I love you." She tried to control the quaver in her voice. "I know you don't believe that, but it's true. I just want you to remember, while I'm telling you my story, that I never meant for you to be hurt."

He didn't move or speak. She dropped her hand, then rubbed her cheek against his arm before she got to her feet and went over to the couch, where she could sit facing him.

"I had a happy early childhood," she said. "My dad was a good-natured Irishman with a good job as a welder at one of the airplane plants in Los Angeles. He had a wife and three small children whom he adored, and a new home in a peaceful middle-class area.

"Everything was great, and Mom was pregnant again when he got sick. It was a severe viral infection with a long name that did irreversible damage to his heart. He was never able to work again."

Briana fought back the memories of that dreadful time. Even though she'd been only six years old, she'd known that everybody expected her father to die.

"At first he had insurance and sick leave, but eventually we lost everything—the house, the car, the furniture—and wound up living on welfare in one of the poorer sections of the city. Mom worked part-time, baby-sitting and cleaning peoples' houses, but she couldn't earn much and still get aid for families with dependent children, and she couldn't make enough to support us without it.''

Briana had Hank's attention now, which wasn't surprising. A sob story like hers was bound to stir his compassion, but she didn't want pity, she wanted understanding.

''There were a lot of kids into drugs and petty crime in our neighborhood,'' she continued, ''but Dad and Mom wouldn't tolerate any of that sort of thing from their brood. None of us ever got into serious trouble...'' She hesitated, then plunged on. ''That is, not until I broke the good record.''

Hank looked sharply at her and she took a deep breath. ''When I was a senior in high school, I got pregnant.''

Even now she could feel the nausea that had plagued her on those mornings five years ago, and the shock she'd experienced when she realized what was causing it.

Hank continued to look at her, but made no comment.

''Dad had been dead a couple of years by then, and Scott Upton and I had been going together for over a year. He was the shining star of the football team in our high school. Scott's parents were on AFDC, too, and like me, his one burning obsession was to get out of the welfare rut and make something of himself. His goal was in sight. He'd won an athletic scholarship to Stanford, and he wasn't about to let me and my 'bastard'—his word—stand in his way.''

Briana's nerves were screaming and she couldn't sit still any longer. She stood up and walked over to look out the window at several children playing baseball in the middle of the street.

''We'd talked about getting married after he graduated from Stanford, but when I told him about the baby, he was furious. He told me to get rid of it. I said I couldn't do that, and he got ... abusive. He swore and hit me...."

She heard Hank's sharp intake of breath and hurried on. "He said it was my mistake and I was stuck with it. That if I made trouble for him, he'd deny that he was the father, and he had friends who would ... would say they'd ... they'd been to bed with me, too."

Even after all this time, she still felt the scalding humiliation at the very thought of such an accusation being circulated among her family and friends.

"I was easily intimidated. My family would have been shamed, and Mom had her hands full trying to stretch the welfare pittance and raise the five younger children alone. I took money from Scott for an abortion, but I put it away to help pay future expenses."

She turned and looked at Hank. "I never saw or heard from Scott again until today."

Hank looked dubious. "Then how did he find you? The odds of you just running into each other today are astronomical."

She shook her head. "No, it wasn't accidental. He knew I lived in Whispering Pines." She told him about her mother's phone call. "For a few days after that, I was afraid he might try to contact me here, but when he didn't, I figured Paddy had told him what he wanted to know, that there was no child."

Hank ran his hand through his hair. "If you didn't have an abortion, then what ... what happened to the baby?"

He spoke hesitantly, as if he really didn't want to know.

Briana wrapped her arms around herself in an unconsciously protective gesture. Well, here it was, the question she'd always known was loaded against her no matter how she answered.

This time there was no evading it. She had to tell the truth. "My baby daughter was born on February first, four years ago." Her voice was ragged with anguish. "I gave her up for adoption without ever seeing her."

Chapter Fourteen

Briana had always considered the cliché "the silence was deafening" to be just an expressive play on words, but now she knew that silence really could be overwhelming. It clamored in her mind and obliterated all other sounds and thoughts except the nerve-wracking quiet that pulsated between Hank and her until, eons later, he finally spoke.

"Why?" The word was more of a cry than a question, and he cleared his throat and repeated it. "Why did you give up your child, Briana? Most single mothers keep their babies. You were already on welfare, surely it would have been easy..."

"Easy!" The sound burst from Briana before she had time to form the word. "You think being on welfare is *easy?* It's a trap. A humiliating snare that feeds on itself from one generation to the next. I wasn't going to doom myself or my daughter to that degrading existence for the rest of our lives.''

She began to pace back and forth. ''I wasn't trained to earn a living, and I had no way of getting training with a newborn baby to care for.

''I was frantic until my mother told me that one of the people she cleaned for was a lawyer who specialized in adoptions. I made an appointment to see him, and after I'd been checked out, I was put in touch with a couple in their midthirties who couldn't have children of their own. The man was a stockbroker, and the woman was a college professor. They offered to pay my expenses until after the baby was born and give me enough money to put me through a vocational-training program, provided I relocate to another region of the country.''

Briana was trembling with the effort it took for her to relive this devastating experience that she'd tried so hard to erase from her mind. She leaned wearily against the wall and glanced at Hank.

He was staring at her with disbelief. ''You mean you *sold* your baby?'' he thundered.

For a minute she simply couldn't believe what she'd heard, but another glance at Hank's unrelenting expression convinced her.

''No!'' It was a scream of protest that bounced off the walls and seemed to fill the room with vibrating echoes. ''Damn you! Who made you God? Where do you get off being so self-righteous? I didn't sell my baby. I sold any chance I had for happiness and peace of mind so she would have a happy and secure life. It tore the heart out of me to have to walk away from that hospital without ever seeing her, and a day never goes by that I don't regret my decision to give her up, but it was the best thing I could do for her. Under the circumstances, I'd do it again.''

She glared at Hank. She'd apologized all she was going to. Admittedly, she'd been wrong for not telling him about this earlier, but who was he to judge her until he'd been faced with the same choices?

"Have you even the faintest idea what it's like to know you have a daughter somewhere whom you'll never see or hold or nurture?" she challenged.

His expression had changed to one of shock at her outburst. He shook his head and admitted, "No, I haven't."

"Have you ever tried to live on a welfare check? Been accused of being a lazy leech when you pay for groceries with food stamps? Been unable to get quality medical care? Heard your mother jeered at for having babies just to get more of the taxpayers' money?"

She could see the alarm in Hank's eyes and knew she was out of control, but she couldn't stop. "Is that what you'd want for your mother, wife or daughter? Would you really have subjected Crystal to that if you'd known when she was born that there were people eager to raise her who could give her everything you couldn't?"

She started pacing again, too wound up to stand still. "There's something else you should think about, Hank. Did it ever occur to you that maybe DeeDee had her child's best interest in mind when she left Crystal with you?"

Hank's reaction was instantaneous. He jerked to attention and his expression changed from alarm to denial. "No, that didn't occur to me, and it still doesn't," he said angrily.

Briana made a massive effort to get a grip on herself and lower her voice. "No, of course it doesn't. You're too busy playing prosecutor, judge and jury to consider that she might have been as concerned about her daughter as you are. You should get down on your knees and thank

God that she didn't take Crystal with her, otherwise you'd be suffering the same hell as I am."

He sprang from the chair and stood glaring at Briana. "You're wrong, I wouldn't have been suffering, because I'd have gone after her. I'd never have let DeeDee drag Crystal all over the country, living in cheap apartments with a man who isn't her husband and associating with people who think doing drugs is a status symbol."

They were standing almost toe to toe, both breathing heavily with rage.

"I see," Briana said heatedly. "I was supposed to have raised my daughter in poverty and privation because she had the bad luck to be born to me, but heaven forbid that a child of yours would have anything but the best, even if it meant taking her away from her mother."

Hank's eyes widened and he started to say something, then he slumped and ran his fingers through his disheveled hair again. "No, Briana," he said, and all the anger was gone from his tone. "That's not what I meant. Do you know where your little girl is?"

Now it was her turn to be surprised, and she stammered as she spoke. "Yes...uh...that is I—I know what the adoptive parents' address was at the time the adoption was final. They had a big, beautiful home. I doubt that they've moved."

He took her arm and walked her over to the couch where they both sat down. "Have you ever considered trying to get her back?"

Briana blinked. "What?"

"Have you ever thought of going to court and petitioning for the adoption to be set aside?"

She was stunned. "You're kidding."

He shook his head. "I've never been more serious. It's not too unusual for a woman to change her mind after giving up her baby—"

She held up her hand to stop his words. "Hank, I gave her up voluntarily. I signed the adoption papers. Her original birth certificate has been sealed and another one issued in her adoptive parents' name. I can't just suddenly appear after four years and say it was all a mistake, that I've changed my mind and want her back."

"I admit it would be difficult," he said, "but if you got a good lawyer and claimed that you were under undue stress and didn't realize what you were doing—"

"No!" She wasn't going to let him tempt her. She had enough grief without that. "Absolutely not. I don't understand how you could even suggest such a thing. I gave her up because I knew it was best for her. I'm certainly not going to mess up her life now by appearing out of nowhere and asking that the adoption be set aside."

"But you're able to take care of her now."

"That has nothing to do with it. Before she was born, her adoptive parents and I were thoroughly investigated by the state of California. They had to qualify medically and financially. We all went through months of counseling, and they took classes in parenting. It wasn't just a case of picking a couple and handing the baby over to them. The state Department of Adoptions was involved every step of the way, and they made sure that all three of us knew what we were doing and were agreeable."

Again Briana stood up, needing a distraction as she swallowed the sobs that threatened to escape. "She's bonded with her new parents now. They truly are her mother and father, and she's their daughter."

Walking over to the low bookcase, Briana picked up a framed wedding picture of her own mother and father and looked at it. "During all this, I came to terms with one indisputable fact. Giving birth doesn't necessarily make a woman a mother. It's the years of love and care she gives the baby afterwards that earns her that honored place in a child's life, and once she has it, it's always hers. No one can take it away."

She set the picture back down and turned to look at Hank. "I wouldn't stand a chance of getting my little one back, and if by some loophole I did, she'd hate me for it. No, Hank, the only gift I can give my daughter now is to stay as far away from her as I can get...."

Her voice broke as the persistent sob finally escaped, and she put her hands to her face. She heard Hank get up and then he had his arms around her, holding her as she sobbed against his chest.

He didn't speak, just held her the way he held Crystal when she cried, lovingly but without passion. It made her cry all the harder, but when the sobs finally stopped, he stroked his fingers in her hair and murmured, "I'm sorry. Sorrier than you can possibly know. I'd sell my soul for the ability to take away your pain, but instead, I keep adding to it."

He put his hands on either side of her head and lifted her tear-ravaged face to look at him. "I do love you. You know that, don't you?" His tone was soft and filled with torment.

She blinked back the new tears that clouded her vision. His face was as ravaged as her own, and she understood what he was going through. Being star-crossed lovers was roughly the equivalent of stumbling through Hades with no road markers to guide them.

She moved her hands up his chest and brushed her finger across his mouth. "Yes, I know," she said tenderly, "but you don't love me enough."

She felt him wince and saw the agony in his expression just before he put his arms around her again and buried her face in his shirt. "I don't know, Briana." His voice was hollow with regret. "God help me, I just don't know."

For a moment more they stood there, neither of them willing or able to break away. Finally, he released her and picked up his hat as he went out the door, closing it carefully behind him.

Briana understood that he wouldn't be back.

For the next week, Briana wandered through the days in a fog of misery, determined to function normally when she was barely able to function at all. The nights were no better, alternating between sleeplessness and harrowing dreams of lost babies and lost loves.

As she'd expected, she didn't hear from Hank, and she was careful not to venture into the vicinity of his home or the lumberyard where she might run into him. If she stayed in Whispering Pines, they'd be thrown together from time to time—it was inevitable in such a small community—but not yet. She needed time to heal, and so did he.

On Wednesday evening, she had a phone call from Scott. She recognized his voice as soon as he said hello and asked if she was alone.

"Yes," she snapped. "What do you want, Scott?"

"Don't hang up." His tone was urgent. "I just wanted to be sure that wild man wasn't listening in."

She looked at her watch. "I'll give you two minutes, so get to the point."

"I'm not going to make a habit of pestering you," he assured her. "I just need the answer to a couple of questions. First, is the little girl that was with you our daughter?"

Briana had already answered that question and so had Hank, but she resigned herself to tell him again. "No, she isn't. She's the daughter of the man I was with. He's divorced and has custody. Everyone in Whispering Pines knows it."

"Fine. Now, one more thing. Did you have an abortion?"

"Yes." The lie rolled off her lips without hesitation or guilt. This man was dangerous. If he knew he had a daughter and liked the idea, Briana was sure he wouldn't hesitate to try to find her. "You paid for it, remember?"

"Okay, babe, that's all I wanted to know." He actually sounded pleased.

Briana was determined to find out what he was up to. "Just a minute, Scott. Now I have a question. Why this sudden interest in my baby after all this time?"

He hedged a little but finally answered. "My father-in-law, the senator, is coming up for reelection, and I wanted to make sure you wouldn't be out for a little revenge by going to the media with the kid and giving them some half-assed story about how I abandoned you. Hell, the old man would have his gorillas break my knees if he lost the election because of me!"

Briana was both relieved and furious. "Believe me, it couldn't happen to a more deserving scuzbag," she said scathingly, and slammed down the receiver, then picked it up again to call the phone company and request a new and unlisted number.

By Friday, Briana was aware of another cause for concern. Not for herself, but for Elly. Maybe it was because of her own grief that she was unusually sensitive to the unhappiness of others, or maybe Elly's sorrow was becoming more noticeable, but gradually, Briana realized that her friend had once again lost the carefree, happy manner she'd regained during her convalescence in New Mexico.

Briana could guess what had happened, and she prayed she was wrong even as she decided to confront Elly. Both women had packed their lunch and were eating in the office when Briana suggested they go to a movie that evening. "That is, unless you're going to the square-dance workshop," she qualified.

Briana had already confided in Elly about her breakup with Hank. Not the details; she'd never discussed her baby with anyone but Hank. But Elly knew they'd quarreled and were no longer dating. She also knew that was why Briana wouldn't be going to the square dances anymore.

"No, I hadn't planned on attending the workshop," she said. "I'd love to go to the movie with you. How about if I pick you up around seven?"

The movie was a new Billy Crystal comedy that kept them both laughing while they stuffed themselves with buttered popcorn. Afterward, they went back to Briana's apartment for beer and pretzels.

They were sitting at the kitchen table when Briana took a sip of her beer and wrinkled her nose. "I don't know why I drink this stuff," she said. "I never have liked it."

Elly laughed. "Must be your masochistic tendencies. I have them myself at times."

"Yes, I'd noticed," Briana observed as she set her glass on the table in front of her. "In fact, that's what I want to talk to you about. What's going on, Elly? Something's bothering you, and don't try to deny it. Are you involved with Quentin York again?"

Elly paled and almost dropped her glass. "Am I that transparent?" she moaned.

Briana reached out and put her hand over Elly's. "Only to me, honey. Damn, I thought you were over him."

"So did I," Elly said, "but then he called me, said he had to see me, begged me to meet him just once more."

She shrugged. "I couldn't resist. I was like a dried out alcoholic taking just one more drink to prove I could stay away from it. I didn't have a chance. The minute he touched me, I . . ."

Briana could feel Elly's pain, and she wished she hadn't brought up the subject. She didn't need someone else's suffering; she could barely handle her own. However, she couldn't abandon her friend now.

"So you mean you've finally surrendered—"

"Surrendered my precious virginity, you mean?" Elly pulled her hand out from under Briana's and her tone was harsh and self-deprecating. "Not yet, but I may as well tell you, I went to a doctor in Cody and got a prescription for the pill. As soon as I'm sure it's safe, I'm not going to hold out any longer."

Briana knew she was fighting a lost battle, but she had to try. "Oh, Elly, are you sure this is what you want? Quentin has a wife and children—"

"Thanks for pointing that out to me," Elly said, her tone thick with sarcasm.

"I'm sorry if I'm stating the obvious, but how can you respect a man who cheats on his wife?"

"Who said anything about respect?" Elly snapped. "I've got the hots for him, and don't tell me you don't know how powerful that attraction can be. I've seen you and Hank together, the tension between you sizzles, so don't try to convince me that you two had separate cabins at Yellowstone last weekend."

Briana cringed. That was a low blow, but she understood that Elly was desperately defending the decision she knew was wrong but couldn't resist.

"I don't deny that Hank and I have been lovers," she said more stridently than she'd intended. "But Hank's not married."

Elly's face seemed to crumble, and Elly shuddered as tears welled in her brown eyes and spilled down her cheeks. "I'm sorry," she said on a sob. "I didn't mean to attack you. I know you're just trying to help, but you don't know Quentin the way I do. He loves me, Briana, truly he does, but he's trapped in a cold, passionless marriage because of his children.''

She swiped at her wet face with the back of her hands. "He's so miserable. I know they seem like a happy couple in public, but that's for the kids' benefit. In private, Janelle hardly speaks to him, and she won't let him touch her. They haven't been intimate in over a year.''

Briana didn't believe it, but she knew Elly did. She also knew that Elly wouldn't listen to any criticism of Quent, but Briana had learned a lot about the seamier side of life when she was growing up in the tenements of Los Angeles. She'd known men like Quentin York before, men who kept their wives barefoot, pregnant and home with the kids while they seduced every pretty young girl they could.

They were pathetic creatures, usually unsure of their own manhood, and with good reason, but Elly was an intelligent adult. There was no way Briana could protect her as long as she refused to open her eyes and take a clear look at what she was getting herself into.

"I wish I could help you,'' Briana said regretfully, "but this is something you have to work out by yourself. Just remember, Elly, I'm here for you if you need me.''

By Sunday, Briana knew she had to get away for a while. She had no intention of leaving Whispering Pines for good. It was her home now and she wasn't going to run from her problems, but she needed a place to sort out her emotions where she wasn't haunted by Hank's presence. Where she wouldn't jump every time the phone rang, hoping it was him calling. Where she didn't have to be careful for fear of meeting him unexpectedly or hearing gossip about him.

If he was dating other women, she didn't want to know it. Not yet.

She had two weeks vacation time coming and called Dr. Wainwright to request a week of it starting immediately. He grumbled about not having adequate notice, but since the tourist season would be in full swing by June, he agreed to let her take it now before they got really busy.

She packed a suitcase, threw it in the car and headed out of town. When she got to the main highway, she had no idea where she was going, but she knew she didn't want to go to Yellowstone, so she turned east.

It was Monday, and Hank arrived at the lumberyard a full hour before it would be time to open. It didn't matter. He couldn't sleep anyway, he thought he might as well check the inventory and make up a list of what needed to be ordered. The hardware salesman was due in a couple of days.

He went into the store and locked the door behind him to discourage early customers, then took off his jacket and Stetson and started checking shelves and bins. His eyes felt gritty and he rubbed at them with his knuckles.

It was Monday, exactly a week since he'd found out that Briana had had a baby and given it away. He was still reeling.

Why hadn't she told him earlier and given him a chance to deal with it while he could still be reasonably objective? He'd aired all his dirty linen for her, and all that time, she'd let him think she was an innocent young woman whose biggest mistake had been in choosing a boyfriend who'd somehow let her down.

Her choice of men had turned out to be a big mistake, all right. A whole lot bigger than she'd let on, and she'd deliberately left out the part about the baby.

He could have understood an illegitimate pregnancy. Hell, he'd been young himself once. He knew about hot teenage hormones and the lines boys used to seduce their girls. He'd done it himself, but he'd been more careful than most about using protection. He'd known a couple of guys who got girls pregnant. One had gone to Cheyenne for an abortion, and the other couple had gotten married, but the marriage hadn't lasted long.

He shook his head to clear his mind and realized that he had no idea what he'd seen in those shelves and bins he'd just strolled past. Grasping his notebook and pen, he started over.

Briana was right when she'd said he knew nothing about what it was like to be destitute and at the mercy of the welfare system. He'd never given it much thought, since his family had always been financially secure.

Hank hated the thought of Briana being mocked by people more fortunate than she. The despair in her eyes when she'd told him about it still haunted him and wouldn't let him rest. She had guts, that's for sure. If it was as tough to break out of the system as she said it was, then she'd come a long way, but it had cost her her baby.

If she just hadn't lied to him; and deliberately misleading him was a lie. She knew where he was vulnerable. He'd been up front with her with his feelings about mothers who abandon their children. He was well aware that he had a blind spot on that subject because of his experience with DeeDee. It wasn't something he was proud of, but it was too deeply ingrained to just ignore.

And if he did manage to come to terms with it and they got married, how could he be sure she wouldn't lie to him again about something vitally important?

Hank had been absently moving around the crowded store, his thoughts racing out of control, when without warning, he tripped on a large object that sent him stumbling backward. He smashed into a display wall and something heavy crashed to the floor beside him.

With horror he saw that it was a double-bladed woodsman's ax that by some miracle had just missed splitting his skull open.

For long minutes he sat there trembling with shock and revulsion as the realization that he should be dead, or at least badly mutilated, set in. Good God, he was a walking disaster, not only to himself, but to others. No one in his right mind would amble around a place like this in a daze. Not with all the sharp knives, blades and saws that were displayed.

What if there'd been a customer walking beside him?

He fought back the nausea that twisted his gut as he crawled away from the wall and pulled himself to his feet by grasping the counter. His head swam, and his body was dripping sweat.

That did it! Any more of this and he'd eventually kill himself or someone else with his inability to pay attention to anything but his own torment. It was damn well time to either forget the past and marry Briana, or else banish her from his mind.

He almost laughed at the absurdity of thinking he had a choice. Hell, he couldn't function without her.

He reached for the telephone and dialed her number. It was still early. Maybe he could catch her at home before she left for work.

It wasn't Briana who answered the ring, but a recorded message. "I'm sorry, but the number you dialed is not in service. Please hang up and try again."

Hank blinked at the phone. God, he really was coming apart. He couldn't even dial straight.

He hung up, then tried again and got the same message. This time his hand shook so bad, it took two tries to replace the instrument in its cradle.

Why had Briana's phone been disconnected? Surely she hadn't . . .

No! He wasn't even going to admit to the possibility that she might have moved away. Not in just a week.

Grabbing up the phone again, he dialed the dental office. After several rings, it was answered by Elly. He identified himself and asked to speak to Briana.

"Briana won't be in today." Elly's tone was chilly. "And her appointments for the rest of the week have been rescheduled."

"Where is she?" Hank yelled. "Is she sick? Why has her phone been disconnected?"

"I don't know where she is," Elly snapped, "and if I did, I wouldn't tell you. She wouldn't say what you two quarreled about, Hank, but she's hurting bad. I've known her a lot longer than you have, and she doesn't deserve the treatment you've been giving her—"

"Elly, don't hang up," he shouted frantically. "She is coming back, isn't she?"

"I don't know. I didn't talk to her. She called Dad yesterday and asked for a week's vacation, then took off. If she had her phone disconnected, then I wouldn't count on her returning if I were you."

Then she broke the connection before he could respond.

Chapter Fifteen

The road sign read: VISIT THE BUFFALO BILL HIS-
TORICAL CENTER. CODY. 49 miles.

Briana settled back in her car and sighed with relief.
That meant it was about seventy miles to Whispering
Pines. She'd been gone a week and she was looking for-
ward to getting home.

Not that her feelings for Hank Robinson had changed.
She still loved him and grieved for their ill-fated romance, but the week away, free of tension, guilt and, yes,
even resentment had been good for her. She'd caught up
on her rest and felt better able to handle the situation.

She'd been on the move the whole time, stopping when
she was tired, eating when she was hungry and exploring
all the things that had caught her interest. After visiting
the university at Laramie where Hank had studied, the
state capitol and museum in Cheyenne and the scenic
drive through Medicine Bow National Forest, there'd been

a stopover in Casper that had proved both informative and alarming. One she had to discuss with Elly immediately—even though she knew it might mean the end of their friendship.

As her mind cleared, she'd also been able to face the fact that there was no future for her with Hank. That love affair had been doomed before it began. Their problems were insurmountable, but that didn't mean she had to spend the rest of her life in mourning.

Briana's past had been a series of knockout blows, but she'd always managed to pick herself up and keep going. She would this time, too. From now on she was through trying to duck problems. She would face them as they came and deal with them before they got out of hand.

She was also through trying to avoid Hank. No more shying away from the places he lived and worked and hung out. When by chance they met, she'd be friendly and outgoing and maybe, eventually, they could even learn to be at ease with each other.

Another of her resolutions was to start dating again. A husband, home and family were important to her, and somewhere out there was a man who would love her enough to trust her in spite of her past mistakes.

A twinge of familiar pain clouded her optimism. Please, God, somewhere there had to be a man she could love almost as much as she loved Hank.

It was a little after three in the afternoon when Briana got home. The apartment was chilly and damp even though it was the middle of June. In Los Angeles, the temperature would be in the nineties by now, hot and dry, but in the high, thin altitude of the Rockies, there was still snow on the mountaintops.

She turned on the heat, then continued on into the bedroom with her suitcase when the phone rang. Dropping the case on the floor, she hurried back into the living room to answer it.

It was Elly, and she sounded upset. "Oh, Briana, I'm so glad you're back. I need a big favor from you."

"Elly, I just this minute walked in the door. I—"

"Sorry, but this is important," Elly said, totally out of character in her thoughtlessness. "I just had a call from Janelle York. She wants to come over here and talk to me—alone. I don't know what it's about, but I'm scared to death. She was insistent, and Dad and Mom are gone for the day, so I agreed, but I want you here, too."

Briana had a sinking feeling in the pit of her stomach. From what she'd learned in Casper, she was almost sure she knew what this was all about, and the last thing she wanted was to be in the middle of it.

"Darn it, Elly, I just got home," she repeated. "And I have a lot of things to take care of before I start back to work tomorrow. Besides, you said Janelle wants to see you alone."

"Yes, but I don't want to see *her* alone," Elly wailed. "I don't see how she could possibly have found out about Quentin and me, but I need you here just in case."

Briana sighed. She'd intended to have a long talk with Elly tomorrow anyway, so she might as well get it over with now. "Okay, I'll come. Give me fifteen minutes."

Ten minutes later, Briana knocked on the Wainwright's door. It was opened by Elly wearing the black-and-white linen dress she'd apparently worn to church that morning. She looked stunning.

The two women only had a chance to exchange a few words before Janelle knocked and was admitted. Quentin's wife looked harried. She wore baggy slacks with a loose-fitting blouse that only emphasized her rotund shape. Lipstick was her only makeup, and her straight hair hung limp and shapeless to her shoulders.

Once the three of them were settled in the living room, Janelle got right to the point. "Since Elly insisted you be here," she said to Briana, "I assume you're aware that she's carrying on with my husband."

Elly uttered a choked cry, and Briana's eyes widened in surprise at the directness of the attack.

"That's not true," Elly said. "We haven't—"

"Haven't been having sex?" Janelle asked. "I'll believe that. If you hadn't been leaving him frustrated, he wouldn't be so passionate with me."

Elly's face was ashen as she jumped up from the couch where she was sitting beside Briana. "That's a lie and you know it," she said angrily. "You don't sleep together—"

Janelle was also pale, but more composed than Elly. "Is that what he told you? We've only got three bedrooms, so where in hell do you think he sleeps if not with me?"

"But you don't make love. Quentin said you wouldn't let him...." Her voice trailed off as Janelle's expression changed from disgust to astonishment.

"You really believe that, don't you?" Janelle murmured. "Well, I hate to burst your balloon, little girl, but you'd better grow up if you're going to run around with married men."

Briana saw Elly cringe even as she started to protest. "I don't 'run around' with married men. Quentin and I are in love—"

"Ha!" Janelle snorted derisively as she, too, stood. "In love, my eye. You're infatuated, and he's in lust. You're going to find this hard to believe, Tinkerbell, but my husband's in love with me. At least as much as he's capable of loving anyone."

Briana was only going to interfere if things got out of hand, but her heart bled for Elly as each of Janelle's challenges hit her like a physical blow.

"That's not true," Elly shouted. "He said—"

"Oh, for God's sake, will you stop quoting him," Janelle shouted back. "He'll say anything he thinks will get you in the sack."

She turned away from Elly and walked across the room. "I used to believe him, too. It wasn't until after our second child was born that I found out he'd been cheating on me for years, not with just one woman, but a series of them. I took the children and left him, but he begged and pleaded and promised to go with me to a marriage counselor, so I finally went back."

Elly sank back down on the couch as if her knees had given way. "But he loves me." Her tone was barely above a whisper, and Briana could see the confidence draining out of her.

Apparently Janelle could, too, because her voice softened even though her words were harsh. "You sound like a broken record, Elly. I can almost feel sorry for you, because I've been where you are now. He's awfully persuasive. He even fooled me a second time, but then I found out he was cheating on me again. That time I didn't confront him, but went back to the counselor, and she laid it on the line for me."

Janelle gazed off into space, not making eye contact with either of the other women as she continued. "Quentin is one of a strange type of men who find the chase more exciting than the conquest. He really does love me and the kids, but he can't, or won't, resist the thrill of a clandestine seduction. There are plenty of women who are willing to play the game, but he's never before picked one as young and naive as you, Elly."

By now Elly was in tears, and it was Briana who spoke. "Janelle, why do you stay with a man like that?"

Janelle looked at her and shrugged. "I love him, and except for his one flaw, he's an excellent husband. He's just as tender and loving with me in private as he is in public, and he adores the children. Besides, I like being a wife, and what other man would want me and my two adolescent kids? I'm neither pretty nor smart, so I've learned to compromise. As long as he's discreet, I pretend that I don't know about his philandering.''

Briana felt compassion as well as impatience with the other woman. ''If you can live with that arrangement, then why are you interfering now?''

Janelle sighed. ''Because his discretion is slipping. We didn't choose to leave Casper—he got caught with one of the teachers. Fortunately the school board was able to hush it up, but only because he agreed to resign and leave town. I told him then that I wouldn't stand for being publicly disgraced and if it happened again, I'd leave him. That's how we wound up here, and I've about run out of patience.''

That got a reaction from Elly. ''You're making all this up,'' she said bitterly. ''Quentin wouldn't jeopardize his job—''

Briana knew she had to speak up. ''It's all true, Elly. I was in Casper a couple of days last week, and I made some discreet inquiries.''

She looked at Janelle. ''I'm sorry to tell you this, but it's pretty common gossip there if you talk to the right people.''

Elly slumped over and put her head in her hands. ''Oh, my God,'' she wailed. ''And I actually believed him.''

Janelle closed her eyes in resignation. ''Just remember that you're not the only one,'' she said raggedly. ''I thought this affair with you would be fairly short like the others, but you haven't given in as quickly as his usual conquests, so he's still interested.''

Slowly, Elly raised her head and looked from Briana to Janelle, then straightened up and wiped her eyes with the back of her hand. ''Well, I'm not,'' she snapped. ''I don't know what you're going to do, but from now on, you won't have to worry about him seducing me. I've never been so humiliated. If you still want him, you're welcome to him."

Janelle shook her head sadly. "I don't have much choice. I don't want to break up our marriage. The children need a father, and I need someone to support us financially. I guess I should have more pride, but pride is a pretty lonely lover and companion."

Janelle left then, and for the next hour Elly was alternately grief stricken and outraged. By the time Briana had her calmed down and thinking straight again, it was after six o'clock.

When she drove down the alley behind her apartment house and turned into the backyard parking lot, all four spaces were taken. Her heart nearly stopped when she saw who was parked in hers. It was Hank's sparkling silver truck, and he was sitting behind the steering wheel!

She was so astonished that she ran her car up on the grass, an action strictly forbidden by the landlord.

What was Hank doing here? And where was all that hard-won cool she was supposed to have gained? Her veneer of self-assurance had just vanished, leaving her exposed and defenseless.

Hank's door opened, and her hand trembled as she fumbled with the latch on hers. He'd started toward her by the time she got out of the car, and she met him halfway. His hat was pulled down low on his forehead, but when she got closer, she could see the lines still etched in his face and what looked like a wary relief in his eyes.

They stopped, facing each other, and he put out his hand as if to touch her but dropped it instead. "I was so afraid . . ." he said haltingly, then he closed his eyes and swallowed but didn't continue.

Her pulse was racing. What was wrong? Could something have happened to Crystal? "Hank, what's the matter? Why are you here?"

"I've been watching for you all week," he said. "I've nearly been out of my mind. I was afraid I'd driven you away."

She put her arm through his and urged him to move with her. "Come up to the apartment and I'll make some coffee." She looked up at him anxiously. "Is Crystal all right?"

He pinned her arm to his side so that she couldn't have gotten away if she'd wanted to, and glanced down at her with a long, penetrating gaze. "Crystal's fine. It's her old man who's falling apart."

Briana was afraid he might be right about that and quickened their pace.

In the apartment Briana started for the kitchen to make coffee, but Hank caught her hand and stopped her. "Briana, I've got to talk to you—now."

A lump of fear settled in her chest as she let him lead her to the couch. He took off his hat and tossed it onto a chair, then sat down, pulling her down beside him.

Now that the Stetson no longer shadowed his face, she could see that he looked ill.

"What do you want to talk about?" she asked.

His grip on her hand tightened, and he showed no sign of releasing it. "I'm sorry," he said. "I know I'm making a fool of myself, but the relief I felt when you finally drove up was so overwhelming that it scattered my wits all to hell and back. I'm having trouble gathering them up again. Just bear with me for a few minutes."

A warm finger of happiness touched her briefly before she repressed it. *Watch it, dummy. Don't be so trusting. Find out why he's glad you came back. He didn't care enough to come to you before you left.*

"I've been in town since about three, but I was over at Elly's," she explained. "Would you like a drink? I have whiskey or vodka."

He shook his head. "No, my mind's cloudy enough, but maybe coffee is a good idea, after all."

"Fine." She stood, then realized he still held her hand. She pulled gently, but his grip only tightened. "You'll have to let go of me," she pointed out.

"I'm afraid if I do, you'll disappear again," he said in all seriousness, and she was jolted by the crackle of electricity that seemed to weld their hands together and slither all the way up her arm.

With a sharp tug, she broke his hold on her and stepped back, shaken and angry. "I'm not going to play games with you, Hank," she snapped. "You've made it abundantly clear that I'm not the type of woman you want so, dammit, leave me alone."

She turned and headed for the kitchen with Hank right behind her. "I haven't made a damn thing clear except that I'm an insensitive, sanctimonious idiot," he thundered. "Lord knows I don't deserve your forgiveness. You're right, I have been setting myself up as prosecutor, judge and jury when I'm not qualified to make judgments in any capacity."

Briana turned to face him, dumbfounded, as he continued. "I only have one redeeming quality, Briana, and that's my overwhelming love for you. I can't eat, I can't sleep, I can't think. Hell, I can't even function without you. These past two weeks have been a nightmare, and it's going to get worse if you send me away."

She wanted to believe him, *needed* to believe him. He certainly looked and sounded sincere, but how could she be sure he wouldn't change his mind once he'd settled down and was thinking more clearly? DeeDee had left him with a skewed image of women in general and mother love in particular. Was it possible for him to differentiate between what his ex-wife had chosen to do and what Briana had been forced to do?

"I'm sorry, but I have trouble believing that," she told him. "If you love me, then why did you walk away from me after I told you about...about my baby?"

She saw him cringe and hated what she was doing to him, but this time she had to be sure he wouldn't change his mind.

"Because I'd just been dealt a stunning blow." His gaze never wavered from hers. "For three years I'd clung to my convenient prejudice against women who abandon their children, because then I could blame DeeDee for the breakup of our marriage and not have to admit that I was a lousy husband."

"But I didn't—"

Hank quickly interrupted. "I know, sweetheart, you didn't abandon your child. You loved her enough to give her up because you couldn't care for her properly, but it took a while for me to get that through my thick head. You should know, though, that I came looking for you before I ever made that distinction. I love you, and I wanted you no matter what I thought you'd done."

She turned away from him and busied herself making the coffee. "I wish I could believe you, Hank. I don't mean that I think you're lying, but, admit it, you've never really wanted me in your life."

Just saying it out loud brought unwelcome tears to her eyes and a lump to her throat. "You've fought the attraction between us every step of the way, so why don't you just give up and recognize the fact that you're a healthy, lusty man and I'm a reasonably attractive woman? What you feel for me is lust, not love—"

Her voice broke, and she spilled a measureful of coffee on the counter.

Hank stepped closer and put his arms around her waist, pulling her back against him and turning her insides to mush.

"It wasn't just you I didn't want in my life," he murmured as he rubbed his cheek in her hair. "I was determined never to give another woman a chance to hurt and humiliate me or to abandon Crystal, the way DeeDee had, but I learned early on that it wasn't just lust I felt for you. The torment I've been going through these past two weeks has little to do with sex."

He held her close, but his hands didn't roam over sensitive areas even when he lowered his head to nuzzle the side of her throat.

"Making love with you is a mind-blowing and addicting experience," he continued softly, "but it's only a part of what I need from you. I need your warmth, your tenderness and your love. Most of all your love. I hope to God I haven't killed it with neglect. You've offered it to me so generously, and I've shied away, afraid to make a commitment."

He turned her to face him and tangled his fingers in her hair on either side of her head. "I can't undo my past mistakes, but I'll spend the rest of my life making up for them if you'll let me."

Slowly he lowered his face to hers and trailed little kisses on her forehead, her eyelids and either side of her mouth. "I need you with me always, in my life, in my heart, in my arms."

His kisses continued down the curve of her throat as his fingers lightly massaged her scalp. "I won't make any demands on you. If you'll marry me, I'll do everything I can to make you happy."

He was making her so happy now that she couldn't think straight. She was determined not to respond before she had the chance to weigh all the pros and cons, but his lips were exciting her to the point of madness. Having lost the battle for control, she wrapped her arms around his waist while her hands caressed his back through the denim shirt he wore.

"I'll make every effort to put a lid on my temper," he said shakily as she felt him shiver under her palms, "and I promise not to pressure you for more children the way I did DeeDee."

Briana couldn't get enough of touching him. She explored his wide muscular back and pressed her breasts against his chest, her stomach against his— Her eyes widened at the strength of his obvious desire.

He lowered his arms back to her waist and clutched her tightly against him. She didn't even try to resist as she leaned into his ramrod hardness.

"I'm sorry," he groaned anxiously. "I didn't want this to happen, but I can't help what you do to me every time you get near. Don't worry, though, I can control myself."

Briana wasn't nearly that certain of her own restraint, but there were still things that needed to be cleared up. "Maybe we should sit down," she suggested, gesturing to the straight-backed kitchen chairs.

"Please, not yet," he pleaded. "It seems like I've waited an eternity to hold you again. I can't let you go, but I promise to be good."

She wasn't going to insist. Actually, she was ashamed to admit that she wished his self-control wasn't quite so strong.

"If I marry, I definitely want children," she said. "Do you?"

"You know I do, but I want you more."

"I want you, too." The confession slipped out, but she wasn't sorry.

He made a sound deep in his throat and brushed her lips with his. "Enough to marry me?"

"Oh, yes," she admitted. "But I have to be sure that you really do love me enough."

"I let you down badly, didn't I?" he said, referring to the last time she'd seen him.

She shook her head. "No. I didn't want you to lie about your feelings. What I'm not sure of is why you changed your mind."

He moved his hands upward to cup the sides of her breasts. "I didn't change my mind. I just wasn't ready to admit how very much I do love you. It wasn't until I discovered that you'd had your phone disconnected and left town suddenly that I realized what a blind imbecile I'd been. I'd blown my only chance for happiness, and I've been quietly losing my mind ever since."

Briana explained that she hadn't had her phone disconnected and why she'd changed her number to an unlisted one.

"If Scott Upton ever contacts you again, my promise to put a lid on my temper is rescinded," Hank growled softly into her ear before caressing it with his tongue and sending tremors down her spine.

"He won't," she assured him, then raised her face and brushed her lips across his. "Kiss me, Hank," she whispered against his mouth.

The words were hardly out when his mouth captured hers and his arms tightened around her, lifting her to fit her softness against his turgid maleness. Her reaction was instantaneous, and her whole body seemed to ignite as her lips parted to welcome his seeking tongue.

She felt his heart hammering against her breast, and his breathing became labored as she squirmed against him, desperately seeking to quell the insistent throb deep in her womanhood.

With a smothered moan he tore his mouth from hers and buried his face in the side of her neck. "Briana, have mercy." It was a cry of frustration. "I promised to control myself, but you have to help me. I can't do it if you're going to tempt me beyond reason."

He was trembling, and she stroked her fingers through his hair. "Then don't you think it's time we quit tormenting ourselves and gave in to the temptation?" she murmured.

He raised his head and looked at her doubtfully. "Are you sure that's what you want?"

She snuggled her head on his shoulder. "Very sure."

He still didn't seem convinced. "Will you marry me?"

This time she raised her head and looked at him. "You mean you want to wait until we're married . . . ?"

The beginnings of a smile twitched at the corners of his mouth. "Oh, God, no," he thundered, "but I want to be sure you understand that the next time we make love, it's going to be a lifetime commitment. There won't be any backing out for either of us."

She smiled and ran her finger lightly down his cheek. "I can live with that," she assured him tenderly.

A grin split his handsome face. "Well what are we waiting for?" he asked as he swept her off her feet and carried her to the bedroom.

He sat down on the side of the bed with her on his lap and pulled her red sweater over her head, then tossed it to the floor. Her bra followed, and he cupped each of her bare breasts in his rugged hands. He kissed first one, then the other before Briana guided his head to the valley between them and held it there.

"There were nights when I paced the floor and wondered how I could live all the rest of my life without ever again knowing the magic of your exquisite breasts in my hands and in my mouth," he said, then planted kisses on her firm flesh.

She returned his kisses with ones on the top of his head. "I'm embarrassed to tell you the part of you I lusted after."

He raised up and looked at her. "Oh?" he said curiously. "Tell me anyway."

She could feel the warm flush to her face. "It was your stomach. You've got the most expressive belly."

His eyes widened with surprise and amusement. "I'm almost afraid to ask, but how does my belly express itself?"

"It—it sort of tightens up every time I put my hand or my cheek on it," she stammered, "and when I kiss you there, it goes into spasms. Do you want me to show you?"

"Feel free," he said, struggling not to laugh as he leaned back.

She started unfastening his shirt. "In order to do it right, it's best if you're not wearing too many clothes."

"By all means," he agreed as she slid his shirt off and reached for the fastener at the waistband of his jeans.

He drew in his breath sharply as she slid his zipper down, and she realized that her hand was shaking and she was holding her breath. The temptation to let her hand slip and cover the long, hard length of him under the fly was almost irresistible.

"Now, if you'll just lie back..." She pressed her hands against his chest, but he stopped her.

"Not until I get the rest of my clothes off." He bent over to remove his shoes and socks. "Something tells me I'm not going to have the time or the patience to do it later."

She removed her shoes, socks and jeans, and pulled back the covers while he stepped out of his trousers and stood before her in only his briefs.

Her fascinated gaze roamed over his magnificent body, all length and breadth and muscle covered with exciting rough skin and blond body hair. She had to force herself to be patient and continue the foreplay she'd started, which had become totally unnecessary.

From the stiff bulge in his briefs, she knew he was having the same problem, but she couldn't resist prolonging the exquisite agony as long as possible.

"Now lie down," she directed, and he got into bed and lay on his back with his arms crossed behind his head.

"Like this?" he asked as he eyed her warily.

"That's fine," she answered, and climbed in on her knees to sit beside him.

Slowly she reached out and put her palm on his flat stomach just below his waist. The firm muscles contracted as she'd known they would and his whole body twitched.

She looked at him and saw that his jaws were clenched. "You see," she boasted. "Responsive."

The best he could manage as a reply was a long, ragged sigh.

"Now watch this," she instructed as, again moving slowly, she leaned down and pressed her open mouth against his bare belly then sucked gently.

His stomach clenched and with a muttered oath, he rolled over. Almost before she knew what was happening, he had stripped them both of their underpants and she was lying under him with one of his knees between her thighs.

"Okay, Briana," he said huskily as he looked down at her with eyes clouded with desire. "You just pushed your luck too far. I'm about to explode."

She wrapped her arms around him and rotated the damp heat of her own desire against his knee. "No, I didn't, my darling," she murmured. "I'm getting exactly what I was asking for. Make love to me, Hank. I can't wait any longer, either.''

With a wildness only barely held in leash, he moved into position and entered her. She uttered a sharp cry of almost unbearable pleasure and arched into him, urging him deeper until his body united with hers produced a friction that blasted them into an exaltation that made them no longer two separate beings, but whole.

*   *   *   *   *